Call Your Steel

By

G. D. Penman

Call Your Steel

By

G. D. Penman

This is a work of fiction. All the characters and events portrayed in this book are either products of the author's imagination or are used fictiously.

Call Your Steel

Copyright ©2017 by G. D. Penman

Cover by Trif Andrei - TwinArtDesign

Published by Azure Spider Publications LLC

1051 NE Pepperwood

Grants Pass, OR 97526

www.azurespiderpublications.com

Library of Congress Control Number: 2017942603

ISBN978-0-9974621-7-3
ISBN: 978-0-9974621-8-0 ebook

First Edition June 2017

Printed
n the United States of America

To Emma

She knows why

Contents

Chapter 1- The Dark Lands

In the sky above there was no sun. Stars illuminated the earth below with their dim and distant light. The moon was a faceless, lifeless, dark circle blocking out the starlight. On the surface of the world there were tiny pinpricks of light. Each bonfire representing a settlement or lonely travellers far from the safety of civilisation. There were four greater lights. Three massive clusters of flame, warm and welcoming. One blue-white light, dazzling and brighter than the rest combined.

Her stage was a pair of planks laid over two barrels by the village bonfire and her wage was whatever scraps the villagers tossed into her hat but even so Lucia felt that the show went well. A troubadour's life was far from untroubled but to see empty faces come to life balanced the cost. She started with a few simple songs. Tapping her foot and strumming along on her sickle-harp. There were a few women and children in the crowd and they were dancing by the time she began playing Four Kings. As the evening dragged on her hat had started to fill up with odd scraps of precious metal and just before the children's extended bed time could run out she decided to risk singing Great Dragons Dance. In the cities where the fear of the Eaters was more pronounced she would have denied even knowing the old piece but out here in the dark it had the children clapping along and the old mothers nodding along approvingly. She gave the children a conspiratorial wink as they were led off to their ash buried hovels and took a quick break to rest her voice.

When she got back on the stage, she broke out a trio of sad old songs of lost love, missing home and a tearjerker about a woodsman who wouldn't light a fire after cold-fall because he didn't want to hurt the forest he loved. There were tears in a lot of eyes after that one so she launched directly into a bawdy song about a farmer's wife who couldn't find a big enough mushroom for an unspecified purpose.

After that one she had to take another break as an old woman in the crowd had hooted herself into a harsh coughing fit. Most of the younger men had flushed with embarrassment under their layers of dirt, soot and ash but there was one standing as close to the stage as he could get. He stared at her with intensity.

Lucia supposed that she was pretty enough but didn't understand the fascination. Her eyes were a little too big for her face, her forehead a little too high, probably accentuated by the latest fashionable hairstyle picked up last time she was in the city. Long and curled on the top and shaved clean along the sides. She ignored him and went on through her usual catalogue before she played a gentle, lilting version of The Time for Sleep as a sort of downbeat finale. There was a scatter of applause from the exhausted people as they lumbered off towards their homes but she knew their real appreciation would be measured in how full her hat had become.

She stowed her sickle-harp in its case first. Then poured her hat's contents into a small sack without counting it. It would be another couple of cycles walking, at least, before she came upon anywhere to spend it. She left the planks on the barrels. Hopefully they would prompt some fond memories when the village folk returned to the drudgery of daily life out here.

She was about to seek out a sheltered spot to snooze until heat-rise when she realised that the ash miner from beside the stage was still waiting for her. She managed to keep her sigh internal as she gave him a polite smile. He walked towards her a little in that odd shuffle that the people out here had acquired to deal with the ground moving beneath them and spoke towards her knees, "I've always thought it would be a fine thing to have a wife that could sing."
Lucia forced her jaw to unclench and asked, "Which lucky girl have you set your eyes on then?" already knowing the answer.
He grunted, "Well I thought maybe you and I could have something to drink and have a talk about that."

She considered playing ignorant but thought it was better to nip this in the bud if she ever planned on passing by this way again. At least this one was being fairly polite about it. She shook her head and said, "I'm sorry lad, but I'm not the settling type."
He glanced up at her and by the bonfire light she saw he wasn't that

bashful, just not all that interested in her face. "Come on now, we've only just met. Let me get you a drink."

She tried to work out what would happen if she called for help. It could be that the townsfolk would shame him into walking away from her or it could be some of his friends who would try to help their friend. She had given them a night of entertainment, but what would that be worth compared to a lifetime's worth of loyalty?

"I'm sorry, but I've met men like you before, you are only interested in one thing. The contents of my purse."
He sniggered, "Well, you aren't wrong. Those fools must have tossed a week's work in silver scrap into your hat tonight and I ain't fixing to have all of that walk away."

By now she had her things together so she slung her pack and instrument case over her shoulder and got ready to run, "No."

His brows drew together. "I tried to make this easy on you. Just remember that when the bleeding starts."

By the time the first word was out of his mouth she had turned and sprinted away from the village. He started shouting at her back but with the wind whipping by she couldn't hear his curses. She was a city girl, born and raised, so the soft ground made her going slow. Not to mention the whole night of standing and hopping and stomping and dancing. If she could get a distance from the light of the bonfire he would lose her. With that in mind she circled around the village's major works. A sifting and mining project to the north of town where they extracted the globules of metal and rivulets of fat preserved by the layers of ash. Then she ran as fast as she could, dropping to all fours and scrabbling forward as the ash and masonry shards slipped away from beneath her and having to fling her pack back over her shoulder. Up ahead there was a particularly high dune of ash. If she could get to the far side she would be out of sight of the settlement.

A half a mile up from the ground, Valerius, Beloved of Negrath stirred from his sleep. He did not need to sleep, and had not needed to for these last hundred years but he found it gave him a peace of mind and clarity that contemplation and meditation did not match. He was clothed in an unfashionably long and loose fitting robe in the same pale cream colour as the ivory the city was carved from, it made him seem less like a man and more like a growth from his chambers' floor. The robe did not press too painfully on any of the bone-spurs starting to rise out of his skin. His long white hair flowed neatly to his waist and his alabaster skin just added to the artificial appearance. He walked out onto his balcony as a wave of heat swept over the city from the east and he looked out across his dominion.

On the horizon little fires burned on the sparse farms and mines surrounding the city and the star light granted at least shapes but the city itself was dark, and would remain dark until he made it otherwise. He considered the lives of the people in the city, quivering in this endless night without him. He set his hands on the two copper rods rising up from the polished ivory of his balcony and he called the storm. Galvanic force flowed through him and out in an ever widening circle, sparking to life the cold blue lanterns throughout his city. The lanterns whined and crackled and gradually accumulated enough power to last until cold-fall and he released his grip on the copper. The city was a blazing white beacon in the dark plains surrounding it. The centre of the world. All was as it should be.

Kaius released his armour and the chill air swept over the bare skin of his arms and head. He drew it deeply into his lungs. His robes were purple, the colour of his city, but they were embroidered at their edges in silver filigree to reflect his rank. Not that colour could be seen so far from the city's lights. They were curious clothes. Form fitting around his torso, absent from his arms and loose around his legs. On a flat plane of stone overlooking the dales he went through the Thousand Forms of Bone. First in order, then switching between them, seemingly at random with a fluidity born of endless practice. From block to strike to grapple and kick. After the fourth repetition of every Form he turned to the east and closed his eyes.

A thin layer of cold sweat beaded on his exposed skin. The wave of heat rolled over the horizon and he was thankful for the clear sky. He saw the dark and ominous shadow of the moon blocking out stars close to the horizon. The flash of warmth loosened his muscles and he enjoyed the ticklish pleasure of his sweat drying. He opened his eyes to the stars above him with a smile on his face, then with a twinge of reluctance he called steel and let the cold metal envelop him again, liquid at first then setting solid. Hiding all of the world from his sight except what was visible through the slit of his visor.

Once it was set he felt neither warmth or cold within his armour, just its comforting weight. He muttered his morning prayers to Negrath and turned to look out across the rolling ash dunes of his duty. The breeze flapped the fabric of his robes around his armoured legs. He drew a deep breath and caught the scent of fear. His pupils narrowed to slits as his senses continued to heighten. He made out moving shapes across to the north-west, nearing the border of the Glasslands.

He called speed and ran across the shifting and tumbling ground towards the source of the scent. Picking out the distinct aromas of stale sweat and boiled leather beneath the omnipresent smell of burnt wood and rancid fat.

A distant light appeared behind Lucia even as heat-rise hit her and she heard a little shout of triumph. Far closer than she would have hoped. She was near the top of the dune and the city coming to life was enough to silhouette her against the white-grey top layer of ash. Over the crumbling summit she tripped and stumbled. She caught her foot on a more solid block of stone and dislodged it to slide down the far side, down the mound and out over the shimmering flat plain of glass up ahead. It slid to a halt after it had left its thick trail of ash behind it.

Looking out onto the Glasslands she hesitated for a moment to take in the alien terrain and wipe the caked ash from her eyelashes. It was for a moment too long. Rough hands grabbed onto the straps of her instrument case and dragged her backwards. She twisted and turned and lost both her instruments and balance for the trouble.

She fell heavily onto her backside then started to skid down the far steeper other slope of the dune, gaining speed until she reached the glass' smooth surface. She slid out across it until she reached the fallen stone. At the top of the hill she saw the shape of a man against the starlit sky. He gaped down at her in surprise. Then she heard a high pitched creak, first from behind her, then from beneath her. It stopped abruptly with a loud crack.

Both the rock and the girl fell as the glass beneath them shattered. She plummeted into the dark. Her hands flailed for purchase at the thick shards of sooty black glass that fell around her. She jerked her head to the side to duck the slab of stone spinning as it fell. She hit a toppled stone pillar after what seemed like an eternity and the air drove out of from her lungs even as the pain made her shriek.

She tumbled off the pillar, falling again into endless darkness, clipping off of sedimentary layers of debris, destroyed buildings and thick crystalline protrusions of glass from the surface above. She lost consciousness before she struck the bottom.

Before he reached the base of the ash mound Kaius released speed and dropped into a crouch to maintain balance as momentum carried him up the slope. Calling speed always made him feel giddy. He released steel for an instant and before his armour withdrew he called it again in a slightly altered form. A curved sword grew out from the side of his arm and shoulder, settling into a reversed grip when it extended and detached fully. The rest of his armour settled back into place, thinner by a minuscule amount.

He halted behind the ash farmer and took in the scene. There was a crack stretching out onto the glass plain ahead that the dune was draining into with a loud hiss. The man before him stared at the damage he had obviously done with a slack-jawed expression. Kaius went weeks at a time without the need to speak so when he did it was rough and echoed back at him within the armour, "Where did you come by that, child?"

The man physically jumped away from the voice behind him. Trying to twist in the air and ending up in a crumpled mess on the ground, starting another slow drift towards the hole in the glass. Kaius took a step forward and put his foot on the strap of the city stitched instrument case. Stopping any further movement. Then he spoke again, "The bag is not yours, where did you come by it, boy?"

Guilt was written all over the man's face, clear to see in the city's distant light to Kaius improved vision. He shook his head as what was obviously a thief stuttered out the beginnings of a lie then plunged his sword into the liar's chest. It was not one of the Forms of Steel, just a brutal thrust.

Kaius released steel after the gurgling and bubbling had stopped, then crouched to examine the stolen bag, he tugged the straps open and looked at the harp and bundled coins inside. While his education had neglected music as a subject he knew that a well crafted instrument was worth a substantial sum, likely enough to kill for if you were a desperate man living out in the dark. Leaving it here for the thief's family to profit from was out of the question so he considered taking it with him, perhaps returning it to some bruised travelling musician.

He snorted at his own brief naivety. There would be a shallow grave somewhere out in the desert of ash with the harp's owner in it. He slid down the dune to the edge of the glass and peered into the hole. It went down too far for him to make anything out except the vague forms of a few criss-crossing pillars of stone.

He cocked his head to the side and listened but the roar of falling ash and stone shards over the edge deafened him. He shrugged and tossed the bag down. As he stood he caught a flash of metal in the distance, out on the glass, moving with called speed. Without a backward glance he called his own steel and speed and darted off after it.

The Glasslands were further still from the city, around the horizon's curve. So Kaius had to rely on the starlight to track his prey. The shimmer of the glass through the soot made it harder to make out the glint of metal but there was no other motion out here. The few settlements on the glass were far further out where the surface glass was broken up enough to be harvested and wildlife couldn't survive here without sustenance. The moving speck of silver stopped suddenly then started to grow bigger.

Kaius had been sighted, so he called the same sword as before and flipped it into an upright grip, adopting high guard, the first Form of Steel. He waited as the speck of silver grew large enough to show a human shape. He breathed deeply to calm himself.

She was nearly upon him when he saw that she wore Negrath's colours too. He did not relax his guard of course. It would be a simple matter for another Eater's Chosen to lay hands on a purple dye. She skidded to a halt, half a head shorter than him and narrower across the shoulders but otherwise her appearance was identical. She had a pair of short straight swords in her hands, the curved one that was Kaius' preference had been out of fashion among serious students of the Forms of Steel for a decade or more. It made his attacks unfamiliar to the younger generation, which had proved helpful on occasion. She released steel while still moving with the juddering motions of someone calling speed and when he saw her face he released steel too.

Metharia was the Chosen who watched over the Glasslands, a wider field than his own duty, but far more sparsely populated and ultimately easier to oversee. It was closer to enemy territory though. She was more likely to see combat against other Chosen. He was almost jealous. She was completely hairless, as all the Chosen were thanks to the vigorous rub-down with bitter vasca oil that formed part of their initiation. The starlight shone off the pale skin of her scalp, she had a strong nose and out here in the dark her pupils dominated her small eyes. Kaius was always uneasy in the city, seeing colours so vividly, hidden even in people's eyes. Things were simpler out here.

She gave him a nod of greeting when his face emerged. Then she released speed and her blurred lines snapped into sharp shadows. She intoned, "Negrath's blessings upon you brother."

He remembered his part well enough, "May his might shield you sister."

She nodded again, satisfied that formality had been appeased, and her stance relaxed, "How have you been Brother Kaius? Are you enjoying your posting?"

"It is well Sister Metharia, the sifters are simple enough folk, a few executions were enough to keep the fear of us in them. How do you like the Glasslands? Have you seen any incursions?"

She shook her head, city born folk always wanted to say everything with body language, they were too used to the lights, "I've seen a few of them on the far-side of our borders but they are just going about their business as I do the same. No trouble from the glass miners, all too scared to so much as twitch in case they break something and lose their money."

Kaius forced his face into a smile, it felt sordid to do it in front of someone else, "It is well that they did not test you, I recall you were adored by the Master of Steel when we were children."

She chuckled, "I think at least part of that was due to him being a perverted old man, but the extra attention certainly improved my forms."

There was a lull in the conversation as they tried to think of some other common ground after so many years apart, eventually Metharia pressed on to business, "You've been out here for three years now. Two years longer than the usual tour. I don't know who you made angry before you left but it seems to have lapsed. I am to take your posting for the rest of this year. The Marked have requested that you return to the city for a new duty."

Kaius flinched but bowed to her dutifully, "My thanks to you for relieving me of my burdens."

He could hear her roll her eyes more than he could see it but she said, "Yes, you are very welcome. Just remember me out here and let me know how the Trials go when you get the chance."

This gave him pause, "The Trials are this year?"

She leaned in towards him as if to prevent her voice from carrying and said, "Why do you think they are calling you back? I bet you are being entered."

He knew that modesty required some deflection of that thought but to his surprise it absorbed him. What would become of him if he fought in the Trials? Would he be Marked if he was victorious and lose his moments of freedom out here in the dark? He half stuttered thanks to her again then turned to face the city directly. A great white beacon in the perpetual void of the sky.

He remembered himself before he called steel and turned back to Metharia who viewed him with a cocked brow, hard to make out with no eyebrow hair, "My thanks to you and fair well Sister Metharia. I will send news of the Trials when I can."

She watched him fade away across the glass and ash. When he passed over the first dunes and out of sight she called her own steel and returned to her final patrol of the Glasslands. They would have to care for themselves until Kaius replacement was dispatched.

Chapter 2: The Halls of Steel and Bone

The city first loomed over Kaius then crept up further still until it dominated both the land and the sky. Soon after he was Chosen, as part of his education, Kaius had travelled through all of the domains of Negrath and far to the south he had seen mountains. Standing at the base of a mountain was the closest experience he had to coming to the Ivory City. The central spire stretched up into the sky, the summit's light shrouded by the clouds. The lesser spires of varying heights, interlinked by beautifully graven balconies and bridges, were home to the city's noble families from which the next Beloved would be selected by Negrath in a few more generations.

The remaining buildings grew up around the base of the spires, constructed from simple stone and wooden planks like any other city. The gates were little more than cracks in the exterior walls and as Kaius walked through he could see the honeycombed structure inside the great bones the city was built from. In the places where spires had been broken over the centuries each air-pocket was turned into a minute vertical slum with a tangle of rope ladders allowing anyone access when the six foot deep cells were empty. It was to the central spire that Kaius walked through packed street markets of screaming vendors and quiet alleys that a man not Chosen by the Eater would have done well to avoid if he meant to keep his silver in his purse and his blood in his veins.

At the end of some alleys there were more furtive vendors with crates and cages of chattering insects, not bred for meat like those in the main-street markets but for their venomous stings and the interesting effects that the stings had on the human brain. Some still tried to peddle the smoking herbs that addicts had indulged in all those years ago when Kaius had been training in the city but they were out of fashion with the nobility, the font of all wealth in the city.

As he passed by the smoke vendors his armour reacted to protect him from what was ultimately a poison, the steel softened and shifted within his visor, it blocked his mouth and nose until he had walked clear. He had forgotten that it was one of the minor annoyances of city life after so long away. The press of so many people and the heat of them all would have been disconcerting but it was the light that he could not adapt to, his eyes were narrowed, his face showed weakness and confusion at every turn, which was of course why he had not released steel before he entered the city. The Chosen had to be infallible for their judgements to be trusted.

In a few hours he would be used to the cacophony, but by then he would be safely insulated within the Spire of the Beloved. It took nearly that long to walk from the city's walls to the spire, even with its base being nearly a mile wide. Some of that was backtracking and moving through check-points and giving meaningful looks to some noble families' house guards. The city was dense, with sedimentary layers of civilisation pressing down the old and uplifting the new, mixing and mingling in strange ways but always, ultimately controlled by the Beloved.

The Spire itself stood open and unguarded, the Chosen dwelt inside, as did their masters the Marked. If anyone was fool enough to attack the stronghold of the Beloved they would find themselves facing men capable of annihilating armies alone, not even considering the raw power of the Beloved himself. A power that made the city a beacon of light in the great darkness.

Kaius made it to the top of the first flight of stairs before he was challenged and politely released his steel. The Marked wore the same cut of robes as the Chosen, albeit all in black and, having been elevated from their ranks, were equally hairless. The Marked that met Kaius was one that he had known all through his life, Atius, the Master of Bone. Neither the Chosen or Marked needed to eat or drink to survive but some never lost the urge and over the years small indulgences quickly added up.

Atius was a tall man to begin with and the years piled on more and more weight until he was more of a wall than a man. Unfit as he was there had been some debate over his suitability to teach the Forms of Bone but a few lessons under his crushing mass and absolute precision silenced every critic. Kaius had been amazed at the looming giant's graceful movements. He had drilled the need for perfection into every student but he only praised the ones he saw it in. His gentle disapproval had stung more than the salted canes that the other masters used to instil discipline.

He rocked back on his heels and smiled broadly now at Kaius, once a favourite pupil, "So you are finally back to finish your studies, eh Boy? Well you are too late. Too late I say. I have more promising students now. They will all be Chosen soon enough and have the good sense to stay here and learn from their betters."

He paused for breath but before Kaius could form a reply he started off again, "Fine, fine. I will teach you. But only for as long as you are Chosen. Do you hear me? When Valerius ascends you after you crush your way through the Trials it would be unseemly. For now though, you are always welcome to return to the Halls of Bone and prepare, although I imagine that it will be the Trial of Steel that you truly need to concern yourself with."

Kaius was staggered for a moment then he broke into laughter. Atius could deliver news like a hammer-blow or with such grace you didn't even know you were being wounded and this time his gusto had carried Kaius along with him.

Kaius finally spoke, "I may bring myself to study under you again before the Trials, thank you for informing me that I had been elected to represent the city."

Atius slapped his gut and pulled a face of mock indignation, "Informing you? Boy, who do you think campaigned with the Beloved on your behalf? Who do you think told him you could rip through the braggart Chosen of Vulkas without breaking sweat? Who do you think told him you would be the greatest addition to the ranks of the Marked in his hundred years of life?"

Kaius had been slowly considering these things as he came to the city, his family had been of no significance and he had not heard from them since the mid-point of his training, they would not have been romancing the Marked and bribing the nobility to support his ascension. Besides, they were mushroom farmers, not the most politically potent of groups. His natural talent in the Forms of Bone, polished by painstaking repetition in his grandmother's garden and recognised by a travelling merchant, was the greatest thing that had happened to them in generations. His acceptance to Halls of Bone had been the talk of their village. Perhaps it still was, he did not know them now. He had taken too long to give his thanks but when he opened his mouth to do so Atius cut him off, "Well it wasn't me you ungrateful runt. I was shocked enough to shit myself when Valerius mentioned you. Didn't even think he knew your name."

With a drawl Malius joined the conversation, "I'm still not convinced that he does."

Malius sidled from a doorway at the centre of the balcony, he was shorter than Atius, thinner too, but neither of these things were particularly distinctive. He had an angular nose and a sallow face, and though he had been Marked at around the same time as Atius he looked considerably older, perhaps in part due to the stressful first few decades when the previous Master of Steel was still in the position he coveted.

It had been a tense period of scheming and backstabbing, culminating in the Beloved's favour wavering, a contrived insult and a short but brutal duel as Malius proved his superiority. The killing blow had been struck with such called strength that windows shattered in the buildings all around the arena. That was in the same year that Kaius was born.

He looked at Kaius appraisingly and said, "It was me, obviously. The Beloved wanted to know who among his Chosen had not gone soft from city living, who had some cleverness to them and who fought differently from the rest of us. And after extending your tour year after year for just such an eventuality, I put your name forward."

Kaius had wondered why he was twice left out in the dark instead of recalled but he had never questioned an order in his career and wasn't likely to start with an order that he liked. "My thanks to you for this opportunity Master."

Malius sneered, "Don't thank me. Win. If you live you will join our ranks and perhaps give this useless lump a kick in the blubbery rear. If you lose, I have not offended anyone of consequence by putting you forward."

Atius took the jibes in good humour, still happy to see an old student, "This one will do us proud Brother Malius, just wait and see."

Malius kept his eyes fixed on Kaius, perhaps hoping he would flinch as he once had. Malius was always quick with the cane, even conducting faux duels with his students using one.

"He still looks sharp enough I suppose," he stepped closer to Kaius, "You were out there for a very long time. All alone. Would you like for me to arrange someone for you? A girl? A boy? After three years I would be needing a few of each I imagine. Shall I send them to your quarters to wait for you? I have some very pretty students this year. All so willing to please."

Kaius smiled in a manner he hoped was polite, not strained and replied, "Not tonight, thank you. I believe I will attempt to follow in the footsteps of our Beloved and rest a night in a warm bed."

Malius face showed a flicker of uncertainty then he

shrugged, "As you wish. Just remember that the offer still stands for as long as you are in the Trials. And perhaps longer if you should be Marked. We can come to arrangements should the need arise."

Atius jovial expression had tightened during what should have been a private conversation but was all to clear to his sharpened hearing. He muttered, "Sleep well little Kaius. I will see you at heat-rise, if you have maintained your sobriety."

Malius smiled beatifically revealing his missing front tooth, "Come and see me at the War Spire when you are done dancing around. We can go through your forms and your itinerary for the next few cycles. You can look over our fresh faced new recruits at your leisure."

Kaius was impressed with his own politeness in bowing to the Master of Steel and walking calmly off to his cloistered room without calling speed.

The room that technically belonged to Kaius had been maintained by servants in his absence but he had never lived here. It had seemed strange to him that people who did not need sleep or food were given quarters at all, but after so long he realised that for most of the Chosen this was a place that belonged to them, just like his morning Forms belonged to him, and while they did not need rest, they still craved comfort.

His room had never been decorated or furnished beyond the simple wooden bed, chair and desk that had been for his use as a child. He knew that he could walk into many fine craftsmen's workshops or even just a simple merchant's shop and ask for anything that he might want and the Beloved would finance it, probably without even realising that there had been a cost involved. Many of the Chosen, kept in the usual cycle of one year out in the provinces, one year in the city, had elaborately painted murals on their walls depicting their greatest triumphs so that bragging slipped more casually into the conversation. Kaius would not be entertaining guests here.

He took off his robes for the first time since he was given them and crouching by a drain he used a pitcher full of cold water, probably intended for drinking, to clean the ash from the crevasses of his body. He folded himself up in the bed meant for a child, feet pressed flat against the foot-board, bald crown pressed against the headboard and eyelids pressed together just as firmly. He slept until he the heat rose in the east, he did not dream.

A new set of robes were laid out on his desk by the door when Kaius awoke and he was surprised that movement so close had not woken him. Back during his training any movement in the room would have had him on his feet and reaching for his wooden sword. He set the thought aside, he would simply stop sleeping again if it left him so vulnerable.

He walked through the early heat as the crackling galvanic lanterns built into near enough every ivory building burst into blue life ahead of him, flooding the city with garish colour again. Seeing it all unfiltered by his armour was even more dazzling but his face was fixed in the impassive mask that was expected of him now, and it would remain so until he was off the city streets.

Perhaps it was politeness in the cramped conditions but he noticed that people walked differently in the city, arms tucked in close, taking careful steps, it made him and the travelling merchants stand out.

He nodded acknowledgement to a group of guardsmen dressed in shocking blue doublets of some noble house Kaius had never learned the name of and it seemed to inflate the egos of the young men. They strutted along like chickens.

He arrived at the Halls of Bone much quicker than he had intended to. His understanding of time had centred on his morning Forms for so long that without them he was having trouble keeping track. The Halls of Bone were once a spire but during some war or another the upper section had been sheared off at a sharp angle. The broken remains of the upper spire were still scattered through the surrounding quarter of the city, dragged around and then buried under the weight of progress.

Inside there was housing for anyone that could prove their knowledge of the Forms of Bone, in theory, had Kaius not been Chosen, he could have travelled to any city in the world and found lodgings among similarly trained men and women. Of course most students stayed close to home and those that didn't would find themselves frequently challenged to prove their mastery.

Knowing what he did now about the purpose of the Forms, he wondered why anyone was allowed to continue their study past the point it was clear they were not going to be Chosen. Some nobles pursued it as an art form, some commoners, if they had managed to pick up enough to wrangle their way in, would act as travelling entertainers, fighting the strongest men in villages and settlements across the provinces.

The forms taught the body the movements it would need to protect itself when the mind could not keep up with events. In any fight where speed was called there was a point, usually early on where you moved faster than the speed of thought. Then all strategy and cunning was cast into the wind and you had to trust in your Forms to win. A moment of uncertainty or doubt would be enough to kill.

There was an area on the roof of the Halls that had been sanded down, following the angle of the split in the spire so that there was high ground and low ground, where the Forms of Bone were practiced through heat and cold and where the supposedly friendly sparring between students was undertaken. With only one or two Chosen to serve Negrath each year it became essential to show your superiority, preferably by removing anyone of similar levels of skill from the immediate area.

It was to this training ground above the noise of the city that Kaius ascended through the bustling Halls unnoticed. It was empty when he arrived and he was shocked. He had never seen it empty in his entire life. Even during exhibitions and furtive duels there were usually dozens of students lurking around. He walked to the centre of the broad circle, turned to face away from the central spire and drew a deep breath.

He moved through the Thousand Forms of Bone slowly and gracefully at first, a formal perfection in every glacial fist and rising knee. Then, without calling speed, he ran through the forms again as quickly as he could. Then in reverse. Then faster. Then switching through the Forms like water. Feeling like he was home again for a moment at least. He spun through the Forms to defend against a sword barehanded, the forms to disarm an armed man, the killing forms.

Sweat ran down his forehead and stung his eyes, his robes clung to him in the unaccustomed heat generated by the thousands of bodies all around him. He moved through the forms until he had forgotten a time when he was not moving. His hands came up to block jabbing fists, he spun and leapt to avoid sweeping kicks and then drove forward with his hands like knives, ripping through the defences of his opponent. He performed the simplest arm lock, applying pressure to the back of the elbow and driving his opponent's face to the ground then stopped dead and remembered where he was.

There was black silk gripped tight beneath his fingers and Atius was on one knee, red faced with exertion and fury. His eyes sparkled with pride, not in his own skill as a Master of the Forms of Bone, but at his mastery of teaching.

Kaius released him and stepped back and only then did he hear the uproarious applause from the students of the Halls lining the edges of the building. Kaius flushed and hated them all for invading his private domain, Atius most of all, as that man at least suspected how deeply Kaius' need for solitude went and had arranged for it to be turned into a spectacle.

Atius brought himself back up to his full towering height, brushed sand from his knee and gave Kaius a polite smile, "I believe that you are ready for the Trials, Brother Kaius."

***

Malius could not be interrupted once he had started talking, "The Chosen of Walpurgan will be flying in as usual and I understand that the Chosen of Ochress will only consent to a single Marked meeting them at the ford of the River Moldan, most likely myself or Brother Atius. But you will need to meet the Chosen of Vulkas at our border."

The two men paced in a wide circle around each other as Malius droned on, "Carry our banner, wave our flag and show how honoured we are to be hosting this great event. Any of our Chosen could be sent to see them of course but I think it will be good for you to meet your competitor early on, try to study their movements, discern what weapons they will call, things like that. It will give you a chance to show them up a little too, you are practiced in walking around on the glass and ash, they will probably be skittering around like beetles on ice."

The students of the House of Steel were diligently moving through the thousand forms of steel with the bare minimum of concentration so they could surreptitiously watch Malius in action. The grace that the man lacked in his manners and behaviour all seemed to have been poured into his swordplay and it was a rare treat to see it in action.

Malius pressed on, "I can tell you that Walpurgan's Chosen will use knives or try to turn the Trial of Steel into a second Trial of Bone. Ochress' servant will use pole-arms; spears or tridents most likely. They will try to keep you at a distance and catch your weapon but a single parried thrust before you close in is usually enough to do the trick."

Malius paused frowning at the closest rank of students as their feet threw up little clouds of dust in perfect synchronisation, "It is Vulkas' Chosen that you need to watch for, they train in as many weapons as we do, probably more, and every one of them has a few favourites to switch between. They grow big over there too. As big as your fat friend or bigger. Perhaps they have more space to grow over there, or better food."

Kaius considered calling steel just so Malius would remember why their meeting had moved from his opulent offices in the War Spire down to the Arena at its base. Kaius persevered in silence, watching the young men and women in Malius' care moving uncomfortably through each of the Thousand Forms of Steel in order.

Over and over and over. He was pulled out of his reverie when Malius said, "You will be meeting Valerius tonight. I know we have no need to eat but do make an effort to look like you are enjoying yourself. It is an extremely rare honour to dine with the Beloved."

Kaius maintained the appearance of disinterest that was required of him but the news left him rattled. He had expected to do his duty, to fight and, hopefully win, then he would assume new duties as were required. It had never even occurred to him that his presence in the city would bring him within sight of the Beloved himself. He supposed that he should feel excited but truly just the jumble of new information left him numb.

Malius had stopped talking to admonish a young girl's poor

form and in the moment of peace Kaius committed himself to the only course of action that made sense. He called steel, wrapping himself in armour and ejecting his favoured curved blade into his hand.

Malius turned back to him and was taken aback for an instant before chuckling, "Of course, we are here to hone you aren't we."

Malius called his own steel, it rippled out from behind his back and engulfed him, settling into the familiar pointed visor over his face and a long straight sword in his hand. His voice came out of it, echoing ominously in the manner associated with the Chosen, "Repetition of the Forms is for these amateurs." he gestured to his trainees, "Let us see if you can score a touch on me."

They bowed to each other politely, eyes never leaving one another, then they moved blindingly fast to close the distance between them. In the beginning they were striking at each other tentatively. Neither was pressing their luck, both obviously had a wary respect for the other's abilities.

Enhanced by the uncertainty of their years apart. They began to fall into a rhythm, parrying and swiping at one another, never over-extending or taking risks. Malius spoke softly, over the clatter of steel normal hearing would not have detected it,

"I hope you understand exactly how much I have done for you. Back when you were first selected for service I had to argue with the other Marked to get you a decent posting away from the city. I had to fight every year to keep them from recalling you. They thought that it was spite, that I held some grudge against you from your training but the truth is you do not belong in the city Kaius."

They broke apart and circled each other slowly, legs crossing behind one another as they side-stepped. Then for an instant Malius called speed to close the distance and his strikes came in a shimmering flurry.

Kaius stopped thinking and kicked out under Malius' relentless hammering strikes. The older man leapt back out of reach and set his blade in a high guard, leaving his legs conspicuously open to attack, he started speaking again as he probed Kaius defences with feints.

"You don't belong in the city. You were born out in the dark and that is where you find your comfort. I saw that from your very first day here. You flinched from the light that the other children were drawn to like moths. I saw your purpose back then. I could see you raised up to the rank of Marked without you challenging my position here. No matter how skilled you were with the steel. How clever you were in your studies. You would never be a Master. Because that would trap you here with the civilised people."

Malius spun forward and when he came around to strike he had a sword in each of his hands, he used them together, one striking after the other, calling strength and shattering the rhythm of defence. Leaving Kaius off-balance just long enough for him to risk his next move.

Malius' arms swept out and then lashed at Kaius from both sides. He ducked beneath the whistling blades and then bounced back up for a vertical cut that Malius scoffed at, catching it in his scissoring swords.

The metal shrieked and sparks flicked off around them as they tried one another's strength. Kaius shuffled a half step forward, squaring his shoulders and bearing down with all of his called strength.

The ground beneath Malius feet began to crack, the solid earth had no choice but to give beneath the impossible strain. It was not enough to break the old man's guard. The pointed visors of their helmets almost brushed and Kaius could taste Malius sour breath. It tickled his face the way that it had back when he was just a boy in the Halls of Steel and it seemed that the heat rise would never come.

He could not see inside Malius' helmet but he knew from bitter memories the man would be smiling his lipless smirk.

The moment of distraction was enough. Malius relaxed his left arm, allowing Kaius blade to slip off to the side. Kaius back-stepped out of reach of his counter attack. Malius circled with his arms spread wide for a pincer attack, speaking softly between the harsh sounds of his breathing, "I could see you raised to Marked by my hand Kaius. I could see you become a powerful tool for Negrath, a leader for war against the other Eaters. I know that you would never turn on me because you would feel obligation to me as the one who raised you up. Because you would rather be out in the field than here conducting politics. Most importantly, because you don't hunger, you don't lust, you barely seem to care what is happening to you. All you hunger for is duty. It is most respectable. Valerius will exalt me for bringing you to him."

The pincer attack came but with a spin of his blade, Kaius caught both thrusting points and turned them aside. Malius had to leap back out of reach as Kaius fist swept through the empty air where his ribs had been a moment before. With that distance and the moment spare the Marked slammed his swords together into one, twisting his body to one side with the new sword set level to the packed earth. Then he snapped back.

The thrust would not have reached Kaius but while over-extending himself Malius called his steel into a great lance of flowing metal. Kaius barely leapt to the side in time, he skidded along in the broken dirt past Malius' side, abandoning his footing and form.

The steel flowed back down Malius' rear leg as he turned, covering his briefly exposed heel. His sword had returned to its normal length and with a blink of called speed and a slap to the inside of the fallen man's wrist   had the tip of his sword set at Kaius' throat.

Both men released their steel, breathing raggedly, and Malius offered Kaius a hand up, which he politely accepted.   On his feet again he found Malius still gripping his hand and pulling him closer.

The older man had a placid smile fixed on his face as he spoke softly, "And this is the final reason that I know you can be trusted. Because no matter how great your triumphs in the Trials or out in the world when we finally go to war, you will remember this moment. You will remember the taste of this defeat and you will remember that I was the one who defeated you. You will remember that I was magnanimous in victory. You will remember that if you cross me then I can destroy you. You will never turn on me," he met

Kaius' eyes, "Will you boy?"

Chapter 3: The Wanting of Things

Valerius sat at the head of a long table carved in elaborate designs of impossible animals and he sipped at a very watery soup that had been served only to the Beloved, the Marked and Kaius. It had a complex and very subtle flavour that Kaius suspected would be lost on anyone without their enhanced sense of taste. There were flavours of plants, actual plants, not fungi, and a meat other than insect that tasted so rich it left Kaius speechless. Even the aroma was enough to satisfy him. It seemed to be mainly for that purpose that it had been served to Malius.

It was not clear if his refusal to eat was because he did not wish to become as large as his rival Atius, who sat opposite him at the Beloved's left hand. More likely it was because it would have interfered in his endless talking with, or rather at, the few nobles that had also been seated at the table.

A great deal of debate went on between him and the woman to Kaius right. Enough so that Kaius wished to swap seats with her several times over. She was Arlia, the Pontifex of the noble quarter of the city, tasked with ensuring that the Eaters and more specifically Negrath were worshipped correctly, with the precise rituals and offerings that would most please them.

Kaius found it interesting that the task was not allotted to one of the Chosen, then the strictures would be applied evenly over the decades instead of being altered to suit each generation's personal interpretations. He considered that perhaps that was the reason that the task was given to someone who would age and die, to keep the public's interest with relevancy.

He wondered if just thinking these things was blasphemous but hoped that Negrath, or at least his most adored servant on this earth, would forgive him in return for his dutiful service. He realised that both arguing guests had turned to him for input. Atius looked up at them from a steamed red beetle that he was in the middle of cracking open with his thumb to reach the sweet white meat inside.

Kaius froze, considering fabricating some generic answer that would move the conversation forward and away from him. Unfortunately he had lost nearly all skill with words in his three years in the dark.

He set down his bowl and turned to face the Pontifex, "I apologise, it has been a long time since I have eaten such fine food and it had entirely occupied my attention. May I ask what we are discussing?"

Malius rolled his eyes, Atius chuckled and Arlia looked exasperated before saying, "The eating of human flesh as a sacrament in loving emulation of the divine Eaters of the Gods. How do you stand?"

Kaius blinked then answered honestly, "I killed ghuls on sight out in the Ashen Dales. They preyed on our working folk. Harassed them, stole their loved ones from where they were buried, snatched children and even killed travellers if they had enough numbers. The few times that beacon fires were lit and villages called for my aid these last three years it was to deal with hidden cults of ghuls, secret encampments of ghuls too close to their homes. On one occasion I was called to settle a dispute over whether a man gone mad out alone in the dark was to be killed as a ghul or imprisoned as a madman after he bit a man to death. After I cut him open we found no human flesh in his stomach so I told them he should have been imprisoned."

The Pontifex was staring at him open mouthed, Malius had his face covered by his hands and Atius seemed to be trying not to choke, his face bright red beneath the galvanic lights that the Beloved had so kindly ignited for their illumination while the rest of the city lay in its cold-time darkness.

The bubble of silence spread further down the table so Kaius tried to fill the silence with a continuing anecdote, "We did find some strange things in his stomach though. He had eaten some little stones, a couple of pieces of polished glass and even a little wooden toy bird. The wings still flapped if you pulled the string."

There was a strange, high pitched wheezing sound from the head of the table then a high pitched trilling that Kaius slowly realised was coming from the Beloved who, until now had been sitting silently throughout the meal. He rocked forward in his seat and pointed an accusing finger at Kaius, then rocked back and the trilling grew louder.

Kaius tensed, waiting for steel to be called against him. If he had offended the Beloved he would accept death peacefully. Atius was the one to realise what was happening first and joined in with the Beloved's laughter. Soon the entire table was laughing like sycophants except for Kaius and the red cheeked Pontifex who had pursed her lips and was clearly waiting for a chance to respond with vitriol.

Valerius spoke, his voice very high pitched but clear, his eyes tinted purple in the galvanic light, "Malius, you should have brought this one to me sooner."

Kaius smiled politely, "If he had done so then I wouldn't have had any stories to tell you, Beloved."

Valerius' benevolent smile flickered as his title was spoken then he replied, "I shall hear more of them from you and share my own. I retire for now. You may attend me at heat-rise if you wish."

Kaius rose too quickly from his seat and it made a screeching sound on the ivory floor, he bowed stiffly as Valerius rose, "It would be an honour."

The Beloved turned away from the table, passed between two steel-clad Chosen by the door to his private chambers and then was gone.

Kaius paused for a moment then moved to head out of the opposite door himself, but the rest of the table had returned to their food except the Pontifex who was staring up at him and tapping her fingers on the tabletop impatiently.

He settled back into his seat and Malius nudged him gleefully with an elbow while Atius wobbled on his chair chuckling. The Pontifex laid a hand on his arm, trying to reclaim his attention and for a moment the level of tension in the room peaked.

Kaius looked at her hand on his arm and then up at her face, resisting instinct and training screaming at him to break her arm.

Atius spoke tactfully, "Wouldn't a Pontifex know that it is forbidden to touch the Chosen?"

She withdrew her hand quickly but the damage to her credibility was done, Malius would not engage with her again. One faux-pas of such epic proportions would cost her her position when the next elections came around. Her lost position would cost her family prestige and opportunities in the future. The system had a wonderful way of enforcing itself.

To show no ill will Kaius tried to continue the debate on the rightness of eating human flesh in attempts to improve yourself but she was too shaken to press her points. Even touching one of the common Chosen in so public a setting would have been scandalous but one of the Chosen who was participating in the Trials, one that clearly had the Beloved's favour, it was unthinkable. Her family may even expel her once her term was complete.

Kaius had forgotten how dangerous the ground was here, how softly they all had to tread so as not to disturb the mechanisms operating beneath the surface. Not to mention the tell-tale tremor that reverberated along his arm when she was touching him.

Malius leaned in close and with a theatrical whisper said, "I have had a few of my students come to speak to me after seeing you fight today and they wouldn't mind risking touching you as long as you could be discreet about it. Of course most of them are a touch younger and prettier than the last one to try it."

The Pontifex was flushed with shame and it was all Kaius could do not to pat her hand where it sat tightly gripping the arm of the seat. So easily any one of them could fall into shame but still the whole table made jokes at Arlia's expense.

Atius and Malius made a series of jokes about trying to dance with the Chosen without touching although the double meaning of the term dancing became apparent fairly quickly. Malius' students were doubly trapped by their Master, if they refused his advances they would be overlooked and punished, if they accepted then they had committed treasonous blasphemy and could be punished when they lost his favour.

Kaius returned to sniffing the porcelain bowl quietly but it did not smell so sweet as before now that it was cooling.

Kaius was standing outside of the Beloved's private chambers before heat-rise. Having risen early from a sleepless night to perform his Forms of Bone in a courtyard that he had found on one of the levels higher than his own cell.

Feeling suitably calmed by his uninterrupted session he was able to disregard several tersely written notes brought by attractive young couriers from Malius on appropriate topics for conversation with the Beloved. He had no such notes from Atius, he assumed that either the man trusted him to conduct himself well or more likely still hadn't sobered up from the hefty carafes of ant mead he had consumed during the dinner party.

Even before heat-rise Kaius found the temperature in the city and the spire particularly to be far too high. In here it was practically an oven. His layered robes, so practical out in the dark had been switched out for the thin ones worn during the fire season. They flowed more smoothly and the parts not sticking to him were very soothing to the touch. He found himself moving restlessly to let the air circulate while still trying to maintain quiet dignity.

When the lanterns along the corridor burst suddenly into light he let out his long held breath and stepped up to the solid brass of the doors. He did not know if he was supposed to knock or just wait to be admitted so he took the third option and pushed the doors apart.

As much as the city was more luxurious than the villages this suite of rooms was more opulent than the rest of the city altogether. A lifespan of centuries, infinite wealth and no voice raised to contradict you did not make for tasteful decoration. There was silver and gold reclaimed from across the Ashen Dales worked into the ivory of the walls and bed-frame, silk wall hangings woven from the finest produce of worm farms across the dominion and at the centre of it all, silhouetted in front of great stained glass galvanic lanterns was the Beloved.

His hair was settling gracefully around his face now that he was in from the balcony. He moved with delicate steps, not quite the normal mincing of the nobles, it had more confidence. He tugged a silk tie from where it was tangled around the bedpost and swept it up to tie back his hair. With the hair out of the way his cheekbones and jaw line were more pronounced, less feminine.

He met Kaius' eyes and smiled softly. He gestured for him to move forward and the two settled at a small table of solid copper, discoloured with verdigris around the top. There was a small smoke burner on the tabletop and for an instant Kaius was taken aback before he realised it was only incense.

They sat silently for a long moment then Valerius spoke, "Your honesty is what distinguished you last night. I would appreciate it if you would maintain that honesty rather than pursuing a course of flattery, self aggrandising and misdirection as my other Marked have done."

It honestly hadn't occurred to Kaius what they would be discussing, he was so overwhelmed that he blurted out, "I am not sure I would know how to do any of those things."

Valerius smirked, "My understanding is that you have been proven intelligent, both in your studies and your counsel, it is the greater part of why a Chosen is elevated."

Kaius leaned forward, "There is a difference between knowing about things and knowing when not to talk about things and I don't seem to have the knack."

Valerius leaned in to meet him, eyes darting over Kaius features, trying to read truth in their movements, "I swear this to you in the name of Negrath. For as long as you tell me the truth I shall not punish you for it."

Kaius nodded, then paused before asking, "What is night?"

Valerius raised an eyebrow so Kaius elaborated, "You said my honesty distinguished me last night."

Valerius chuckled absently, "Ah. I forget how young you all are sometimes. Night is just another word for the cold half of the cycle. Day was the name for the warm half, and for one complete cycle for some reason."

Kaius smiled along with the explanation then decided, as he would in the duelling circle, just to press on and trust the truth to protect him, "Was there something you wanted to speak to me about, Beloved?"

Valerius thought for a moment then said, "Tell me about the ghuls. I hear pieces of reports filtered through councils and the Marked but I do not hear what they are really like."

Kaius composed his thoughts and settled back onto the hard back of the small chair, "They look much like any person out in the dark, their skin is colour sapped, their hair is brittle. You can recognise them in their movements and sounds after they have been feeding for some time. Fresh ghuls are indistinguishable but the older ones or the ones born into ghul families, they move around as if they are calling speed but not using it, they are always twitching and moving. They giggle and cry for no reason too. It is very difficult for them to be silent and hidden so they rely on quickly unfolding ambushes even when it would be more tactically sound to let an enemy pass."

Valerius held up a hand. "Who do they consider to be enemies?"

"Everyone," Kais replied without hesitation, "The moment you stop thinking of people as people and start thinking of them as fodder to pick over and dish out, everyone becomes your potential prey. Most ghuls tear themselves apart before too long if they do not have ready access to supplies of food."

Valerius cast a glance over to the balcony and asked, "If there were ghul living in the city, operating in secret, how would you ferret them out?"

Kaius looked hard at the apparently disinterested profile of the man before him, "Are they truly operating in secret or do you already have suspicions about certain groups? Perhaps religious groups?"

Valerius scowled back to him, "Do not overstep yourself. If we had no knowledge of them, what is the best way to destroy them."

The problem was too complex for Kaius to consider, he thought of a half dozen partial solutions then answered, "The best way would be to remove the source of food."

Valerius sighed, "Emptying the city is not an option."

Kaius shook his head, "If they are hidden in your population then they will just travel with them and feed in a new location. You need to make the meat inedible."

Valerius gestured for him to proceed after a moment, "Poison everyone. Not lethally. Not even with enough poison to make them sicken. But with a poison that lingers in the flesh. That builds up in the body and sickens you once you have too much. I recall hearing of certain heavy metals that could serve the purpose."

Valerius face remained impassive as Kaius outlined his plan then cracked into a genuine smile when the younger man was finished, "You would have made a great Beloved if you had been born correctly. I feel like so much of my work is poisoning our people for their own good."

Kaius was unsure if that was meant to be a compliment. Valerius moved on. "You are to be my champion in the Trial of Steel. I understand that you would have been better suited to the Trial of Bone." He paused to see if Kaius would argue then went on. "I have been told that your skill with the sword would have been sufficient to win out against the last few years crops of contenders, excluding Vulkas' beasts. The prestige of a win in the Trial of Bone would not justify your ascension. Something that dear Malius has been campaigning for the entire time that he was simultaneously fighting to keep you out in the provinces instead of here, protecting me from harm as is your duty."

Kaius interrupted, "I am still protecting your interests when I am out among your people Beloved."

Valerius swatted at the air, "Not Beloved, not here. Valerius. It is my hope that we can form a bond of friendship as well as servitude Kaius. Titles and inequality will stand between us," he conceded, "I acknowledge that you were doing good work out in the Dales. I do understand the value of having Chosen out among my people. I do understand the value of those people who live out in the dark. But I have so many years weighing down on me and so many more still to go. I am surrounded by these sycophants. These deceivers would tell me anything they think I want to hear if they thought they could curry my favour for even a moment. How they do not realise that all deceptions crumble with time, that I will always see through them in the end, I do not know."

Kaius remembered to shrug his shoulders, "Sometimes people can't see beyond what they want in the moment."

Valerius licked at his thin lips and finally asked, "What do you want Kaius? What makes you happy?"

He considered it for a long moment, it was not something that he had ever given much consideration to, "I want to do my duty in service to Negrath. I want to serve you to the fullness of my abilities."

Valerius set his jaw, narrowed his eyes and snarled, "I do not want platitudes and flattery, tell me the truth or I will have you cast back out into the dark for the rest of your days."

He glowered across. Watching Kaius' face as it shifted from surprise to a flash of anger then confusion. Valerius called speed and snared Kaius chin between manicured fingers, he looked up into the taller man's eyes and slowly his expression softened into surprise, "In Negrath's name. It is true. Isn't there anything that you want in the world?"

He released Kaius chin and let him speak, "I have never had the opportunity to want anything since I was Chosen."

Valerius stalled him, "Before you were Chosen, when you still had need for things, what did you want then?"

He realised the answer even before Kaius gave it and they said it in harmony, "To be Chosen."

The heat had grown oppressive as time flitted on. Valerius had asked questions throughout their time together. Ostensibly it was always to learn more about Kaius, to understand his position on the issues of ruler-ship but in reality he was gaining perspective on the things that his other advisers withheld.

As cold fell the heat in the room just went on rising. Valerius casually discarded the upper half of his robes and lay on the bed. Kaius let his eyes trace over the strange patterns of Valerius torso. The odd ridges of bone protruding amidst the carefully sculpted planes of muscle. If you had no knowledge of how a human body was meant to look then they were quite beautiful as delicate decoration. If you were attached to the traditional notions of beauty without mutation then they would have made your skin crawl.

Kaius felt nothing. Not in the usual, deep cold way that he felt nothing at all. Aesthetics were not an area of intense study for the Chosen and Kaius could not recall much of his time before coming to the city. He could recognise the layout of anatomy that was meant to be attractive through observation of the reactions of others but he had no strong feelings about them himself. Valerius watched him for a reaction and seemed halfway to disappointed that there wasn't one.

The conversation continued until heat rise was approaching and they were both laying, propped up on their elbows as servants fetched in more iced water. The conversation had come full circle by this point.

"I have been enjoying our conversations. I believe that we shall continue to have them for as long as possible," Valerius held up a hand before Kaius could interject, "I am aware that Malius wants you back out in the field as soon as you are Marked, waging war on the other Beloved. But it is not Malius' wants that you serve. It is mine."

After so long it seemed unconscionable to Kaius to be less than honest, "I would be more comfortable waging war than in the city. I enjoy the solitude."

Valerius pointed at him and smiled, "I knew that there must be something you liked. Just a shame that it excludes me so completely."

Kaius moved to apologise but Valerius overruled him swiftly, "What is your favourite thing about being alone out there in the dark?"

Kaius closed his eyes and pictured it, so far from the luxurious linens he was stretched out on now, "It is nearly silent without people to make their noises. The natural sounds become part of the silence. Around this time of day when others are sleeping I can release my armour and feel the wind on my skin. I can perform the Thousand Forms as they were meant to be performed, moving closer to a better understanding of them each time. It is peaceful."

He opened his eyes to find Valerius' face mere inches from his own, staring at him intently, "All that you wanted was to be a warrior for Negrath and all that you enjoy is complete peace. I understand that many of my nobles have similar tastes to you, they find a willing partner to chain them and beat them and make them act as slaves. They enjoy the pain, just as you must."

Kaius leaned away from Valerius slowly, under the pretext of reaching for his glass of water. He shrugged a shoulder, trying to be nonchalant about his discomfort, "If I wasn't Chosen I don't know what I would be, I have no trade or skills beyond war. Perhaps I would be dead by now, or working to sift gold dust from the ash in the Dales."

Valerius smiled warmly, "I am glad that you are here with me instead."

The heat within the sweltering chambers increased once again and Valerius seemed startled, "I seem to have lost all track of time. Excuse me while I light the city."

He rose from the bed in a fluid motion, walking to the balcony and exposing his back to Kaius for the first time since he had shed his robes. There were lumps running down the sides of his spine and out along the ridge of his shoulder blades, some were larger and brighter red while some seemed more subdued. There was no logic to which grew where although the ones closer to his head seemed uniformly larger.

He glanced back to the bed over his shoulder, his hair was working its way out of the tie and hanging loose about his face, "I imagine you have never seen someone call anything but steel, would you care to watch?"

Kaius followed Valerius to the balcony where the Beloved of Negrath grasped hold of a pair of copper rods and smiled widely, "Stand back please."

He called the storm. His arms shook as the galvanic force pulsed through them and blue sparks crackled and fluttered all over the uncovered parts of his body. This was why the servants of Negrath were feared by the other Eaters, this lightning could pass through called steel and cook you within its shell.

The called storm could bring down enough rain to wash away the Ashen Dales or to irrigate enough farms to support a dozen standing armies. The city beneath them came to life and lit up in layers, starting from the central spire and rippling out.

Valerius turned away once the city had been awoken and gave Kaius a mischievous grin, stepping closer he pressed his hand flat onto the younger man's stomach.

Kaius shuddered as everything around where Valerius touched tightened and hardened for a moment.

Valerius bit his lower lip and giggled like a child made large.

He reached the hand up to run it over Kaius bald pate still laughing, "Don't worry, it is quite safe now."

Kaius did his best not to flinch at the unwanted contact. When Valerius realised that he wasn't enjoying himself he took a half step back and wiped his sweat slicked hand on the silk overhanging his belt. He pursed his lips and said, "You will be meeting Vulkas' Chosen at their border of the Glasslands two days from now. You should devote your attentions to your training until then. Following that, you will be tied into the events of the Trials for several days at least. After all is said and done you will return to me and I will raise you to the rank of the Marked. Then we can resume this conversation. My friend."

Both men bowed formally to each other but their smiles were genuine. Kaius was relieved to find the Beloved to be all that he expected from the highest mortal servant of Negrath and he was honestly relieved that he had not been found wanting himself. He enjoyed the illusion of friendship but in his heart he knew it was probably just a ploy to control him, as he had no particular vices to exploit. It was a most pleasant illusion. Kaius had never had a friend before.

Chapter 4- The Silver Scale

Lucia decided after feeling the cycle of heat and cold pass over her several times that she was not just going to die in her sleep, however much she might have wanted to. Thirst and hunger had reared their ugly head despite her situation. Neither her legs or one of her arms could function and she could see bone protruding by her elbow.

There was pain in every part of her body, and when she tried to move it reduced her to shrieking as her bones ground together and her bruised flesh dragged along the floor. Her one good arm was enough to prop her up and gradually her eyes adjusted to the diffused starlight coming through the distant glass above.

She was in some sort of courtyard, surrounded by carved stone arches, at one side there was a fountain depicting the victorious Eaters, finally ending their war on the gods by consuming them. Whatever mechanism had once pumped water up to spray from the great dragon at the centre's mouth had been long out of use but a short length of copper pipe protruded and she could swear that she heard a trickle of water.

She left a red trail behind her as she pulled her way agonisingly slowly across to the fountain. In the basin there was a slimy mould growing but in between its putrid swirls she found little pools of moderately clear water. She drank her fill, mouthful by sour mouthful. Then she just rested, leaning against the side.

It was an old carving, older than any she had seen in the cities. She recognised Negrath of course, with his lightning bolt in hand. She saw Vulkas with his great sword held up in triumph. She saw Walpurgan, hands hooked into dripping talons, although she had a strange sickle shape carved in the sky above her that Lucia didn't recognise. She expected the next to be Ochress, riding a great wave with a spear in hand but it was not. She realised that she had not dragged herself around to the far side of the structure yet so it had to accommodate more than just the four Eaters.

She frowned and forced herself to move around. "Not like I have anything better to do," she muttered through cracked lips. The next eater was clad in colossal armour with extremely harsh edges, the one after that was clad in flowing robes and had her hands raised up to what looked like a ball of fire in the sky. The final Eater, before she came around to Ochress with a fishing trident, was little more than a child elevated from the ground on what may have been a gust of wind or a cloud.

Lucia's stomach cramped and when she curled herself around it, she pulled on every injury across her back and body. She whimpered for a moment before she got control of herself. Terrible injuries were no excuse to complain, she thought to herself.

Looking at the dragon at the centre of the carving, its wings torn and its scales broken she started to sing the chorus of Great Dragons Dance to herself. It was her favourite part, before the brave Chosen came to drag them down from the sky and bury them in the ground forever more so that the people could mine their metals.

When the song was just about fire in the sky and the beautiful beasts that the world would never see again. Her eyes were drawn back to that ball of fire above the robed woman and she tried to let her mind accommodate the idea that once there had been seven Eaters and now there were four.

It was blasphemous, obviously, but it left her fixated on a single idea. This meant that the Eaters could die. It was a chilling thought, without the Eaters to protect them, who would keep humanity safe. Her stomach, full of cold water and nothing else twitched again. She was going to starve down here in this cavern under the glass, she was going to starve and there wasn't anything that she could do about it.

She was still singing the refrain to herself, "Dance dragons, dance. This is your last chance. So dance a dragon's dance. Their steel is called for you."

She stopped herself, both because she didn't want to waste her energy and because she didn't like the end of the song with the Chosen triumphant and the dragons lost from the world forever. It had a melancholy note to it that she did not need right now.

She dragged herself to the far side of the courtyard as a comet soared past overhead, lighting up the entire cavern with shifting green tinted light. There had been a city here, all turned to ash and rubble, some buried down here and some left on the surface. The cavern was a great bowl that she had landed on a distant edge of and at its centre there was a great star-burst shape of soot. She crawled through one of the open archways in the direction of that great explosion but something stopped her.

Wedged, tip down between two flagstones was what looked at first like a pitted shield but as she drew closer she saw that the tapered shape was not dented, it merely had a grain running through it. She reached out a hand to touch the scale as it glimmered. She touched the side and traced an edge sharp enough to slit her hand open.

Something gave her pause, she brought her fingers to her face and sniffed at them. She could smell cooked meat. Her stomach growled and gave her a jolt so she pulled herself towards the scale, then past the scale to look at its rear side. Growing from the rear side of the scale, charred and blackened near the edges and juicy and tender near the centre was stringy meat.

She had torn a handful away before she even realised what she was doing. This cavern had not seen a human being in so long that it was impossible that this meat was still safe to eat. But as he hunger grew she brought it closer to her face and sniffed it again. It smelled delicious, not like the beetle meat that they had to subsist on out in the dark, it smelled red and ripe and before she stopped herself again she moved it from her nose to her mouth and took a bite. Clear juices ran down her chin and she moaned at the taste.

She ate the rest of the handful, then eagerly pulled more of the stringy flesh off of the scale, even tugging on a ragged tendon that seemed to stretch down between the flagstones to dislodge a hunk of meat that was hiding there, barely harmed by the fire. It was still a bright red and she could feel it pulse in her hands before she bit into it. The sweet salty flavour of life ran down her throat. She ate every piece of meat that she could tear from the scale then she pushed her face against it and scraped her teeth over the metallic surface to remove any last remaining scraps.

Her stomach was distended by the time she had finished eating and she realised with horror that she had finished it all. There would be no rationed food to keep her alive as the cycles went on. She didn't understand what could have so completely overruled her reason. She lay down on the flagstones and fell asleep until the heat rose again.

Lucia was burning in a shell of steel. A cocoon of it was wrapped tight around her in her fever dreams. She was being roasted inside it and as she grew hotter and hotter her skin cracked and peeled, revealing the shining scales beneath. She pressed against the cocoon as she grew larger and larger and when she burst free her wings spread so wide that the shadow covered the entire world.

It was a disappointment to open her dry eyes to see the ash covered flagstones. She pulled herself, hand over hand, to the fountain, dampened her fingertips and rubbed them on her lips and eyes. Her skin was hot to the touch and her vision slipped in and out of focus. She stood up in the centre of the fountain and sucked a slow trickle of water from the copper pipe in the dragon's mouth. She wished that she had a light so she could at least tell if what she was seeing was real or a blurred imagining.

Her eyes slipped further out of focus and she saw some sort of ragged script on the stone, glass and ash laying around her. She saw little fragments of words she didn't know drifting through the air, then duller than all the other words she saw one that seemed familiar to her.

Pressure built in her head as she looked at the word intently and the pressure was suddenly released as the word lit up in the air. The pupils of her eyes had divided into two, connected tenuously in an hourglass shape but as she returned her focus to the real world, so too did her eyes return to normal.

There was a flicker of flame hanging in the air where she had conjured the word, barely larger than a candle's wick. Some of the foul smelling gas drifted through and caught alight with a flash. Her body gave out, emptied of energy, and she toppled to the floor again. She was dimly aware that some part of this impossible thing that she had done was missing.

The power flowed from her, emptied her, but it did not flow into her. It was like realising for the first time that something valuable had been stolen. She drifted back into her fevered dreams, steam rising from her skin wherever water had touched it, without ever having realised in her feeding frenzy that her bones had set and her wounds had closed.

Chapter 5- The Girl in the Glass

Still harbouring a quiet resentment to Atius for his involvement in the shaming of the poor Pontifex, Kaius went through his Forms of Bone in his private courtyard. The Beloved had gifted it to him for what was ostensibly the rest of his stay in the city, but could very well be the rest of his life.

The ivory pillars that surrounded the central square had phosphorescent lichen coiled up them, dousing the packed sand of the floor in an ambient green light. He had moved through the forms around twenty times since being dismissed so casually by the Beloved. His mind churned as he went through each of their conversations until it was just a confusing blur, so now he took to the Forms. Running through them until his mind was silent.

Malius approached the courtyard and waited politely until Kaius had finished his last set.

Back when Kaius was learning the Forms of Steel under his

tutelage there was always an extended sarcastic commentary after he had finished. Malius seemed to be reaching for something to say even now but eventually he gave in and fell silent, allowing Kaius that moment of respect before moving on to business, "Has the Beloved informed you of our schedule?"

Kaius smiled, "I am to meet the Chosen of Vulkas at their border. The Beloved did not inform me if I was to travel alone or in company."

Malius scratched at his upper lip, "If one of the Marked go it shows we have no faith in your abilities. If you travel alone then it might be a little too tempting a target, the two of them could work together to eliminate you from the contest before it has even begun. Seek out Sister Metharia as you are crossing the Ashen Dales, she can accompany you, give you a bit of fun too I will wager, such a sweet girl."

It was Kaius' turn to look uncomfortable, "I had promised to bring her news from the city when I was next in the Dales, this will be a good opportunity."

Malius smirked, "Well, you can tell her that her favourite instructor is looking forward to seeing her when her assignment ends. You can tell her that her family still fares well although the city is abounding with rumours that her grandfather has taken a new lover and has been devoting cycles of attention to him while neglecting the affairs of state."

Kaius looked perplexed and Malius pinched the bridge of his nose, shaking his head and explained slowly, as if to an idiot, "The Beloved is her grandfather."

Kaius still looked perplexed and Malius had to assume it was an affectation, that Valerius was trying to keep him secret very poorly. The Beloved must have wanted it known or he wouldn't have been so blatant in giving his attentions.

The possibility that Kaius genuinely hadn't become the Beloved's latest acquisition did not cross Malius' mind so he side-stepped the issue, "Shall we begin with your training again?"

Kaius took a long moment then shook his head, "Our last session made it clear to me that once our level of skill in the Forms of Steel has been reached it becomes less about training and more about cleverness, about tricks and misleading your opponent. And with all due respect, I believe that was the lesson you were trying to impart on me and repeating it will not help me further."

It was the longest sentence that Kaius had ever said to Malius and he was surprised at the hidden depths of understanding under the younger man's simple facade. He seemed pleased, "Very good. What shall you do with yourself until it is time to meet with whatever slab of meat Vulkas has furnished us with this year?"

That was simple, "I am going back out into the dark. I need to find Metharia before the day and the Ashen Dales are a very large area to cover. If I am very lucky I shall be attacked by some ghuls and add their dirty tricks to my repertoire alongside yours."

It took Malius a moment to realise that he was making a joke and join him in a smirk, "Kaius my boy. I may have taught you all the dirty tricks that you know, but I haven't taught you all the dirty tricks that I know."

It took only an hour or so to lay hands on proper robes

again and make his way out of the city. Now that he was known he did not need to delay at checkpoints or have to snarl at the pushy insect vendors. One of the smoke vendors, possibly the one from before, possibly not, had his back to him as he walked through and struck him with a censer full of his product.

Kaius called strength almost without thinking and crushed the perforated brass orb in his hand. The vendor had greasy hair cut in last season's style, shaved up the sides, and she flicked it back out of her face with an angry pout on her face before she followed the censer chain to his fist, then up past his purple robed chest to his face.

She let go of the chain and Kaius dropped the still smoking mess onto the ground. "Such sorrow, Chosen. Forgive me. Let me drown in my sorrow."

She dropped to her knees and he stared down at her with impassive eyes, he looked away, across the pots arrayed on her barrel's top and asked her, "Which of these begins to smoke the fastest when lit?"

Her terror was quickly transformed into avarice as his words penetrated the drugs haze, she thought for a moment then pointed to a large green urn. "Morton's weed burns up the fastest but it is a weak flavour, I could make you a blend of some of the strongest, finest herbs from across the.."

He cut her off with an upheld hand. "Blend something slow burning with the Morton's weed, I want it to produce instantly when I set it alight and clear within a few minutes. Can you do that or do I need to seek out a more competent apothecary?"

She poured a dash of what smelled like vasca oil into a wooden bowl, dropped a handful of the Morton's weed then sprinkled in a few dried clumps from the other clay pots before crushing it together into a dirty little grey-green cube that she held out to him.

He lifted it up from her palm without their skin coming in contact and tucked it away inside the waistband of his robes. He nodded politely to her still outstretched hand and said, "My thanks."

Then he walked out of the city gates without looking back, calling steel and speed the moment he was past the press of people moving along the roads by the city.

He passed the mushroom and insect farms that fed the city. Their soil enriched by the ash blowing in from the west and kept moist by Valerius' summoned storms. Then he reached the first great grey dunes of ash piled up on the dark soil. His passing threw up a cloud of dust and dirt behind him. He casually leapt the soot clogged river that marked the official border of the Dales and skidded to a halt, looking back at the city with a moment of wistfulness, the feeling surprised him.

He built up speed again before he hit the shifting desert. It took him half of the cycle to cross over to the Glasslands, at their border he saw the first signs of Metharia's work. The village by the border was burning, the plume of smoke disappearing into the empty black sky, it had been home to a ghul two years ago and he assumed it was home to the thief he had killed just before being recalled. The hovels were mainly underground, reinforced against the weight of constantly shifting ash with salvaged wooden beams that were now burnt away. The entire village was collapsing under its own weight, the bodies buried unseen and the fires smothered.

Kaius mounted the tall dune by the Glasslands and looked out for the tell-tale glint of steel but even with the extra height he could not make Metharia out. He released his steel and closed his eyes, sniffing at the air and cocking his head from side to side. The shifting ash was the only sound for a moment then he heard a distant whisper from behind him. He walked down to the plane of glass, his feet slipping a little on the smooth surface, he listen for another long moment, then crouched, putting his bare hand against the glass, feeling the vibrations.

He peered down through the blackened glass and he could swear that he saw a flicker of firelight beneath it. He walked across the glass, listening and looking for any other flickers.

Through the soles of his feet he felt a rhythmic pulse. He saw the shimmer of light again and he called steel into a heavy blade in his right hand. He drove it down into the glass and with a twist of his arm sent cracks off in every direction. He hauled it back out with a shriek and transformed it into a war-hammer of such great proportions that he needed to call strength just to hold it. He leapt into the air and brought the hammer down on the point of weakness he had created, punching a great hole into the glass.

He called the steel back around him as he fell, called speed, held onto strength and used the combination of his three gifts from Negrath to transform a deadly fall into an acrobatic display of beauty, leaping from one great shard of tumbling crystal to the next before he landed with a crash amidst the splinters of falling glass.

Little flickers of fire came to life and died in the dust filled air. He was in the midst of a courtyard, a stalactite of solid glass pierced the ancient flagstones behind him, sending something metallic clattering away into the night and bursting some buried plumbing into a quiet shower around him. It fell quiet as the last of the glass settled in place, then he heard a trembling voice making sounds he had never heard before, rhyming words with shifting cadence.

The music that he had heard in the city was nothing like this, it was all rhythmic clanking of metal and ethereal wails and he had been informed at a very early age that it was beyond his intellect to appreciate. He came around the side of the block of glass and saw the girl lying with her back propped against a fountain.

There had been a lot of noise for a few minutes there, but Lucia was well past the point of believing everything her eyes and ears were telling her. Sometimes she could see something like writing, sometimes it was more like tangled threads woven from starlight. Other times it was nothing at all but she could hear footsteps on top of the glass a few miles away.

She waited until the worst of the noisy hallucination had past and went back to singing The Ballad of Kurgan Hall. The brave Chosen had just barred the door to the village hall with all the people inside and the demons were circling. His steel sang against their armoured hides and the tempo of the song kept building until there were no more breaks between the lines, only an endless stream of colliding words.

It ended abruptly when she saw the shape of a man come

into her line of sight. This was a new delusion. She perked up as it approached, the fever might still be raging but at least it had brought her some company, or an audience. She wished for a little light to see him by and a whisp of flame appeared to his side. He was wearing armour like the heroes in her songs. It had a pointed visor that hid his face but it was so simple, interlocking plates of steel without engraving or decoration.

She had always imagined it would be beautiful to see one of the Chosen in their blessed armour but this armour seemed to have been made solely for function. The only thing that could truly be called decorative at all were the skirts of purple cloth hanging around his waist and even they had practically nothing except a thin strip of silver worked down their edges.

His armour shivered and peeled back from his face then poured away out of sight. He crouched down and she saw him clearly for the first time. His brow protruded with no eyebrows over his narrow hooded eyes. His thick jaw set beneath an oval shaped face, as bare as a babe's and honey toned.

His face was an emotionless mask as he asked her, "What happened to you child?"

Her lips cracked as she smiled and said, "Slipped and fell."

He looked around her little pit, the fountain where she drank, the squalid corner where she squatted to pass the water back out again. He stared up at the broken glass above and took in the gap that he had not made. He pointed, "You fell from up there?"

She craned her neck to see, then nodded. He leaned closer, took her by the shoulders and shook her. She startled back to reality for the first time in many cycles. She was still hot but the shimmering threads all around her had disappeared and she could focus, a wild thought came to her, "Are you here to rescue me?"

He almost smiled, shrugged a shoulder and said, "Why not?"

He hauled her to her feet. Taking in their surroundings, he asked her, "If I throw you up to the hole, will you have the strength to hold yourself on the ledge until I get there?"

She looked down at herself, taking in her emaciated condition for the first time, "Um. Probably not."

He thought for another long moment looking at the great spikes of glass, bursting up from the sandy ground and hanging at chaotic angles from the thick sheet of glass above. He looked at Lucia then grabbed her by the waist, lifting her up off the ground and holding her there. He hefted her, judging her weight.

She stayed very still but asked him, "What's the plan?"

He grumbled at the interruption but she continued to look at him querulously until he answered her, "If I lift you and jump from one spike to the next before they break we will be able to reach the surface."

He realised that he was still holding her up and set her back on her feet, "But..." she prompted.

"The glass may be sharp, without my armour it may cut my feet too badly for us to continue, then we would fall."

"And you can't wear your armour because..."

"I cannot call my armour because it throws up sparks when I am moving quickly and there are gasses in the air that may ignite.

Which would most likely kill you."

She glanced around at the air as if she could see these burning gasses. "I haven't seen anything to make me think that there are any gasses."

He looked her up and down, "I have seen flames appearing in the air. What you might call marsh lights."

She looked at him for a long moment, then asked, "You saw them too?"

He cocked his head to the side, "Yes."

She started breathing faster, the world spun around her as she tried to decipher the meaning of this but before she could say anything he stepped forward and said, "Hold your breath and close your eyes. It will be easier."

Before she could think, he called steel, strength and speed once again, he seized her beneath the arms and he launched her towards the hole in the ceiling. Her eyes were still wide open and she screamed as she flew through the air.

Down in the dark she saw a blur as he moved, leaping from one shattering piece of glass to the next as he sped towards her and caught her around the waist. They soared up towards the hole in the ceiling and reached the apex of their leap just above the ash covered surface.

He landed gracefully on his feet while she dangled limply under his arm like a sack of root vegetables. He dropped her onto the surface of the glass with casual indifference.

He looked down on her with disdain. "Will you survive from this point on or do I need to waste more time on you?"

She laughed out loud and rolled onto her back to look up at the black faceless expanse of the moon overhead, the great round hole in the stars. "I will be fine now. Thanks. My hero."

He turned to walk away from her, looking back towards the Ashen Dales, hoping to catch a glimpse of Metharia. She rolled over and got up onto her knees before calling out to him, "Actually. Which way is the nearest city?"

He pointed towards the distant glow on the horizon, "The Ivory City lies ten cycles of walking in that direction. If you leave today you should miss the worst of the foot traffic surrounding the Trials," he paused, "Do you require food?"

She staggered to her feet, shaking her head, "Not very hungry. Thanks anyway. Is there a village any closer?"

It was his turn to shake his helm from side to side, "There was one, just on the border. But it has been destroyed. If you want to head further onto the Glasslands there will be mining camps."

She snorted, "I think I have had enough of the Glasslands for now."

Inside his helmet Kaius was smiling despite himself. He walked back to Lucia, "You are some sort of performer. Would you like to trade a song for my assistance?"

She pulled herself up to her full height and set her shoulders, looking up into the slit of the pointed visor, "I am a trained troubadour with a writ of free travel from the Beloved of all four Eaters. I have performed in the courts of the greatest houses in this land. You think I am going to sing for you just because you ask?"

He remained immobile, "Was that a yes or a no?"

She smiled again, "You don't strike me as a supporter of the arts."

His reply was still cold, "I have never yet had the opportunity."

In all his time out in the dark Kaius had never had cause to make a fire so it was with some degree of fascination that he watched Lucia building one out of the pieces of half charred wood he had hauled out of the ruined village.

When she demanded kindling he found a bisected body and pulled the woolly underclothes from under the boiled leather clothing. She saw what he handed to her and he watched as she wilfully ignored what it was while building the fire.

As she put the pieces of the fire into a cone she started to see the threads of light again and she recognised that same duller shape from before, growing brighter and brighter as she put the pieces into place until the pattern of fire had almost formed entirely of its own accord.

When Kaius looked away she applied a touch of concentration and the little bonfire sprung to life. Exhaustion washed over her again. She was coming to realise that each time she did this she lost some small part of herself and it would not return without some outside assistance.

When she glanced back Kaius was watching her intently, he had not seen or she was sure he would have reacted. He brushed past and sat on a half buried log opposite her.

He gestured casually with a steel clad hand, "You can sing now."

She tutted, loudly, "Lets try that again shall we?"

She stood up and gave a theatrical bow, "My name is Lucia and I shall be your entertainment. What is your name brave hero? That I might remember you in song."

He smirked, the first time she had seen his face move, "I am Kaius, Chosen of Negrath. I saved you from certain death beneath the surface of the earth. Sing now."

She scowled at him, "You are being rude."

He glowered back, "You are being disobedient."

She set her jaw and said, "A song isn't something you can demand. It is a gift that the singer gives you."

He stared at her blankly. She rolled her eyes and said, "Eaters save us. If you want me to sing you need to be nice."

He continued to stare at her, "Was saving your life at risk to my own considered to be nice?"

She sighed and said, "Yes. That was nice. Thank you Kaius."

He continued looking at her expectantly so she cleared her throat stood staring into the fire and sang Four Kings as best she could without accompaniment. When it came to the end the Four Kings went their separate ways to rule their separate kingdoms, their friendship over forever. He held up a hand, like a child in a classroom, when she acknowledged him. He asked, "Was that song about the Eaters?"

She was taken aback, "I suppose it must be."

He continued looking at her, confused, "If you do not know the meaning of the songs, why do you sing them?"

She was struck by the question and sat down to think it over.

"Most of the songs are so old I don't even think about what they mean. I know which songs are happy, which songs are sad. But I don't always think about the context. We have sung these songs for hundreds of years, I guess that they meant different things to the people that sang them back then."

He stared at her with some intensity now. "The words still mean the same things. Sing another."

He gestured for her to stand and she did, head still buzzing with the idea of meanings that never change. She thought of the coiled lights and the words, and the more that she examined them the more similarities she saw. To cover her confusion she began to sing Great Dragons Dance.

It was only when she came to the first chorus that it hit her like a cold weight dropping into her stomach that she was singing this blasphemous song to one of the Chosen.

She faltered for a moment then sang on proudly. If she was going to die after everything else she had just been through she was at least going to finish.

Her song came to its end and she stood silently with her eyes closed. Her lips trembled as she waited for the bite of steel but there was no way that she was going to show fear now. Time stretched out.

She cracked open an eye and saw Kaius still sitting across from her. There were beads of moisture on his cheeks that she would have called tears if the face beneath betrayed any emotion.

He swallowed hard, then said, "I am not familiar with some of the words that you used in that song."

She started shaking with relief, her voice quavering as she spoke, "Yeah. There are some old words mixed in to the older songs to make sure the rhymes still work. What didn't you understand?"

He cocked his head to the side for a moment then carefully said, "Betrayed."

Her mind raced as she tried to answer truthfully without compounding her blasphemy, "It means that someone you trusted has turned against you."

He stood utterly still as she spoke, "A word for when it is unexpected. I understand. And what is the meaning of valour?"

She thought back through the song, "I didn't sing the word valour."

He wiped his cheek and looked at the liquid there in confusion, "You sang it earlier, when we first met you were singing about a Chosen protecting a village."

Her jumbled memories were not availing her so she mentally ran through her repertoire of songs and said, "Were there demons? The Ballad of Kurgan Hall?"

He nodded and she pursed her lips, "Good memory. One word in a song you only heard once.""We are Chosen for our minds."

She looked at him, really looked at him properly, on his bare arms and beneath the tight section of his robes she could make out clearly defined muscles, but he was smaller than many farmers that she had seen and much smaller than most smiths and miners. He was strong enough to throw her around with ease and jump dozens of times his own height but it wasn't under his own power.

She supposed that it made sense to choose a man for his mind if everything else could be added artificially. She said, "Valour means... I don't know. It means behaving in a heroic way? Doing the right thing even though it is difficult. Maybe it means..."

Kaius was on his feet and moving towards her with armour flowing over him and a sword extending from his hand. She sighed and bowed her head. Blasphemy was punishable by death of course. But it seemed like such a waste to have escape from the certainty of the pit only to face it again now. Lucia was genuinely startled at the sound of clashing steel behind her. She stumbled away and a shower of sparks hit her.

Kaius was in motion, driving their attackers twin swords up then hammering them down towards the pointed helm facing up at him. Over the clattering of steel he heard shouting. A boot caught him on the knee, driving him back a step. He drove forward again with a powerful thrust and gouged along the steel covering his attacker's ribs.

The would be assassin released steel and he saw Metharia's furious face scowling out at him as she staggered back and landed on her backside. He had called strength without even thinking, it was a dangerous habit to develop.

She cursed at him, "What are you doing back here you fool? I thought you were rutting ghuls picking over the useless drizzle that used to live here."

She scrambled to her feet and kicked him again. There was a quiet clunk when it connected with his midsection. She yelled at him, "What are you doing out here Kaius! You are meant to be drinking and whoring your last days away in the city. Not drinking and whoring around my protectorate."

Kaius released steel and gave Metharia a half bow, "I have orders for you. You are to accompany me to the border of Vulkas' lands and escort me and their Chosen back to the city for the Trials."

She deflated a little and in a flat monotone said, "As the Beloved commands."

She pointed past him to where Lucia had turned away and was staring up into the sky. "What are you doing with her? Finally work out what that thing between your legs is for?"

His face was impassive once again, "She is just a traveller. I was seeking information. I was looking for you in fact."

He glanced back at Lucia where she had flung herself face-down in the ash and said nothing. He walked away with Metharia without a backwards glance.

They called steel and speed together and disappeared from sight. Lucia uncurled after silence had fallen, propped herself up by the weak warmth of the fire and tried to decipher the tangled bands of power that had been flowing across from the distant horizon. She sat there by the dying embers until heat rise.

Chapter 6 – The Titan in Steel

Now that he knew the relationship, Kaius could not help but see Valerius in Metharia's face, without the long hair her features seemed harsher and without the added centuries of practised grace her movements were rougher, although some of that may have been residual anger from the fight and what she considered a surprising defeat.

They sped all through the cold cycle across the diameter of the broad circle of the Glasslands. Coming to a halt they continued to slide until they ploughed into the ash-banks built up at the far side. Technically encroaching on Vulkas' lands.

They didn't scamper back onto their own land but they didn't wait around any longer than necessary to antagonise anyone. They released steel at nearly the same time and with an irritated grunt Metharia sat down on the cold glass. She scowled up at Kaius until he followed her lead and sat cross-legged, albeit with more grace. He was positioned himself to overlook as much of the border as possible. She stared at him and eventually said, "I guess you were picked for the Trials then?"

He nodded, eyes still on the horizon, "I have been granted the honour of representing Negrath in the Trial of Steel."

She continued to glower at him. "Why you? My steel was always better. You were the one obsessed with the Forms of Bone."

He shrugged, "I understand that it is a political decision rather than one of merit."

She fell silent for a few long moments then spat, "I could take you, you know. If you didn't spring up out of nowhere. If I knew I was going to be fighting you. I could take you."

He glanced at her sidelong, "If only real life afforded us such equal chances as imaginary scenarios."

Her face crumpled with anger and she looked completely unlike her serene grandfather, "Do you want to try me? I will cut you to pieces."

He looked away from her again with an enforced calm and said, "But then Negrath will have no champion in the Trial of Steel and dishonour would be brought to his name. To satisfy your anger you would do this?"

She snarled, "I could be his champion."

Some heat crept into Kaius voice as he said, "But you were not chosen," he turned to stare at her with wide eyes, "You were not chosen and I was. Do you think that this was an accident?"

She called steel and speed and was roaring across the shining plane of glass before he finished his sentence, she skidded to a halt with her blades crossed under his chin. He looked at her with disdain and said, "Stop being ridiculous."

Enveloped in steel he could not see her arms straining as she tried to contain herself. She stepped back from him and released her steel. Her cheeks reddened and her hands coiled into shaking fists.

He disregarded her completely and turned back to look at the great mounds of ash on Vulkas side of the Glasslands. He idly wondered what name they gave their version of what he still considered to be his lands.

Time passed. Perhaps an hour before he turned to look at Metharia again. She was still glowering at him with murder in her eyes. He sighed and rose, giving her a formal bow and saying, "Call your steel. Blunted, if you please. I do not wish for either of us to be harmed over such a trifling matter."

Excitement flashed over her face as she rolled to her feet, he held up a hand to halt her, "If Vulkas' Chosen arrive we must end this. Do you understand?"

She tutted,then shouted, "Come on! Stop talking. Lets do this."

They called steel and took their stances opposite each other. She called both speed and strength and came at him without hesitation or thought. She flowed through the forms of steel and fluttered into the forms of bone intermittently to take him off guard.

Malius had treated Kaius as an equal, assumed that his mastery of the forms was sufficient and that only superior cunning would win out. Metharia wanted to prove that she was better at a fundamental level, she wanted to prove that her skill alone would prevail. She was faster than him and the pair of swords kept him constantly on the defensive, whenever he was parrying one the other was already spinning around the other side of his defences. He held his ground against her, his feet planted in place.

Kaius watched her and wondered if this was how her grandfather would fight. He was rewarded for the distracting thought by narrowly avoiding a thrust towards his midsection. She was faster than him and she kept increasing in speed, she was well past the limit of called speed and sacrificing the power of her strikes, intent on getting past his defences and landing a touch, however light.

She was getting frustrated but she focussed that intensity into her tight movements. Kaius leapt away and she charged in once more, giving him no time to think, no time to counter-attack. He made one feinting thrust at her as she charged and she skidded to a halt, making a half dodge to the side, expecting Malius' ridiculous over-extension.

He danced back across the glass, keeping his footing but staying well out of her reach, denying her the contact she was obviously desperate for until she did exactly what he expected of her, bringing her two swords together in a shimmering blur and stripping the steel off her back to extend the blade in a great rippling spike towards him.

He set his feet again and slapped the flat of his blade against the side of the lance. He dashed forward, blade scraping along the side and throwing up a shower of sparks. She was recalling the steel around herself rapidly, trying to remake her weapons and armour, but with speed called, Kaius was faster than the quicksilver. He spun around behind her and playfully smacked the back of her thighs with the flat of his sword.

Echoing out of her helm he heard a squeal of surprise that twisted into a growl of fury.

He took a step away and released everything, taking deep slow breaths. Metharia spun at him with her swords back in hand, she swung them cleanly under his chin one after the other a hair's breadth from his throat.

She released her steel and turned away to spit onto the glass, her eyes were watering and her cheeks were red. She pointed a finger at him and tried to articulate her anger but it just came out as a loud grunt.

He bowed to her politely and watched her hands as they clasped into fists then released. Eventually she bowed back. They heard the Chosen of Vulkas approaching before they saw them and were both in full formal armour and facing towards them as if they had never been fighting.

The first of Vulkas' Chosen came over the dune, their armour had a solid face plate and the decoration seemed to be composed primarily of solid looking spikes, either designed to catch blades or to impale attackers. He bowed to Kaius and Metharia and gestured back across the ash dunes.

The head appeared first, then the shoulder spikes. The body took much longer as it rose up. It was only when its waist drew level with the top of the dune that perspective re-asserted itself.

The second of Vulkas' Chosen was close to nine feet tall and six feet across its shoulders. Its armour seemed to bear marks of its great muscles pressing outwards, curvatures and dips that normal called steel would not produce. It was so tall that the light of the Ivory City glinted off of the top of its helm.

Kaius could not think of it as a he, only as an it, no human was so large. In the Trial of Steel, calling speed and strength were forbidden. This beast would shatter his steel and bisect him with a single blow. This creature could crush him between its thick fingers without calling even a touch of strength.

Both Metharia and the first and smaller of Vulkas' Chosen released their steel and gave formal greetings. Kaius had never seen the people of Vulkas lands outside of their armour. They had even darker skin than Kaius but their eyes were larger and more rounded. Those eyes reminded him of Lucia's for a moment, then he set all thoughts of her aside. They would not help him now.

***

Lucia barely noticed that Kaius was gone now that she saw the thick cords running across the sky. As he left with the other Chosen, she watched the cords swell and pulse with light, different intensities and patterns played out and she realised that she could replicate them.

These were a simple weaving that she suspected she could create without even conscious thought. It would drain her, as every action she took in this other reality did, but she was still convinced that her new-found power would return in time. It made no sense otherwise. If you ran, you became tired. After rest, you regained your strength.

She lashed together the patterns that she had seen soaring overhead. She learned how to tether them to herself and then she drew on them gently. She looked down at her hands, her strength still draining away in a trickle and she forced the double pupils of her eyes back into their normal shape so she could make out the shape of her own flesh beneath this new pulsing tangle.

Her hand was flexing and twitching spasmodically. As she looked closer she could make out a cloud of dust and ash drifting away from her as her entire body minutely vibrated. Lucia rose to her feet, looked to the glow on the horizon and ran faster than she had ever moved in her life.

She made it over a half dozen dunes before she looked down at her feet for an instant, saw the blur and then tripped over herself. Falling forward and tumbling until she rolled up onto the packed ash of the road's surface.

Still shaking and flailing around she rose to her feet between the wagon tracks. Bit her teeth back together to stop their chattering and ran again. By heat-rise she was in the city. Having finally shattered the new weave before it completely drained her of life, she staggered through the city gates, utterly ignored. She was just another girl from out in the dark, here to see the show.

She found an empty shop on the edge of a slum and collapsed into the doorway to sleep. She gave a quiet prayer to any Eater that was listening that she wouldn't be disturbed until her energy came back, but she wasn't confident that anyone was listening.

The weave was still there. She could feel it burrowing under her flesh like an intrusive vine, but without her power flowing into it there was no more shivering. Just the dull ache of having changed.

**

Each step that Kaius' colossal opponent took made a clanging and clattering sound. He had not even made the pretence of conversation, he just watched as it walked along beside him. It had no fault in its balance, its movements were free and easy, unhindered by any old wound he could exploit. He appreciated the simplicity of its tactics.

It did not even look at him. It did not acknowledge his existence, much less that he could be a threat. It would be overwhelmingly demoralising if he had not already lost all hope. His only real chance would be for one of the other Chosen in the trial to fight this mountainous creature and kill it in the first round. The odds were not in favour of that particular outcome. So they walked and he watched and after several hours they began to gently call speed to get them to the city by cold-fall.

Atius greeted them on the plain before the city gates. He was chewing on a thick strip of dried meat, possibly some sort of proof that Negrath's servants were better fed. He bowed deeply to the visitors but his eyes only left the giant for a moment as he nervously sized up Kaius in comparison.

They were about to pass through the city gates, formalities fulfilled when Kaius and Metharia both sensed something wrong and came to a standstill, both cocking their heads from side to side before calling their weapons. Kaius shouted out to the circle of curious onlookers,

"Get inside or get on the ground. Now!"

Most just looked confused, a few, more educated, more scarred and more obedient subjects fell to the ground dragging their families and neighbours down with them as the piercing, all enveloping screech echoed off the city walls and across the plains.

Kaius and Metharia dropped into low crouches, eyes darting around the pitch-black sky, seeking their attacker.

Before they were even spotted, the owls fluttered down to land amongst the prostate crowd. Their great talons carved up the cobblestones of the road and drew blood from those unfortunate enough to have been beneath them when they landed.

With their wings spread, the owls cast shadows out across the farmlands. The people from out in the dark, far from civilisations safety, cowered in terror at the gigantic apex predators looming over them with their huge golden eyes and their dusky feathers.

Kaius moved to put himself between the pair of owls and the mass of people pushing past towards the safety of the city.

Metharia was circling around behind them, seeking a better position to strike from. One of the owl's heads swivelled to follow her as she moved until it was facing directly behind itself.

Kaius turned to look for Atius and found him bowing politely to the owls. A pair of women dismounted from the complex looking saddles attached to the owls' backs. They wore tattered grey robes in the cut of choice for the Chosen, the colour, or lack of colour, marked them as servants of Walpurgan, the Witch Queen.

They both had pallid skin and eyes like ice. They were so similar that Kaius would have gambled that they were twins.

One made a clicking sound with her tongue and the owls spread their wings wide once more and launched themselves into the air. They came to roost atop one of the towers spaced around the city walls and then were forgotten in the cavalcade of greetings and politeness that followed as each of the Chosen was introduced to each of the others.

Kaius groaned internally at both the endless prattle of it all and the depressing knowledge that he would have to do it all over again when the Chosen of Ochress finally arrived. He cast a longing glance first out into the dark then up towards the central spire of the city.

He had never been so far from home. He nervously hummed a tune to himself before he noticed the attention that it drew to him and stopped abruptly.

They marched through the city together, all eyeing each other carefully as they went, with the exception of the gigantic Chosen of Vulkas, who strode on as if the streets were empty. They arrived at the great courtyard in front of the city's central spire. Up on his balcony, Valerius looked no larger than a flea, a distant dark mark on the side of the ivory.

Through some trick of acoustics or called power, his voice echoed and resonated through the city. "Chosen servants of the Eaters of the Gods. I welcome you to our city. When heat rises next on this world, you will prove your master's strength in the strength imparted to you. You will prove their wisdom for choosing you to represent them in these trials. And of the four Chosen in each contest one of you will prove that your master deserves our respect for that choice. Die well, Chosen, and bring glory to your Eater and their Beloved."

Kaius was certain that Valerius was looking at him as he said the final line of his well-practiced speech.

Through the cold cycle Kaius was essentially confined to his quarters, followed around by the other Chosen of Negrath to ensure that no mischief befell him. He moved restlessly from that room out to his courtyard and ran through the forms of Bone over and over and over. He thought that he should probably be in steel, moving through those forms. But that didn't calm him and it was peace of mind that he required. The clarity to think when heat-rise came.

At one point, he heard Valerius' voice echoing through the throbbing streets once more and he knew that Malius had returned with the Chosen of Ochress. They were all here now, there would be no delay. Only the public drawing of lots while he was confined in the gladiator's cells, and the inevitable Trial of Steel.

Chapter 7- The Bloody Circle

Lucia woke twice in the night, startled by a booming voice that she took to be another hallucination. She was still feeble and aching all over, so she drifted away again soon enough.

When the first heat came, she was nearly blinded by the crackling blue lights bursting to life all around her. She saw a pattern within the lightning, similar to the one she called in flame.

She wondered where the power came from, enough to light a city. It would kill her to light a quarter of these lanterns. The power that she had found inside her was not returning. It was finite and she had squandered so much of it in her fever and madness, both down in the dark and rushing to the city for nothing.

She felt like weeping, damned her foolish hopes and let rage settle into the base of her stomach. She made it to her feet although she seemed to be carrying a leaden weight on every limb.

She shambled along with the crowd, following them

through the packed streets and crushing bodies. There was an unfamiliar structure ahead that they were dragging her into. A great round building made up of ivory arches with no roof. Inside the moving tide of bodies, she twisted around, taking in the knotted bands of light all around.

Throbbing veins of power burst up from the packed sand floor of the arena, coiling off over the distant horizons. But as she watched, being jostled along towards the cheap wooden seats, a dark coil wrapped its way around each one of them, dragging them together and constricting them until only a faint silvery thread was left.

The seats up here in the stands, so far from the ring, were practically splinters. She saw some man in robes at the centre of the arena, calling out the names of the Eaters in pairs in the same bone rattling voice that she had heard rolling over the city through the cold time. She had no idea of its meaning until she saw steel-clad men emerging from either side of the arena.

They ran at each other. From up in the stands it was hard to make out the exact action taking place but one of them seemed to be a woman and the other seemed to be a man wielding a spear. Lucia was distracted again by the silvery threads leading away from the contenders, she could make out the patterns and pulses that covered the contenders in steel. As she watched one fluttered and then snapped back over the horizon, untethered from the man in the ring. She did not know how much time had passed but the crowd around her had screamed itself hoarse.

One woman was weeping openly, another a few rows down

from her was handing out little bags of silver talents to grinning gamblers. There was blood on the packed sand and the victor was walking in a wide circle around the corpse.

She held her red tinted daggers up to the empty sky then released her steel. She was as bald as all the other Chosen, but it was hard to notice under the complex patterns of floral tattoos that covered her head and exposed arms.

Lucia's vision snapped back to normal and she staggered back and landed on the bench. Exhausted beyond reason, aching and confused by the visions that haunted every moment she was awake, she tilted her head back and open her eyes to the peaceful sky. Here in the city it was a flat black colour with none of the depth of the stars.

It all spun around her and when she looked back down she knew that some part of her mind must have broken because instead of two men entering the circle there was only one. Entering from the other side was a creature from the oldest songs. She started humming the Giant's Lament and the crowd around her soon picked up the tune.

Music in the upper classes of the city was a complex affair of discordant notes and overwhelming complexity but the common people had close ties to the farmers and traders. They knew the old songs and the Giant's Lament was one of the oldest.

***

If there was no hope then all that mattered now was for Kaius to die well as Valerius had so passively requested in his speech. He still held some hope. If the beast was slow or stupid he may find his way around it. It was a small hope, you were not Chosen if you were slow or stupid, no matter your size and strength. Vulkas' Chosen had already called a great-sword and was waiting for him to come with the massive slab of metal slung casually over its shoulder.

Kaius called his steel, trying to ignore the hundreds of faces staring down at him, trying to take deep breaths and relax. He cleared his mind as if he was about to go through the forms. Kaius called out his simple curved sword and took his stance.

Nothing so huge had any right to move so swiftly. No sooner had Kaius called his blade then the great-sword was already lashing down towards him. He stepped to the side, out of the forms of steel, already off balance. He didn't have time to regain his footing before the sword was already coming back across at his head. He ducked underneath then let his perspective shift.

He fell into the Forms of Bone where attacks were avoided, not countered with force. It gave him enough control to dance around the next three mighty, impossible swings. His breath was already coming hard and ragged, echoing strangely in his helmet, deafening him.

He released steel and without the armour's weight the next strikes seemed to slow. With the power of the weapon being swung at him his armour wouldn't save him anyway. The attacks seemed effortless, the giant's strength was so overwhelming that he could handle that great slab of steel like it was weightless.

Kaius watched closely as the blade swept past his face again, the broad centre tapering to a razor edge. Step by step, strike by strike, the giant drove Kaius back over half the length of the arena, almost to the gate by which he had entered.

One last overhead hack came down at Kaius and he sidestepped. When the blade stopped a hair's breadth above the packed sand, he knew for certain. He kicked the side of the blade as it was rising up and stepped inside the reach of the sword. His face pressed against the jagged front of the giant's armour.

He called his own steel as the Chosen of Vulkas back-handed him away casually. He heard the hollow metal echoing in his ears. The front row of the crowd saw his head snap back, his body fly and a savage grin appear on his face before his helm reformed over it.

He rolled to his feet and side-stepped another vertical slice. In his left hand he formed a sword-catcher, a sort of two-pronged fork. In his right he formed a hammer. His armour trickled away and thinned as he added more and more mass to the hammer.

He leapt back out of reach of another slice then stepped forward as the gigantic blade swept down towards him. He caught it with the sword-catcher and the impact rattled up his arm. Then he swung the hammer and snapped the hollow sword in half.

The crowd fell silent after the scream of metal. On the back-swing he struck the inside of the giant's knee. It toppled to the ground with a clatter.

Kaius reformed the two weapons into one great sword. Then he drove it point down into the centre of the fallen titan's chest. Blood burst up out of the hole in the armour, staining his sword, warming his hands, and spattering over his boots.

The armour melted away revealing a small woman of no

more than fifteen years at the heart of the false body. She was gasping and reaching a hand up to the empty sky, eyes wide, blood running down her cheeks.

The triumphant grin vanished from Kaius face. When he released his steel his face was back in its usual placid mask, he bowed politely to the crowds then went back down the stairs to his waiting room.

The rest of the day was occupied with the Trials of Bone. All of the city's students competed to be Chosen by Valerius. In the brothels around about a reduced rate was on offer as the courtesans tried to perfect their own arts in the unofficial Trials of Flesh.

Several of the city's noble men and women took time out of their busy schedules of languorous parties to attend some of the more upmarket establishments in vain attempts to improve upon their own skills. Some were judged to be at least the equals of the professionals.

In the arena, twelve new Chosen were selected from the line-up. They were the only ones still standing after the relentless brutality of the Trial of Bone. Negrath's servants had swollen by almost a quarter of their numbers. The finale of the event that had so thoroughly captivated the minds of the entire city would happen at cold-fall. Negrath's champion and Walpurgan's would battle in the Trial of Steel to prove their supremacy. Another Chosen would die for the favour of the commoners, though not one of them seemed to be aware of the event's purpose.

***

Lucia sat as still as a stone on her bench, though she was

jostled by the constant comings and goings of a whole city's people. She watched as the net of power knitted into the flesh of the new Chosen, she saw the new threads stretching down into the packed sand. She saw the broad, pulsing cord of power travelling from the pale robed man to the same subterranean source. He was incandescent with all of the cords woven into him, bound so close to the source of his power that he was practically becoming it. He had more of that vital energy bound inside him than Lucia had ever held within herself.

Reduced as she was now, he was like a beacon of light in a dead world. She briefly recognised Kaius early in the day after his triumph over the huge man and foolishly called out his name, though it was luckily lost in the tidal screams from all around her.

He had disappeared soon after and though she strained her new eyes to take in every detail of every face she did not see him again for the rest of the event. It was only as the stadium grew more and more densely populated, with nearly every person in the city trying to force entry that she realised he would fight again, and soon.

The pale man stood once again at the centre of the arena, dazzling in the directed galvanic lights. He held up his arms and the city fell silent. Some of the cords of power bound around him lit up and he rose from the ground on a round platform of steel, balanced on a pin-like post until he was hanging level to the middle rows of seating. He lowered his arms and spoke with a sonorous voice, "Walpurgan herself has sent us a message."

The crowd burst out into murmurs. The idea of one of the Eaters, walking amongst their people, speaking and writing, was all so alien to the people of the southern lands that the idea was almost blasphemous.

Valerius raised a hand and they all fell silent, "She says to us that when her champion defeats our own she will be Marked by Walpurgan. She will be ascended. Let it never be said that our master lacks the generosity of his sister. Negrath spoke to me as I watched the trials this day. His voice echoed in my mind. And the voice said to me, 'when our champion slays the feeble offerings of Walpurgan I will mark him before the heat can rise again.'"

His voice had gained in volume and intensity as he made his declaration, practically shouting by the end of it. The crowd was on its feet, roaring.

Lucia smiled bitterly. At least Kaius would have plenty of people cheering him on as he murdered someone else for their amusement.

***

Kaius walked up the stairs and this time he heard the crowd roar in approval. He saw them all in the blazing galvanic lights and up in amongst them he picked out Valerius' face, smiling down at him.

He called his steel as he walked across the rust coloured sands, armour and sword formed around him. He took his stance and faced the Chosen of Walpurgan, the visor of his armour hiding his wild grin.

Over the screams he heard the thumping of his heart and his own breathing echoing. A comfort now rather than a distraction. After all, he had almost lost that breath earlier.

The Chosen of Walpurgan were always women and this one

stood almost a head shorter than him. Her armour was infinitely more complex than Kaius' own, the faceplate was shaped like the face of a wolf. Further up, the helm transformed into a tangle of steel antlers. There were complex designs worked all over the steel itself and it seemed to be composed of far more plates than were necessary. Each scale was worked with a design of vines around the outer edges. She had a pair of straight daggers in a reverse grip and she crouched down in a wrestler's Form of Bone.

Malius' advice was holding true in that regard at least. In the dense forests and the warrens of tunnels that the people of Walpurgan called home, the daggers were the most sensible choice, but out here in the open his weapon's reach would easily outweigh the benefits of their speed. She gave a mocking bow to him and waited for him to approach.

A cry reverberated over the city, driving the screaming crowds to silence, an owl's shriek that made the first few rows cover their ears. The individual plates of Kaius armour chattered together. The sound stayed within the armour, crushing his head like a vice.

He felt his skin quiver and in that long moment of pain and confusion she was out of his line of sight. Her dagger pricked the skin above his kidney before he could move. He rolled away from the other Chosen but she stayed close, pressing her advantage with a speed that seemed impossible without calling upon her Eater's, and a ruthless efficiency.

She was inside his guard and it was only frantic movements that kept him from the dagger's thrusts. She kicked out twice, and hooked his feet back in closer when he tried to stagger away.

He abandoned his sword, seeing its futility and letting it fall to the ground as he danced back. It turned liquid as it hit the sand and began its slow creep back towards him. He brought his hands down to catch her wrists but he was always a moment too late and he narrowly avoided losing the tips of his fingers twice before he gave in, clenched his fists and tried to knock the knives far enough out from her tight routine to allow for some sort of response.

She was having none of it. If anything, her blows came faster, gashing along the inside of Kaius' arm on one side and a moment later slashing a line across the front of his chest.

It should have burned each time. The pain should have been sharp and every movement should have made it sharper but instead he felt numb. The cuts, shallow as they were, felt cold. The cold was spreading. Kaius moved slower now. Even if he could call speed he would barely have kept ahead of the knife darting in at him again and again. His thoughts slowed and the arena grew grey in his sight.

The knives hit him with a rough tug at his skin but there was no pain, there was no world outside of his breathing and the forms that he still moved through faster than thought.

A knife slashed his cheek to the bone and in his distant state the pain reached him. Still clad in full, useless, armour and unthinking from the poison he called his steel. The puddle of quicksilver still trickling across the sand in pursuit of its master leapt like an arrow to his hand as he toppled backwards to avoid the last slash at his throat.

He hit the ground with a clatter of steel and waited patiently, listening to his heart's slow beat, for the final blow to be struck.

The Chosen of Walpurgan had fallen to her knees a few feet away. Blood flowed hot and rich down the details of her armour, catching in every crevasse on its slow descent. Where the steel of his sword, had passed through her there was a small hole, only as wide as two fingers.

It had punched directly through her sternum. Kaius lay on his back looking up at the blackness above, all sign of stars stolen by the encircling lights.

With the Trials finally over the restrictions were released. He called strength and it was enough for him to rise up, first to sitting, then to one knee and finally with one last burst to his feet. The poison chilled him to the bones but he lived.

The crowd was roaring and cheering, then just as suddenly the sound disappeared into another brain rattling shriek. Kaius fell to his knees again, facing the wrinkled corpse of his opponent and the owl swooping down to protect her body.

***

In the stands, still propped up by the wailing crowd, Lucia watched the events unfolding. She saw the thick cord of power tangled in the owl's head, stretching off over the horizon. She saw the complex tangles surrounding the Beloved light up, dazzling bright compared to the dull glow of Kaius.

He moved between the owl and his servant in one graceful fluid motion. Lucia saw the patterns crackle to life within his robes before a dazzling blast of lightning lanced from the palm of his hand towards the owl, charring its feathers and drawing out another shriek. The crowd was moving now, running for the exits or pressing forward for a better view. The bird raked its talons through the air scarce inches from the defiant man as he gathered his power again, the beating of its great wings sent great circles of sand out around them and made the dead woman's body twitch on the ground with each sweep.

The screaming and lightning dragged on, moment after moment. Lucia never doubted that the beast would be defeated. If the man would just strike at the cord piercing its skull it would all be over. The owl, beneath the crushing weight of some greater mind, was terrified of this place, it wanted to be away in the sky. Lucia raised a shaking hand as the crowd pressed and swelled around her, she pinched two of her fingers together around the cord and tugged gently.

The thread of power snapped loose. It lashed around the arena then recoiled over the horizon. The end looked charred. The owl rose up only for another bolt of lightning to burst through its chest. It fell to the ground, the round golden eyes empty.

Valerius blasted it away with the flick of his wrist then turned to lift Kaius back to his feet. His voice resonated across the city, it swept out over the plains and farmland outside and he cried out,

"Your victor!" then he half dragged, half carried Kaius out of the arena with an arm gripped tight around his shoulders.

The city was silent.

Chapter 8- The Mark

Kaius woke up to a stinging sensation just below his eye. His hand snapped up to grasp whatever creature had wandered onto his face while he was resting and instead found soft skin and softer silk in his grasp. A trickle of water fell from the cloth in Valerius hand and ran down over Kaius lips, he tasted an odd blend of herbs in the mixture.

He looked up to the older man with his breath catching in surprise at the warmth in the Beloved's expression. Valerius spoke softly, "Do not worry, the scars will not last many years. You will be beautiful again in no time at all."

Kaius knew that he should have some response to this but instead he only felt a great discomfort. He was lying on the Beloved's bed, stripped of his clothes and bound with bandages in many places, predominantly his arms. He took it all in and risked a smile to

Valerius, and a small, "Thank you."

Valerius rolled his eyes dramatically and tutted, "Well I could hardly let my champion lie rotting in the streets now could I?"

Kaius face returned to its neutral position and he said, "It would have been disrespectful for me to rest in a gutter while my Beloved still works tirelessly."

Valerius raised an eyebrow, "Indeed. Of course I am working tirelessly now and there you lie."

Kaius began to pull himself up onto his tightly bound elbows only for Valerius to push him flat on the bed with a smirk, "I command you to rest here until the morning. Until heat-rise. Then you will accompany me about my business until I take you to receive your Mark. Are my orders clear?"

Kaius lay back gratefully and let his eyes close as he whispered, "Yes my beloved."

If Valerius noted the change in tone he did not acknowledge it as he tended to the remaining scratches and Kaius slept easily.

***

Lucia had found a silver piece underneath the stands, fallen from some merchant's pocket. She brushed past the vendors hawking their overpriced and dubious wares and made her way as far as she could from the arena before giving in and buying a fire blackened mushroom from a small shop.

She made it around a corner before she started stuffing it into her face. The first bite was delicious but then the next was overpowering. She retched while still trying to force the food into her mouth. She had to regain her strength somehow. She went on retching until she had brought up the entire mushroom and a great deal of bile that burned at her throat.

Tears ran freely down her face as much from despair as from the pain. She made her way further out of the city proper, into the tents and cobbled together shacks nearest the walls. The odd structures made mostly of outcroppings from the walls. She dragged herself into the gap between two of them, her knees wedged against her chest, and she sobbed herself to sleep.

***

Far to the north where snow swept through during the cold seasons there was a forest of petrified trees. They could have been pillars of stone, but they were still known as a forest by those that lived there beneath their crumbling boughs. Ensnaring them, binding them all together and preventing them from collapsing to the ground as they probably should have centuries before.

The vines were not natural. This too was known to the people of the forest. When exposed to a fire you could see that they were a green so dark that they were practically black. Of course, you would have to be quick about it. The vines did not tolerate fire in their presence for long and the traveller who offended them could very easily find themselves dragged down into the roots to feed the forest.

All of these things could still be explained by nature, as animals could move, kill and feed so too could plants, albeit slower. The reason that the Strangled Forest was disturbing was far more subtle. It could pass a traveller by for days without them realising what was setting their nerves on edge. Air swept in and out amidst the trees in a constant gentle breeze and the thick pods on the vines would pulse in time to that coming and going.

The forest was breathing. Rhythmically sucking in all the poisons in the winds and exhaling clean air. It was no wonder the people of these lands lived under the ground in their tunnels rather than suffer to feel that breath tickling over their skin each day.

Deep beneath the Strangled Forest on an old throne of what was once brass and was now verdigris, wrapped and bound down by thick vines of ivy, sat Walpurgan. While the others worked through their agents, she alone still spoke to her Chosen and her chattel. She looked for the most part like a woman, though a woman of unusual height. Her skin was grey, tinted in places with patches of white like a sickened elm.

She spoke in a rattle but there were always Chosen close by, using the pinprick of light from their lanterns to illuminate the bark and charcoal that they used to scribble down her every utterance. Her constant litany halted when the owl died, halfway across the world. She shrieked and stood, tearing without thought through the cocoon of ivy and bending the old metal of her chair as she rose up.

The rotten tatters of her garb fell away and with a clawed hand she took hold of the wrist of the nearest Chosen who froze in place and watched Walpurgan with terror in her eyes. The hag hissed and grasped at her head with her free hand then snarled out, *"Send word to Ochress and Vulkas. We are betrayed. Negrath has eaten of the Burning One, he turns that power against us even now."*

The bald women surrounding her frantically scribbled this down and one started to run for the door and the messenger owls when a root burst down suddenly from the ceiling and snared the woman by her collar. Walpurgan snapped, *"No. Wait."*

The crowded room shuffled in discomfort. Never had they seen their Eater in such disarray. Something of terrible importance was happening before their eyes.

Walpurgan's lips moved as she flitted through the options then she stopped as still as a statue once more. She released the bruised arm of the girl she had been clinging to, settled back into her seat and resumed her usual position and tone, *"Send no word to Ochress or Vulkas, but have letters ready for each of them warning that Negrath is destroyed and his destroyer will soon turn his attentions to them. Then send a note to Negrath. Tell him... Tell him that the one who burned him walks within his city. Send it to that boy of his. See what reply we get. And have the messenger fly the moment the message is handed over. I would not have her tortured for information that she doesn't have. Tell her to circle the city for a few days, stay well clear of Negrath's servants, but watch for the outbreak of chaos."*

A smile creaked across Walpurgan's face as her orders were carried out. She was living again in interesting times.

***

Static discharged onto Kaius exposed stomach a moment before fingers brushed over it, trailing up across his hairless skin to check the bandage there. The air in Valerius room was dry and hot as usual so Kaius had no way to judge how much time had passed, though the fact he could think clearly again told him the venom had left his system.

He flinched away from Valerius' touch, muscles across his torso contracting minutely and tugging on his fresh scars there. He opened his eyes to the brightness of the room. He was lying on silk sheets and he could not shake their clinging feeling. The discomfort ran to the bone. Valerius withdrew as Kaius sat up, fetching a cup of water for the younger man then muttering, "It is time."

Kaius dressed quickly in his new robe of black, more silk. His old robes had been disposed of, torn and shredded as they had been by the Trial. His other meagre possessions, all that he could carry in his belt pouches, remained, though the ash stained leather of the belt hardly matched his new station.

He moved with less grace than before he was cut and that was all the more apparent when he was so close to Valerius, who could have put a cat to shame. They left the guarded suite at the top of the tower and progressed down the great spiral staircase carved into the outer wall. They passed through the luxurious quarters of the Marked where Kaius would soon find a room.

Down through the stark barracks of the Chosen and then deeper still, past the kitchens and store rooms and the surface of the earth itself. Down here on the lowest floor the galvanic torches were replaced with burning oil lanterns, maintained by whichever Chosen had been the most spectacularly unimpressive in their duties.

There was a solid double door when they reached the lowest floor, it looked to have been made of solid, seamless steel. Valerius prodded Kaius forward, so he approached the door and then pushed against the impassive surface. It had no effect.

Glancing back at the Beloved who merely shrugged, Kaius called steel and tried again. The cuts on his arms, only just closed, stung as the muscles beneath them strained. The steel remained.

Valerius gave a smirk then laid his palm flat on the door and called lightning, just a small shock. The metal of the door rippled away at his touch like any other called steel. They proceeded along the corridor for a short distance before they came to the second, more conventional door. Before it stood one of the Marked, fully clad in armour, with a spiked mace in each hand and no indication that he was going to move. Valerius breezed past him without a second glance and pushed open the door. It opened into total darkness.

Valerius took Kaius by the wrist and led him through. The Marked outside pulled the door back into place behind them. It was cool down here beneath the earth, and from the hollow echoes all around, Kaius could tell that they were in a sizeable cave. The floor beneath seemed to be flat solid stone so he followed Valerius blindly instead of creeping forward as he would have preferred.

Eventually something brushed against his face. There were thin curtains hanging at odd angles across the room that they brushed through without comment. Down there in the dark Kaius could feel the air moving as something, something huge and hidden, drew in rattling breath. Valerius stopped and knelt, seemingly at random, but he tugged Kaius arm as he descended and soon they were both kneeling together.

His voice echoed strangely amid the curtains and stone, "Lord Negrath, this one was Chosen for you but in this time of conflict we ask that you Mark them as your own that they may better serve you into eternity."

There was a sound like the creak of leather, a wet sound and a groan. Valerius grabbed at Kaius and pushed him forward, still trying to stay bent over in supplication. Kaius crept forward alone with his hand outstretched until he touched something in the dark. His fingers scraped across twisted skin, hot and stretched over an infected mass. It gave away a little at his touch, lumps and fluids shifting around beneath the surface.

Kaius leapt back, dropped to his knees and shuffled away backwards in what he hoped was the direction of Valerius. He panted. He bumped into something and his heart nearly stopped for a moment before Valerius' scrabbling fingers brushed up and over his face. His face was held between Valerius powerful hands and the Beloved whispered, "Did he touch you? Can we go?"

Kaius nodded, the oppressive fear of the room now mixing with the smell of corruption. Valerius, feeling the movement, took a hold of Kaius bare upper arm and dragged him back towards the door. They emerged on the other side and Kaius was unconsciously rubbing his hand against his robe, trying to remove the sensation of oiliness.

It was only when they were back in the light that he saw his fingertips, discoloured and pale. He looked up into Valerius face and the man was grinning, their breath could be seen in the air.

Valerius clapped him on the shoulder and said, "Let's go and celebrate," and Kaius pretended that he could not hear the quaver in the Beloved's voice.

There was another feast, even more luxurious and even more wasted on Kaius than the first. He sipped at a liquor that Brother Atius had forced into his hand on arrival. It was stronger than ant-mead and he couldn't quite describe the flavour. It was sour where the mead was sweet, cloying where the mead was smooth.

The vapours rising from its surface had made him sneeze when he held it beneath his nose for too long. Atius had let out a garbled speech about how the booze of the Chosen would not affect his now mighty constitution but Kaius was unsure who the speech was directed at as none of the nobles in the room would have had any inkling of what he was talking about and both Malius and himself had abstained from alcohol since before they were Chosen.

The noble men and women were cavorting by the time Kaius was ushered through, a dull ache still lingered in his fingers. Valerius had disappeared into some ante-room to change into more flamboyant dress for the occasion. The drinking and eating had started immediately after his victory in the Trial and had been going on ever since, with the less dedicated party-goers slipping away to nap and the more dedicated ones slipping away to get stung, detour to a brothel in the final stages of the Trial of Flesh or even just staying here to bask in the reflected glory.

It had been several years since Negrath's last victory and this party could stretch on right until harvest time if the cards were played right. After harvest, when the cold settled more thoroughly over the city, the nobles would hole up in their own estates for the most part. Some would travel by carriage to visit one another, and generally there were spare bedrooms in every one of their homes to provide the appearance that the visits were not purely carnal in nature.

Malius had approached soon after Atius had been distracted

in pursuit of what looked like a large bird but may have been a rotund beetle with some dyed grasses arrayed around it for the baking. He had drawn Kaius into a fraternal hug and whispered to him, "As I predicted, Brother. Now the real Trials begin," he glanced at Kaius impassive face and added, "And I am sure you will not be found wanting."

Kaius replied cautiously, "Thank you... brother."

Malius turned to stand beside Kaius at the wall where he had sequestered himself. They both looked at the crowd throbbing through the chambers of the palace. Were it not for Negrath's gifts it would have been impossibly unsafe to have so many people in close proximity to the Beloved, with the gifts it would be almost comically easy to clear the room. Unless an enemy had Chosen one of Negrath's own nobles and somehow hidden that fact from Valerius, the Marked could tear through any assassin like paper, not to mention any noble foolish enough to stand too close.

Malius glanced at Kaius circumspectly then said, "The Halls of Steel have been filled with the sound of dropped swords since heat-rise. The noise is getting deafening, I shall have to make other sleeping arrangements for this evening to keep me as far from the place as possible. Every one of my students is trying to recreate your trick. Every one of them, clad in steel and calling steel. I never taught you that trick. I have never seen it done before. Can you explain yourself?"

Kaius shrugged, "I was poisoned and bleeding. I cannot recall what thoughts led me to that course of action."

Malius pursed his lips, "An accident then. An accident that

has young fools trying to call steel as though it were a pet. Capering around with quicksilver chasing them. It is not a part of the forms and it looks ridiculous. I do not believe I shall ever forgive you for your accident. Entirely new forms will have to be drawn up and taught. You have given me a century of work at least."

Kaius inclined his head in mock sorrow and said, "I am glad that your time will be gainfully occupied."

Malius huffed then wandered off in pursuit of a young couple, barely teenagers. Kaius returned to nodding politely to the overenthusiastic nobles, every one of which had either been seated within a few feet of him during the combat or had a vividly detailed imagination.

Valerius burst into the room with a crackle of power that caused all of the galvanic lanterns to brighten for a moment. His robes were golden and reflective, cut in close to his body around his mid-section like one of the Chosen but with flowing sleeves that concealed his hands.

He smiled benevolently to the crowd who began cheering his victory, but he gestured to Kaius and the applause all turned his way.

Kaius shifted uncomfortably at their attention but kept his face placid. Valerius strode across with his hidden hands still held out to Kaius and a broad smile on his face. He cupped Kaius' cheeks again as he had down in the dark but this time he leaned in close enough for his too hot breath to tickle over Kaius lips.

He raised his eyebrow in what might have been a question but never waited for a reply before his lips were pressed ever so softly against Kaius.

Kaius froze in place, feeling the soft sensation of the Beloved's lips on his own. He leaned minutely forward, thinking it was how such things were done and the tip of Valerius' tongue traced across where his lips met, drawing a shiver in reaction.

Valerius leaned back with a smile and Kaius tried to return it. Doing your duty even when it was not appealing, when you did not understand why your Beloved would want it done so, was the entire creed of the Chosen.

This duty was like the silk sheets and Negrath's touch. Kaius restrained himself before he stepped away from the uncomfortable closeness of Valerius, who had now wrapped an arm around Kaius waist and was smiling around at the crowd.

None of them were foolish enough to look scandalised at the Beloved's new interest. There was only some light hooting, blushing and giggling in parts of the room. Kaius filed away the images of the scowling faces in his mind. They may not move against the Beloved for anything so tawdry as a romance but they would be the ones gathered into conspiracy by one of the more intelligent nobles who was acting as though they approved.

He gathered his courage and placed an arm around Valerius, his hand resting on the slim hip opposite him after trailing over his lower back in a deliberate motion that he knew Malius was observing with hawk-like attention. Atius was currently standing on a table at the far end of the hall, holding a barrel of the milky liquor over his head and threatening to drink the entire thing. Kaius leaned over to whisper in Valerius ear, too soft for the nobles to hear but well within the capabilities of the Marked, "Please let me know when you are ready to retire to your quarters. I do not take pleasure in events like this."

There was a hunger on Valerius face now when he spoke, "Let me walk among my people for a time, then you and I shall return to my rooms. We can celebrate more privately."

Kaius smiled at him again and hoped that the numbness would be enough to carry him through to heat-rise.

Chapter 9- The Hunt

The dry heat of the chamber did nothing to help. Kaius resisted the urge to flinch as Valerius swept into the room behind him, positively radiating his happiness and excitement. With luck, it would be mistaken for another shiver. Kaius had very few illusions about what would happen next. He had lived from childhood to Trial in the extremely communal Halls of Bone. The only rule placed upon the students had been to have no children of their own and there were herbalists in the city who saw to that with ease if you could get a moment free or could trade some favour to an older student. Despite the atmosphere of the place almost all of the interactions between the students were consensual, the application of force was a significant part of every student's training. Triggering any kind of violence was a good way to end up dead. In the cots lining dim-lit rooms, pretending he was asleep and trying to ignore the sounds, he had seen nearly every combination of teenage fumbling, and more than a little experimentation.

The human body held no mystery to those who would be Chosen. Their studies covered anatomy in great detail and their training showed them that anatomy in lethal motion every day. Kaius had watched it all through half closed eyes, filed away the information but never participated. It all seemed so tawdry, so bestial, the grunts and fumbles and squelches. He suppressed the shudder this time. Kaius walked to the bed as Valerius flitted about the room, removing the outer layers of his garments, poured himself some water, heightened the level of lighting in the room and from a chest in one of the alcoves pulled a bundle of cloth that held a perfumed mixture of aromatic oils inside. Kaius stripped his robes with the same efficiency as he had dressed himself. He had undone them from his chest and they were hanging loose around his waist, he was trying to decide if Valerius would prefer him to remove the bandages too. He was not certain, some of the students had appreciated the aesthetic of nudity. Others, he presumed, had preferred the difference in textures.

There was a rustling of paper behind him and he ran rapidly through a mental check-list, trying to insert paper into the required actions. He turned to see Valerius, pale-faced and all pretext of composure gone, holding a lichen stained scroll in one hand and clasping at the front of his robes with the other. For a moment Kaius felt like he was back down in the dark chamber beneath the tower. He could smell the foulness again, catching in his throat. Valerius shuddered then whispered so softly even Kaius could not hear. Valerius looked up at Kaius with fear on his face, "I am sorry my dear, we shall have to conclude the celebrations later. I have a very important task for you."

The mask of dignity slipped back over his face as he swept out of the door and began rattling off instructions to the Chosen on guard outside. He glanced over Kaius' exposed upper body and bit his own lip. Then he sighed, "You had best make yourself presentable. I have just sealed the city. There is an enemy within our walls."

Atius and Malius burst through the doors at a run, skidding to a halt and falling to one knee before the Beloved. Malius barked, "Your orders?"

Valerius had calmed himself now, he spoke with his usual voice and Kaius wondered if the others saw the man's hands shaking as he took a sip of water. "There is a creature within the city walls, the Beloved of another Eater, possibly another Eater itself. It will most likely have the appearance of a merchant or some other traveller that would not look out of place coming and going through the city. It will isolate itself to prevent detection. I require that you search the city for this creature and destroy it. I require that you do this personally, I would not have word of this spreading among the Chosen and I want no rumour of it to reach the commons. Do you understand?"

Malius nodded tersely as Atius shook his head in bewilderment. Valerius turned to Kaius last, expecting a response but the man was already lost in thought. Without due reverence, he asked, "Is there some way that we can detect this creature? Is there some distinctive mark upon it? How can we expect it to defend itself? Should we evacuate the area before we engage with it?"

Valerius turned a stern gaze at him, "We know nothing yet. Get out of the tower. I would feel its presence here at least. Search through the city with all haste. Find the thing. Destroy the thing. Then return to me with any further questions."

He turned away from Kaius with a sneer and was startled when the man spoke again, this time to the other Marked, "We should split the city in three. If the creature is trying to remain hidden it will stay as far as possible from the tower. We should begin our search at the outer walls."

Malius bristled but Atius bobbed along. Kaius strode across to the door, pausing only to give a formal bow to Valerius before heading down the stairs with the other two following close at his heels.

He turned his head to Atius as they moved down the stairs, "If it would please you to search among the merchant's quarter and the houses of such noble houses as may take in strays. I shall focus on the abandoned areas and the slums."

Malius interjected, "And what are my orders? What are you going to command me to do boy?"

Kaius did not break his stride. "I believe that while I am not going to be very useful in the more populous areas of the city. They would suit your unique skills perfectly Brother. You have a memory for faces and a talent with people. You alone among us may be able to pick out the stranger infiltrating the city."

Malius sneered, "Do you think to flatter me? What right do you have to bark orders? You who has been Marked less than a day?"

Kaius did not even look at the man, "I am trying to determine the best course of action to complete the task given directly to us by the Beloved of Negrath. A task given with the sense of urgency. If you have a suggestion as to where our unique talents are better applied I would be happy to fall in line with your wishes."

Malius laid a hand on Kaius shoulder and spun him around, "Was this always your intention all along? To slither into the Beloved's bed and usurp the position of your betters?"

Kaius' hand snapped up faster than even he had expected

and he struck the older man in the jaw, lifting him off of his feet and sending him tumbling down the stairs ahead of them. He turned to Atius again, "Do you have a better suggestion with regard to the use of your time?"

Atius shook his head, looking more than a little concerned. "I will blend in nicely and raise no suspicions in the places you suggested, oh yes. Just as Malius will fit in fine where you are sending him, when he gets up. Um, perhaps that was not your wisest move there lad."

Kaius shrugged, "I do not have time for the jealousy of petty men. I have my orders and we must move quickly. The gates are being sealed as we speak."

They came to a halt on the landing where Malius sprawled. Kaius knelt dangerously close and spoke clearly, "I apologise for striking you Brother, but I cannot tolerate you speaking ill of the Beloved or interfering in our progress. Please search the areas that I suggested or I shall have to report your behaviour."

He rose up and had started walking away before Malius called steel.

The lance was completely expected and rather than his frantic roll last time Kaius simply slapped the back of his hand against the side of it to knock it off its path into his lower back. It lodged in the wall but would have taken just a moment to free. A moment that Malius did not have in a battle with called speed. The heel of Kaius' boot struck the front of his helmet, then again, and again. He watched the metal collapsing in, sharp edges turned in towards his face and visor slit blocked. Malius released steel with a roar and the final stamping kick broke his cheekbone. Kaius looked down at him and shook his head, "I will not ask so kindly again.

Brother."

Atius went away to his business in silence masked with joviality. Kaius called his steel the moment he was out of the door and launched himself onto the rooftops, able to clear much more distance without the risk of crushing someone in the crowd. He moved over the ruins that composed the slums peering down at the terrified faces looking up at him, reaching down to lift the rust scarred corrugated metal when it hid them from his view. He dropped down onto the mud of the streets only when there was solid stone blocking his view.

He walked through homes holding three generations of a family, and brothels with the same. Through open air restaurants that were little more than a pot of questionable soup or stew over a fire and those scared and huddled people who had scraped together the silver required to buy a bowl to share. He went onward into the alleys and warrens of tents and piles of rubble until he reached the honeycombed wall of the city itself. He closed his eyes and listened, letting his heightened senses soar for the first time since he returned to the city. He heard the screams and gibbering of a thousand voices and he flinched under the weight, nearly as bad as the owl's shrieking in the arena. He closed his mind to thoughts of the arena, thoughts of the blood soaking into the sand for nothing but applause. Some of the blood had been his.

He shook his head again and listened for something out of place and then with his head cocked to one side he laid his fingers against the city walls, felt rather than heard the sounds vibrating through them. He searched for the sound that did not fit. His fingertips, still lifelessly pale within his glove, stung as though they had been singed. He flexed his fingers then raised his hand again, the stinging heat was most pronounced towards the east. He began following around the curve of the wall in that direction, casually hopping the odd building that had latched itself on to the original structure.

Eventually the stinging sensation eased so he turned his hand in towards the city and almost immediately the heat returned. He moved through the nearly abandoned streets, streets that became much more abandoned at the sight of him. Up on top of the wall he caught the familiar glint of steel and he waved his arms to catch the Chosen's attention. The armoured form dropped from the wall like a rock, then instead of crashing into the ground it rebounded and sprang across to meet him. Kaius halted the woman with a hand on her shoulder. He could feel her tense as he leaned in closer,

"Contact the rest of the Chosen. Have them find Brother Malius and Brother Atius. Tell them that I am here and I do not wish to proceed without their oversight."

She nodded rapidly, leaning away from his touch.

"Go quickly now."

He turned back, trusting Negrath's other servants to do their duty, and immediately his hand burned as though it were aflame. He released his steel now despite the prying eyes on him from hidden niches. Then he dropped into a half-crouch and crept forward letting the growing pain guide him. He came to a halt beside a building that was more hole than wall, all raw stone and spit for mortar streaked with ashen rain blown in from the Dales.

He called a touch of strength, more than he really needed to numb the pain in his hand. It was strange to find it flowing so easily now where before Negrath had always withheld it. He eased off until he could feel the beginnings of the burn again. He didn't want to start ripping the buildings apart by accident and lose all element of surprise. He glanced around, expecting to see the other Marked, more than willing to let them take the lead, take the credit and defuse the situation with both Malius and possibly Valerius too. It had been only a few minutes, they were not yet found by the searching Chosen. Kaius did not know what form this creature would take nor the nature of its power. Valerius had told them far too little, but so close to the heart of the empire they could not tolerate any enemy running free. Kaius called his steel and dashed around the corner of the building with a blade drawn.

Lucia was still there wedged between the buildings. Kaius' fluid movements faltered. He reached into the gap and grasped the back of her clothes. She hung limply over the mud and compounded filth. Bile was still crusted around her chapped lips and her hair was caked in ash and filth. Her breathing was shallow, her eyes were unfocused when Kaius pulled them open. The pupils were not so much dilated as they were multiplying, there were three pupils to each eye, drifting in slow circles.

He dropped her in shock and when she hit the ground she awoke gasping. She didn't even have the strength to do more than roll onto her side and groan. Buried deep within Kaius was the solid core, the place that duty had always spoken to him. Now in the place of its steady drum beat all he could hear was a song.

He backed away slowly and released his steel. His senses were nearly overwhelmed with the reek of corruption. His hand ached where he had been marked. He heard a whisper in his mind and understood Valerius' look of horror when Negrath had touched him in the same way. The voice was not clear, it was wailing and scratching behind his eyes, muttering, squealing, and ranting, *kill it, kill it, kill it*, over and over.

Kaius' grip on his sword quavered as Negrath tried to tighten its hold. Kaius dropped the sword and immediately Negrath withdrew. His absence was like the strike of a hammer. The sword hit the mud and burst into a splatter of quicksilver. It did not move back towards him. He looked down in horror at his hands, the colour had returned to his fingers and he immediately tried to call steel again and found his connection blocked. Not just blocked, gone. He looked down at the helpless girl in the mud and he began to shake as he realised all that his hesitation had cost him. A moment's doubt was a moment too long.

Behind him he heard Malius drawl, "Is this the creature, Brother Kaius?"

Kaius halted the quaking to turn with all the false confidence he could muster. Both Malius and Atius stood at the far end of the path, by the rubble of a collapsed aqueduct support, in full armour, with their favoured weapons called. He did not hesitate, to hesitate again would have made the loss for nothing, "She is nothing. Listen to me Brothers, my mark burns here. I feel that great Negrath is trying to speak to me. What can you feel?"

Both men stood impassive for a moment then said Atius said,

"Negrath speaks to us Boy. That is the fate of the Marked. To hear his will."

Malius took a half step forward, face hidden but spite bursting from his lips, "Why can't you hear him now Brother?" Malius flipped the swords in his hands and started to walk forward. Atius tightened his grip on his mace and started to circle around Kaius. Malius roared, "Why can't you hear him tell us to cut you down. Why can't you hear him traitor?"

Kaius fell into the first defence of the Forms of Bone, tightening his fists as his teachers approached. Atius shook his head, "Stand down boy. We won't hurt you. Everyone has moments of... confusion. You have had a busy few days, no wonder you are getting mixed up."

Malius laughed when he got a proper look at Lucia still lying in the mud. "For this Kaius? This is what you finally work out what your cock is for? Some skinny little ash farmer? This is what you throw your eternal life away for?"

Without speed of his own to call, Kaius only had time to flinch as Malius slashed both of his cheeks in quick succession, hissing, "Tell me why Kaius? For some little whore? Did one of the other Eaters get to you out in the dark? Make you a better offer?"

Blood ran scalding hot down Kaius' cheeks as he looked back at the defenceless woman and then turned to two of the three most powerful men in the city. Malius blurred into motion again but this time Kaius was moving first, the flat of his hand smacking against the hard steel of Malius armour, driving the thrust out wide. He was afraid now, his hand ached and his muscles twinged with atrophy after years of relying on other strength. He smiled at Malius, "Valour."

Malius, still shaken by his interrupted strike cocked his head and said, "What?"

Kaius took a controlled step to the side, still in his stance, and said softly, "For valour."

Then Atius charged in from the right and Malius slashed at his legs. As skilled as he was he was only human. He kept his legs, in no small part by luck but his ribs cracked under the mace strike and he tumbled to his knees gasping for air. Malius laughed and kicked him in the face with a steel boot, breaking his nose with a wet crack.

Despite the pain, he twisted as he went over to land on his hands and knees. His body shielding Lucia from the sight of her enemies. His breath rattled and blood rolled down his face. Her eyes were open and fixed on him. Malius sword had lengthened into a heavy chain covered in small hooks, a complex feat. He lashed Kaius back and the silk of his fine new robes tore away leaving trails of blood. This was Malius standard punishment for disobedient pupils, they were rarely disobedient again, even if they lived.

Kaius held himself up even as the chain lashed right over his shoulder and a hook lodged under his collarbone. Malius cackled and pulled at the chain, it dragged Kaius back up onto his knees before the hook jerked free in a shower of blood. He toppled back over Lucia, she was lying on her back with tears in her eyes. Agonisingly slowly her hand reached up to cup his marred cheek and she whispered, "My hero."

Strength flowed through him, dulling the pain, and steel flowed over him, blocking Malius' next strike. He drew in an unsteady breath.

Then he rose.

Chapter 10- The Shortest Path

The steel was light around him and he was off balance when he moved far too quickly out of the whip's path. With almost casual ease he reached out and caught it. With a tug he sent Malius off balance and when Atius rushed in from the other side Kaius snapped out his other hand and caught the mace by its handle. Their faces were covered but body language showed through the armour.

The Marked were beyond shock. They were trying to understand the meaning of the impossible armour and the sudden strength. To decipher the will of Negrath.

While they thought, Kaius moved. Snapping the whip to tangle its barbs around Atius and kicking the feet from under him. Only when both men were stumbling did Kaius scoop up Lucia and run for his life. He still moved too fast. He stumbled over obstacles he thought he had plenty of time to avoid. He crashed through half-built walls and shanty houses when he could have jumped them.

Every step, he twisted and turned to keep the girl cradled in his arms safe from the showers of mortar and stone. They burst into a square amongst the slum houses and skidded to a halt by the abandoned cooking pot. He laid her down by the fire, hoping that it would bring some vigour back into her cooling body.

Some blood trickled out of his visor when he was looking down at her, dripping onto her cheek and prompting a startled moan. Kaius took a sticky bundle of herbs from his belt pouch and tossed them under the cooking pot. Then he jerked to his feet abruptly, kicking the cooking pot at Malius as he entered the square.

Malius deflected it with a flash of steel and scorn. Kaius called his usual sword, then adjusting for the situation, called a second. Atius burst through the wall behind him, hefting a hammer as big as himself and roaring. Kaius did not turn, just thrust one sword point back towards the man, who reversed his charge so suddenly that he nearly fell.

Atius feared him, that much was clear, he had seen this warrior's skills in action and found his own wanting. Malius still moved with a confidence born of many victories, many of them over Kaius. Malius took in Kaius position in the square, noted the way he stood over the husk of a girl on the ground. He was rooted in place if he wanted to protect her.

Inside his visor Malius lips peeled back from his yellowing teeth. He merged and extended his swords into a spear as he approached Kaius. He used his reach and mobility to strike at Kaius from a variety of angles. Even launching a few thrusts in the direction of the huddle of rags on the ground. Kaius deflected them with more force than necessary. Malius kept it up, certain the boy would tire soon.

Atius found his courage and swung the hammer down at the same time as Malius' latest attack. With one sword above him Kaius managed to deflect the hammer, letting the curve of the blade on the pole angle it away but while he was doing so Malius made another flurry of attacks and he had only the one sword to parry them away.

For the first time Kaius consciously called speed and the sword moved so fast that he missed two of his parries, having to snap the blade back for a second attempt that was successful due more to luck than skill.

Atius came on again. He discarded his hammer after a horizontal swing was thwarted by another parry and launched into a rough amalgamation of the Forms of Bone, snatching at Kaius' wrists.

Malius still demanded Kaius full attention. He could not turn to face Atius so he released his armour and took a lumbering step forward with the heavy man pressed hard against his back. He kept his swords up and moving.

He ignored the sharp edges of Atius armour cutting into him. Ignored the tightening grip as he tried to twist out of Atius arms. Kaius took another step forward, feeling the heat of the cooking fire on his legs. His sweat and blood dried in the heat as he went through the motions of the Forms of Steel against their Master.

Atius locked his arms around Kaius and started to crush the breath from him when suddenly the world went dark and he could not breathe either. The herbs in the fire pumped out an oily black smoke now, enveloping the struggle and cloaking them from Malius' sight.

Malius' next spear thrust hit solidly and when he pulled it

from the smoke Atius staggered out with it. The winged tip of the spear caught in the jagged rend in the armour over his stomach as Malius withdrew it. The fat Master's armour fell away in a shower of silver and Malius could do nothing but gape as Kaius strode from the smoke. Kaius' face was the same emotionless mask it had always been through his years in training. Through his years out in the dark, and through those darker times when Malius had offered him up as a morsel to delight whichever nobles' favour was being courted. Kaius' sword lashed out in a perfect horizontal cut, true to the Forms as he had been taught, and Atius' head tumbled from his shoulders.

Malius took a half step back then found his courage, retracting the bloody spear and reforming his straight swords. He snarled, "You have never bested me boy. Not once. How do you think this will end for you? How do you think it will end for your little whore?"

Kaius did not charge as Malius had hoped, his face remained impassive as steel formed a plate over his features, one of the swords disappeared into the moving mass of metal and Kaius was left with his favoured weapon. It was still strange in his grasp. The new strength flowed through him without needing to be called. It made the sword seem too flimsy so he called more steel and made the blade thicker and heavier. Then he flipped it around his hand with a twist of the wrist and took his stance. The herbs and oils tossed in the fire had all burned away. The air cleared. Malius waited for the charge but it never came, Kaius stood perfectly still, almost peacefully, between the Marked and the musician.

Malius ran forward with all of his speed called and slashed

straight for Kaius' throat. He did not trust in the element of surprise so his other sword was already moving to parry the expected counter-attack. Kaius leaned just out of reach of the first sword's swipe. He called strength for his answering strike and Malius sword was bent from the force of the blow and wrenched from his grip. They parted for a moment and Malius tried to circle around, to put Kaius between the bent sword and his quaking hand.

Kaius stepped sideways to block his path, shaking his head in what Malius took to be disdain for so obvious a move. The steel leapt back to Malius hand and was reforming when Kaius brought a heavy double handed blow straight down at him. It hammered both of his swords down so their opposite edge dug into the armour of his faceplate.

Kaius lifted his sword a fraction to bring it down again and Malius flung himself backwards, rolling through a wall before coming to a halt in a low guard. He glanced around at the terror in the eyes of the peasants living there. Crammed in so tight that the walls were practically made of flesh. There were so many he could not count them but he knew they would not interfere.

Kaius had moved from his spot by the fire to inside this hovel. Malius could not see where he had gone until the tin roof collapsed above him in a shower of sparks under the plunging weight of Kaius colossal blade. Malius managed to dodge aside again, crushing a few of the inconsequential slum-dwellers into the wall. The falling roof obscured the other side of the room from view but he heard childish shrieking. The cacophony of the city was a constant distraction to the highly-attuned senses of the Marked.

Malius caught the next thrust between his two blades and turned it away to pin a filthy faced girl to the wall. Kaius simply released the weapon and closed the distance too fast for the eye to see. He moved through the Forms of Bone, switching through their motions impossibly fast. Already inside Malius guard. A well-placed kick knocked Malius off balance into a wall and the punch that followed pushed him through that wall and back out into the street in a shower of bricks.

Kaius recalled his sword as Malius rolled to his feet and charged in a fury, both blades dancing in and out in carefully measured thrusts. Testing Kaius' defences from every angle of attack. Kaius' speed, balanced by the weight of his sword kept his parries more consistent and he gradually upped the pressure, deflecting each thrust with more force, striking the tips of the blades earlier until there was a hole down the centre of Malius defences. Until his swords were driven out to the sides and a simple step forward and thrust pushed the huge curved sword through armour and sternum to burst out of Malius back.

They stood like that for a long moment as the family in the ruined building behind wailed and ran for their lives. Kaius withdrew his sword. Savouring the vibrations as it grated against bone and armour on its way out. He released his steel as Malius fell to the cobblestones and made sure the man saw his smile before he punched him. The strength he had called was well beyond any that he had experienced as one of Negrath's Chosen. The force of the blow snapped Malius' neck and spun his head around to face away. Malius' steel trickled away and Kaius left his broken body kneeling in the street. Kaius drew a quaking breath then retraced his steps back to Lucia.

The fire's heat seemed to have brought some life back to her and she had pulled herself up into a cross-legged sitting position. She greeted him with a feeble wave. He took a knee beside her and gave her a forced smile. She was staring into the fire and her eyes seemed more reflective now, he saw the flames flickering in them. Now that she was coming back to awareness she was shaking. She turned her alien eyes to him and whispered, "You killed them."

Kaius smiled with a swell of satisfaction but Lucia did not seem pleased. She whimpered, "You knew them and you killed them. You didn't even think about it. You just killed them."

Kaius shifted uncomfortably, morality was not taught to the Chosen, only obedience. They might debate how best to serve their master but never whether it was right to serve their master, he muttered, "It was them or us. In battle that is the only choice."

Lucia shook her head, "It shouldn't be like this. What are we going to do now?"

Kaius looked across the city to the tower. Then he spoke with confidence, "You have Chosen me to serve you and my old master has abandoned me. I will serve you until my final breath if you will have me."

Lucia seemed more startled by this than by anything else, "I don't need you to serve me. I just need to get away from here. I need to find a cure or some way to restore my strength."

He glanced around and spoke softly, "I am yours to command in all matters but if you wish I will also offer you advice in matters which you may not be familiar."

She shivered,"Such as?"

Kaius answered, "The arts of war. "

Lucia rolled her eyes, "No. No more killing. I am not at war with anyone. I just want this to end. I just want things to go back to the way they were."

Kaius paused for a moment then came to his feet and looked along the length of the outer wall, searching for the tell-tale shimmer of silver. Over his shoulder he asked, "When did you change?"

Lucia shuddered, "I... I ate something. Some sort of meat. Down under the glass, when I thought I was starving. Things have been changing ever since then."

He turned back to her, "By the arts of war, I also mean the philosophy that has been imparted to me in my studies. If your goal is to gather information about your condition then I recommend that you seek someone with the same condition."

She scoffed softly, "You know someone else who this is happening to?"

He met her gaze and she saw his face was back to an emotionless mask, "I know of four creatures that this has happened to. One of them lives within this city."

Lucia returned her gaze to the fire and her eyes widened as she tried to comprehend. Her breathing came faster and faster. Kaius went on, "In war and in life it is always best to take the shortest path to your goal. Negrath can tell you what to expect. How to rejuvenate yourself. It can guide you. Even its lies will help us discern the shortest path to your goals."

Lucia shook her head frantically, still looking into the fire, "Absolutely not. No. No. Under no circumstances do I want to be in the same room as an Eater."

Kaius sighed, "You are already in the same room as an Eater. I am only suggesting that we talk to another."

She didn't reply, still staring intensely into the fire. He went on, "If you wish I will take you from the city. We can run and hide out in the dark lands and wait for the hunting parties to come. I am very skilled in combat and tactics, I can say this without pride as it is merely fact. I shall hold them off from you for as long as I can."

She glanced up at that, "How long would that be?"

He slumped back down beside her, "It depends how many they send. Not long. Weeks. Perhaps months."

She sagged and wept, her shoulders heaving. Kaius sat uncomfortably by her side, glancing around nervously. Eventually he shuffled over slightly and put an arm around her shoulders. She practically flung herself into his arms, sobbing and gasping as he looked into the middle distance and tried to calm his own discomfort. When she seemed to be running out of tears he asked, "Imagine that you did have the power of one of the Eaters. What would you change?"

She snorted. Everyone in the world had complaints. Nobody was allowed to speak them, but they all carried with them in their mind a perfect world where everyone was kind and there was no hunger or pain. But there was no use in dreams. Dreams that could never be fulfilled turned to poison. They made you forget how the world really was. Dreams could trap you just as surely as having no hope at all. She wondered at this. Her tears dried on her cheeks in the fire's heat. She thought about her entire life and the paths she had walked. She said, "No more killing. Real laws that would protect people. The real people. The ones who live out in the dark and work themselves to death trying to feed the lazy sots in the cities."

Kaius smiled at that, and with that small encouragement she pressed on, "No more wars. No more abuse of power. No more using people like pieces in a game."

Kaius bowed to her, "It is within your power to change things with this gift you have been given. With your power, you could remake the world to protect those who are weak."

She shook her head sadly, "Life isn't a song, Kaius."

Kaius stared at her then, long and hard, "Nothing changes that we do not change. Let life be a song."

She returned to staring into the fire and he interrupted her reverie, "What is your decision?"

She nearly started crying all over again but gradually got control of herself. When her breathing had evened out she replied, "Let's take the shortest path, Kaius."

He smiled softly and squeezed her gently against the side of his body with what he hoped was appropriate warmth. He helped her to her feet and kept a grip on her hand. Together they walked towards the tower, past the ruins that they had made.

Chapter 11- The Burned Ones

Kaius wore the robes of the Marked. His new armour looked the same as the old. He walked through the streets with Lucia stumbling along beside him. He walked into the tower unchallenged and carried her quietly down the stairs until the torches turned to oil lamps.

He settled her in a dark alcove far from the stairs then retraced his steps from the visit before. With called speed he moved up the stairs in between the patrols of the chosen and with called strength he tore a galvanic lantern from the wall, twisting it free of the copper wire that tangled up through the ivory walls. It was still glowing brightly, so close to the source. Kaius rushed down the stairs and shattered the glass against the steel door. The tiny spark of Valerius' power discharged into the metal and it melted away. He retrieved Lucia and dragged her on through the corridors.

Every time Kaius called on her powers that thin cord connecting them lit up and she felt her strength trickling away down it. She fuelled the fire that glowed around him, but if she severed that connection they would be defenceless.

The last of Negrath's Marked stood guard before the final door into the darkness, weapons at the ready. Kaius did not know this man. He had been down here since before Kaius had even come to the city, since before he was born. He could have been here for a hundred years and nobody above would have known. There was no point in bluff or bluster, only the Beloved of Negrath was granted audience beyond that door.

Kaius called his steel and came on hard. The Marked was stronger and faster than Kaius had expected but the wellspring of power now at his disposal was beyond anything he had ever known. There was no time for subtlety with a tower full of enemies above. He struck with all of his strength, snapping the mace heads from the Marked's weapons and then following through in a plunging strike to the man's chest. The armour flowed away, trickling into the cracks in the flagstones. The body that hit the ground was nothing more than a torso and head. This man had given all of his parts in Negrath's service. His face was missing a nose and what was left of him was criss-crossed with scars. Kaius could not even begin to guess at his age.

With one arm tucked under Lucia and an oil lantern sizzling away in the other they pushed through the great wooden doors. The floor was rough-hewn stone, barely worked by human hands. This place was more cavern than room. Walking in deeper, the sounds of their steps echoed strangely. They existed in a tiny bubble of light with darkness pressing in all around them.

They came soon enough to what Kaius had taken to be curtains but now looked like very fine but tattered leather, so thin that the light passed right through them, revealing a pattern of veins within. Spasmodically pumping not blood but something putrid and yellowish. The curtains twitched and shied away from the heat of the torch as they approached and Lucia shuddered. They hung from what may have once been bone but were now eroded down to twig like thickness. There was a bramble of these bones running across patches on the ceiling. All interconnected and growing denser the closer that the interlopers got to the creature at the heart of the cavern. They moved past the things that were like arms, the rotten things with too many branching points and fingers that had brushed over Kaius. They moved past the tendrils of ragged, putrid flesh that reached out towards them like the arms of deep sea creatures.

Whenever any part of the ruined flesh mindlessly reached for them, the light and heat of the lantern rebuffed it. They walked towards the strangled sound of breathing and came to what had been Negrath's head. It was too long to be human, even if it wasn't so many times larger. The flesh was blackened along the upturned side with glimpses of bone revealed. Sickness had swollen the flesh of the other side to make it a pallid mass of lumps, leaking fluid that had congealed on the floor, running into the drains carved there and clogging them. In the black mass of burned flesh three eyes opened, one was white and blind but the other two lit up brightly. Exposed muscles twitched all over the face and by some deep-rooted instinct, it tried to pull away from the heat and light, to retreat to the cold darkness it had made for itself.

It lacked the strength. Its destroyed body weighted it down and, after some straining, it submitted to their attention. The eyes narrowed and Kaius toppled to the ground like his strings had been cut, nearly hauling Lucia with him. He could not move for the massive weight of his called steel. What Negrath lacked in raw strength, he made up for in experience, it had reached out and pinched Lucia's connection to him shut. Lucia staggered forward and then toppled to lie, propped up against the sticky side of Negrath's head. It grunted at the impact. Then a wretched sound echoed through the chamber, a gurgling that it took Lucia some time to recognise as laughter.

Her hair became matted against Negrath's exposed flesh and liquid trickled down the back of her neck. The laughter gradually abated and the air in the room shifted as Negrath inhaled. The sound of its voice was sickening, a gargling shrieking sound that ratcheted up and down in volume without logic. *"You came all this way to finish your murder and you fail. Your power fails as I knew it would. Starve, Sun-Eater. Starve. All these years. I knew you endured. All these years. I could still sense you somewhere. Out in the ruins of your kingdom. Even as I wiped your name away from memory and we rebuilt the world in our image."*
Kaius groaned from where he lay and Negrath snarled, *"Silence. Monkey. I speak to the organ grinder."*

So many of these words were alien that Lucia sat in silence trying to piece them together. Negrath knew that she was powerless. He knew why. He thought she was another Eater. One that had tried to kill him and had eaten his son. If that was the secret, eating other people, Lucia would just starve. And the way that the other one had killed and eaten... She could not imagine why you would grind a person's organs. Lucia was not familiar with the makings of sausages, only with the end product. The silence became oppressive until she whispered, "I didn't do anything to you. Please help me. You think I am someone else."

Negrath lurched and roared, *"You did this to me. You burned me. Do you know how long eternity stretches? How long pain will endure as your body rots around you. Do not think I cannot see through your eyes. But I have won. Our alliance destroyed you and our power block the light from you and you... You have lost. I have won."*

The last words were a pained whimper from the great beast. Lucia's head lulled to the side. She saw Kaius dragging himself to his knees, inch by painful inch under the weight of metal with no strength but his own. Then her eyes slipped out of focus, the pupils separating out to show her new spectra of colour and motion.

She saw the huge tangled mass of cords flowing out of Negrath, stretching out in every direction. Power flooding through them, enough to have drained her dry in a moment. Some were the simple weaves she had seen attached to the Chosen but others she could not guess the purpose of. She saw the raw information of Negrath's thoughts pumping through the connection to his Beloved. She saw a few cords so deeply ingrained that Negrath did not even think of them, stretching out to touch the other Eaters. They were thicker than all of the others, dense and complex, and Lucia did not know whether they were attacks or the bonds of alliance. She doubted that Negrath knew either. She caught a glimpse of her connection to Kaius, pinched shut by a twist of Negrath's will. She saw one small strand outside of his grasp and poured the last of her strength into it. Warmth spread through her as she fell unconscious.

Fire poured from Kaius fingertips and Negrath squealed in terror. Whatever hold it had over him released. He rose to his feet and stopped holding back. The flames lashed out. Igniting all of the paper-thin skin hanging from the roof. Negrath rolled and tore parts of itself away, trying to escape the flames. Lucia toppled to the ground, her cheeks becoming hollow before Kaius eyes. He stopped the flames and drew a ragged breath in the superheated air of the cavern. He pointed to Lucia, "You fix her now or I burn you. I burn every part of you. The Eaters are eternal, or so they say. Do you think you will still live if you are ash? Do you think that you will want to?"

Negrath wailed, *"I cannot undo what has been done. All four of us hid the sun away. It cannot be broken. She will wither. I will prevail."*

Kaius eyes narrowed, "You will prevail as ashes or you will save her. Where have you hidden this boy? I will fetch him out from anywhere in this world."

Negrath laughed again and it rolled through the cavern, *"You know nothing. She will wither. My servants will carve her into pieces. They will slide her down my throat. I will be master of fire and storm. I will remake myself. I will wage war on all of the others and bring them to heel. Those that cross me shall be my fodder. I shall be the all in one. There shall be no other. No one, but me."*

Kaius' mind spun out the paths ahead of him and then he spoke softly, "There cannot be so much of you that is still alive. If I carve you. She can eat. Whatever sustains you can sustain her until we find whatever you have hidden."

Negrath chuckled, *"I think not."*

With a crack of thunder Valerius hit Kaius across the back of the head.

Chapter 12- The Lessons of Youth

Kaius did not see Valerius move, he only felt the impact of steel boots in his side. His armour, so crippling a moment ago, probably saved his life. Rolling across the room got him out of striking distance and positioned him between Negrath's greatest servant and the girl. He spun to face Valerius and startled at his armoured form.

Valerius armour was not smooth and simple, it had a mess of sharp spikes jutting out from the joints and the plates were asymmetrical in shape and size. His face was still visible, as though it were growing out of the barbed metal. He had tears flowing down his cheeks, reflecting the dull red glow from the embers of his still burning master, "Why would you betray us? After all that I have done for you."

Kaius was silent for a long moment, considering, then he spat, "After everything you allowed me to do for you?"
Valerius' face contorted in disbelief but Kaius snapped at him before he could refute it, "I killed for you and your master. I gave you my entire life. And you took it. Without a moment of doubt or care."

A blade snapped into Kaius hand and he advanced. Valerius expanded his gauntlets and reformed them so that his arms ended in great spikes.

Kaius snarled, "I do not belong to you Valerius. I do not belong to Negrath. There are higher goals than obedience."
Valerius froze, stunned at this sedition. Then he whispered, "But I loved you."
Kaius brushed the words away with disdain, "You wanted me. You do not know love."

The Beloved raised the great spike of his arm. His face contorted in hatred and a bolt of lightning lashed out from the tip. It struck Kaius in the chest and passed through his armour. The steel carried the lightning all over him. He could do nothing but twitch and burn.

After what seemed like an eternity the lightning stopped and Kaius fell to the ground gasping. His armour fell away and the burns and cuts of the day were exposed to the ashen air. The sudden heat hanging all around them made him groan. Sweat trickled and stung his many injuries. Valerius tensed and shook his head as Kaius rose to his feet. Kaius called his sword again and charged. The result was the same as before. The lightning blazed through the room blinding bright and rolling thunder through the cavern. It was briefer this time and the impact flung Kaius back. Electricity still crawled over his sword and his once sure hands trembled.

Drawing a quavering breath Kaius said, "I do not wish to harm you. You are ignorant to the injuries that you have done to me. You are kept ignorant so that you may serve your master better. All I ask is that you stand down."

Negrath had up until now held silent, terrified by the lash of flame, but now it squealed out, *"Kill him. Kill them both. Quickly. Do not let him speak his lies. He seeks to twist things."*

For the first time Valerius eyes left Kaius, first to glance at the great bloody mass of Negrath, then to the girl lying by his side. He shuddered, then his eyes narrowed bitterly, "Now I see how it is, my love. What lies did she offer up to turn you from the true path?" Kaius looked down and whispered, "It doesn't have to be like this."

Valerius scoffed then leapt back in startled surprise when Kaius unleashed a roiling mass of flame between them. He startled back another step, blinded by the sudden light, then cast lightning out wildly into the room. He struck his master and the roof with two of the more frantic bolts.

Gouts of fire blossomed up over the roof, searing more of Negrath's dangling skin and leaving thick clouds of smoke in its place. Visibility in the dark cave could be measured by the length of your arms and even that only barely. Negrath pressed down into Valerius' mind, the ancient will beating down on him constantly. The crooked face on the slab wailed again, *"Kill him. Kill them both."*

A great torrent of fire lanced out from the dark and struck Negrath. It roared in anguish as the infected flesh of what remained of its torso bubbled and burst into reeking chunks. The ribs blackened in the sudden lash of fire. Valerius charged off in the direction the fire had originated to find nothing but an expanding cloud of choking smoke that his armour nearly smothered him trying to protect him from. He released his steel and roared, "Stop running you coward!"

A kick to the back of his knee sent him tumbling to the ground but with a burst of called speed he was on his feet and swinging the pointed metal of his arms at the space Kaius had so recently occupied. More flames rolled over Negrath and its wailing intensified, shaking the walls with its volume, *"Kill. Kill."*

Valerius charged again to find emptiness but this time he spun around and unleashed a cascade of electricity through the room. Kaius' fist caught him at the base of his neck and his head filled with a bright white flash of pain. He was lost to the pain for a moment too long before he recalled his armour and swept his bladed arms around him wildly. He staggered back and forth and screamed in impotent rage. Kaius called out from the distant end of the cavern, "Before you became this creature, this servant of that vile beast, what were you?"

Valerius stomped forward a few steps then realised his mistake. He froze in place and unleashed a succession of electric bolts in different directions, illuminating the room in blinding white sections and punching further holes in Negrath's still breathing corpse.

He spun around looking for any sign of Kaius and listened for his breath. Then he spat on the ground from between grit teeth, "I was a scholar and a poet. I wrote great verses praising Negrath that the Halls still teach to their children. I was a genius and the nobles loved me. I was the greatest man in the city. There was no question, when the time came, that I should be the Beloved. Known by all as the greatest man in the world."

He walked backwards as he spoke, eyes darting around the room as he moved towards Negrath and the helpless girl by its side. A useful hostage. He backed right into Kaius chest. A dagger's curved blade pressed softly into his cheek. A drop of blood rolled down the razor-sharp edge.

Valerius barely moved, he whimpered, "Kaius, please."
Then the young man whispered in Valerius' ear, soft as a lover, "I was a warrior."
He jerked his arm and slit Valerius' throat. The Beloved of Negrath toppled to the floor like a rag doll. Kaius spoke calmly to the silent room, "I am a warrior."

He advanced on Negrath and jammed his gore slick dagger into one of its eyes. It roared in pain and Kaius twisted the curved blade inside its skull. He screamed in its ruined face, "Any more tricks?"

Kaius dragged out the blade and thick white pus poured from Negrath's latest wound. The stench of it in the dry heat of the room was sickening. Kaius dragged the blade along Negrath's hide and when the scales rattled off onto the floor and the flesh separated, yet more corruption poured out. Negrath hissed and moaned deep in its throat. Kaius spoke calmly again, "Tell me everything that I want to know or I will carve you like a beetle. When I slice all the dead flesh away, how many mouthfuls do you think will be left. How many moments will it take to slide them down her throat?"

Negrath hissed as he approached again then whimpered, *"What do you want?"*

Kaius made a show of smiling to the one eye still remaining, "First, tell me how to fix her. Then tell me what made you this way."

Negrath snorted in disdain, *"I ate of the god flesh. As the god died I ascended. The more who ate, the weaker each was. So of each god, only one of us fed. The gods were gone and only the eaters remained. All mankind was freed from their tyranny."*

Kaius stared at the creature, so ancient and powerful, but so completely unaware of the significance of its actions. It rumbled on, *"Then that one turned on us. Slaughtered us. Burned us. Twisted brothers and sisters to each other's throats. Only through our power combined did we starve it out."*

As Negrath spoke Kaius moved around Lucia. Lifting her eyelids and feeling for her breath. Patting out the little flames still clinging to her ruined clothes. He placed a soothing palm on her head and then reluctantly pulled her back up into a sitting position. Kaius released his steel. His entire body was covered in bruises, rising up under his skin from every vein the lightning had touched. The parts that were not bruised were bleeding. If strength was not constantly flowing through the link he would have been immobilised or dead. Instead, he moved freely and life was draining from Lucia. Negrath snarled and sprayed mucous as it spoke, *"Each is possessed of infinite power. So long as we dwell within our element. From the moonlight Walpurgan drew her witchcraft. From the earth Vulkas drew his might. From the sea Ochress drew its boundless life. From the sunlight this filth grew bloated and blinding."*

Kaius frowned and interrupted the ranting for the first time, "The moon has no light. It is the absence of light"

Negrath let out another gurgling laugh, *"Walpurgan thought herself so clever. Starving the usurper. Leaving her kin mutilated and feeble. She thought to rule us all. She did not know. She blotted out her own power in the same stroke.*"

Kaius cut it off again, "This is not answering my question. How do I help her?"

Negrath gasped in a sickly breath and then gargled and laughed at Kaius again, *"You cannot. All four of us are bound in Walpurgan's work. It is eternal as we are eternal."*

Kaius seemed to be ignoring the creature now. Working his hands over Lucia, rubbing life back into her limbs, bundling her up for travel and slapping her gently on the cheek in a vain attempt to rouse her.

Sighing, he hefted her over his shoulder and started walking towards the door. Negrath's laughter rolled and echoed through the chamber. It cut short when sparks and then five tiny flames began to trail from Kaius' fingertips. He laid Lucia down carefully by the door. With a mournful look at the sallow skin of her face he turned back to the dark beneath the city and flooded it with scalding light.

Chapter 13- The Rise

Far out in the dark lands, steel fell in thick rivulets from every one of Negrath's chosen. Their strength failed them. Their speed failed them. One died under a ghul's cleaver as he faltered.

One fell to her death as she was leaping over ravines and lost all velocity. Everywhere the Chosen became mere humans again. Some for the first time in decades. The effect rippled inward as Negrath drew all of that power back in to protect itself. The Chosen on the city walls stumbled and fell to their knees, bereft. Without a Beloved or Marked they were the last true draw on the Eater's strength, except for one. Flames caught and spread through the ruined body. It charred, burst and dried out in quick succession. The heat grew and grew until Kaius had to back away from the temperature of the air in the room. He still poured out more and more fire as Negrath wailed and flailed feebly on the grand altar of stone it had used as a pillow. The Chosen in the tower upstairs were now snatching up what furnishings they could use as weapons and scattering outside. They searched for the source of the attack with fearful faces. They searched for their commanders in vain. The people of the city watched them in confusion.

Smoke began to pour out of the tower, rising up from below the earth. The Chosen did not understand the significance of the smoke. They assumed that the lower levels of the tower were turned over to servants. So much was hidden from them that they did not know that their master burned. There was less and less of Negrath left. Its eyes had burst in the heat. Its dead flesh had sloughed away. Its bones blackened and cracked. It called a thick shell of steel around the charred remains of its head. Wrapping layers after layers of metal, spaced out for insulation. The heat rose once more and the outer layers began to trickle and melt in the temple that had now become a furnace. In the throne room that was becoming its grave. Kaius was at the door now, standing over Lucia's prone form as he drained the life from her. The thick cord of power between them was swelling as he drew more and more from her.

Her eyes lolled open. They were vacant but for the constant

orbits of her many pupils. In what had been a vast tangled constellation of Negrath's will, there remained only the frantic scramble as it tried to protect itself and a single band stretching off towards the horizon. She reached a hand up for it, brushing against Kaius leg and startling him. He halted the inferno and turned to her with smoking hands. He crouched over her and supported her head as she tried to lift herself up. She did not see him. The whole world was dark except for that one dazzling bright cord. She reached out and pinched it between her fingertips. Then, feeling its cool power throbbing, she snapped it before lolling back again, seeing only darkness.

Kaius abandoned his attempted murder, trusting in the still blazing fires within the room to finish Negrath, if such a thing could even die. It pained him to do it, but some things took precedence. Things that included not being roasted alive himself. He dragged the door shut to keep in the heat. Then he lifted Lucia up in his arms and carried her slowly and painfully up the stairs, releasing all of the strength that he could bear. Her cracked lips were still letting out the laboured sounds of breathing and that gave him comfort. He kept on past the ground floor and the scampering masses of Chosen and servants.

They did not recognise his face, as ruined as it was by the events of the last few hours. He passed safely up to what had been Valerius' chambers. They were empty and unguarded. He laid Lucia on the bed before the great ivory archway. She was not dead but she was so close he did not think she would notice his absence. He walked out onto the balcony overlooking the ivory city. Soon chaos would descend. The other eaters would march on the city and slaughter any defenders, but he had no illusions that he would live that long. When Lucia passed and he could not draw on her strength, his injuries would most likely kill him. If that did not finish him then his former comrades in arms would be happy to finish the job once hey realised what he had done. He stripped the tatters of his robes from his upper body, gasping and wincing as they passed over his cuts and bruises.

He moved slowly through the Forms of Bone on the balcony, ignored by the people below and aching with every movement. He had broken a sweat with just the walk up the stairs but this left his skin damp and tight. He turned to face the coming heat-rise and closed his eyes. This would be the final time he got to experience this moment of peace. He tried to block out the press of sound rising up from the city. To imagine that he was back out in the dark lands that he loved. Not dying here in a nest of vipers. He raised up his arms and everything became bright.

Heat swept over him and his eyes snapped open. A white-hot sphere rose up over the distant mountains. The people of the city began screaming in terror. Kaius' pupils narrowed to slits and he staggered backwards into the room trying to shield his eyes. On the bed, Lucia shimmered silver. Every inch of her skin taking in the light and shining bright. Kaius fell to his knees before her and bowed down, to protect his eyes as much as to give obeisance. Light touched every part of the world outside. The ivory city cast its very first shadow and it stretched out for miles.

Day spread out and caught in the ash and dust still drifting through the air. Mushrooms on the farms and in the gardens that fed the city exploded in clouds of spores at the sun's touch. The herds of insects broke free of their corrals, seized by sudden terror, and started burrowing and scattering in search of safe darkness. Lucia drew in a breath and all of her pain washed away, replaced by perfect warmth. Within her eyes the pupils split once more. The bones of her face, so pronounced when she was withering, took on sharp edges.

When she spoke, her voice reverberated, *"Get up Kaius. I am no different now than I was by the fire when we last spoke. I am still myself. Just... More so."*

Kaius dared to look up into her face and was startled to see the glow dimming to reveal her skin, still smooth and pale for the most part, now showed tiny silvered scales across her cheekbones and around her eyes. Her hair had regained its lustre and now hung gracefully down one side of her head. The filth and deprivation had all burned away. This new form that she took, strange as it may have been, was beautiful to his eyes, at least.

He looked ragged by comparison, all scratches and soot. His clothes in ruins and a branching tree of bruises running across his bare torso. She smiled down at him and he rose unsteadily to his feet. She said, *"Not so bad being treated as an equal?"*

With a small effort, he curled up the sides of his lips, "It will take some getting used to."

Her smile never wavered as he re-opened their connection and started drawing strength again, he wondered for a moment if she could even feel it now that she was so swollen with power. There was a metallic ring to her voice and every word seemed to echo up from inside her, *"What happened while I slept?"*

She looked out over the city and heard the wailing from below for the first time with concern, *"What is happening?*

Kaius shifted uncomfortably, "I killed Negrath and its Beloved. Then this light appeared in the sky. I believe that the Eaters were keeping this light in the sky hidden to prevent you from regaining your strength."

She glanced back at him with wide, alien eyes, *"You killed... Wait. You can see it too?"*

He nodded, "We all can. You need to consider your next move. The other Eaters have already shown their hostility. I recommend a pre-emptive strike against them. Many of Negrath's Chosen will fall into line if given the correct incentives. Or if you would prefer, you can select a new crop from the Halls of Steel and Bone. There is no immediate need to select Marked, or Masters of the Forms. Though we should consider replacing the latter, a necessity if we are to engage in a prolonged conflict."

She waved her hand to silence him with an imperiousness that would have escaped her only a few cycles ago. A few days ago. He took a mental note that while she spoke of equality between them she found it easy to fall into her new role. *"How can you speak of such things when the entire world has changed? Look. Look at it there in the sky. We no longer need bonfires to guide us. The city no longer needs lit as a beacon. The darkness is gone."*

Kaius flinched at that last statement then said, in the measured tones that he would use with a child, "The world has changed for you in more drastic ways than an oversized torch. If we do not take action, there will be riots in the streets and armies marching on us before the heat-cycle has passed by. What is your command?"

Lucia stared at him blankly, *"Why do we have to do anything?"*

Kaius sighed, "Because if we do not, then many of the people of this city are going to die and you made it clear that your goals do not include widespread death."

There was more screaming outside as chaos spread throughout the city. She looked at him then back to the open archway and with pursed lips she said,

"Stop them from hurting each other. Fix this."

He nodded curtly then headed out onto the balcony. He tried to call strength to his throat only but the muscles around his chest and the back of his skull started twisting in protest. He called as much strength as he could and then started shouting out his proclamation to echo out over the city and plains, "I am Kaius. Beloved of Lucia. Negrath is dead by my hand."

In some quarters the screaming and panic became more widespread than before. He roared, "Silence!" and the city fell still.

"Negrath is gone. His servants are gone. Lucia is all that remains. By her order every one of you will be protected. Every one of you is promised safety as long as you are obedient. Every one of you is promised agony if you betray her in word or deed."

The words echoed out and met with a weighing silence.

"Chosen of Negrath. You served well and now a time of great opportunity is upon you. Any of you who wish to end your service are free now to do so. Go forth if you wish. If you still want to fight, to be more than mere humans. Present yourself at the base of this tower. Lucia will look upon you and judge those who are worthy of serving her."

He looked out over the people crammed into the streets to better hear the announcement. It had clearly captured their attention to drag their eyes away from the still rising sun. Kaius looked into the sun and his face broke into a momentary grin before he composed himself and resumed his firm tone, "To any who would make themselves our enemy I say this unto you. Look to the sky. By the limits of Negrath's power and artifice a city was lit. By the will of Lucia alone we bathe the entire world in light."

He turned his back on the people and strode back into the tower smiling. It was like being out in the dark again, not a sound to be heard.

He almost walked into Lucia. The metallic shimmer made it more difficult to read her face but it seemed obvious she was unhappy. Kaius cocked his head, "What is wrong?"

She stared at him, *"Why did you make it sound like I was going to kill anyone who disagrees with me?"*

Kaius shook his head, "If anyone requires killing then that duty shall fall to me."

She grabbed him by the shoulders, the skin on the palms of her hands was hot enough to make him wince, *"I don't want any more death Kaius. We have had generations of people dying at the Eater's whims. I am not going to be like that. I am not another tyrant."*

Steam started to rise from Kaius skin and he tried to maintain a steady voice, "I am trying to ensure the minimum of bloodshed. You made your wishes clear."

She snapped, *"You threatened to kill everyone!"*

Kaius nearly rolled his eyes at her naivety, "Yes. That threat is what is keeping us safe. If we were attacked I would have to defend us with force. People would die, the very thing you wish to avoid. Those words will keep conspirators and rioters at bay. They will give us time to form a plan."

Lucia walked back to the bed and flopped down, face first and groaning loudly. Kaius stood watching her and shifted uncomfortably from foot to foot. Eventually she rolled over and said,

"What am I meant to plan? I don't know what I am meant to do. Nobody should have to deal with all of this."

Kaius agreed dutifully, "This is the first time that an Eater has successfully destroyed another and seized their base of power. From what Negrath said before, I believe it was more common before history began being recorded. There is no precedent set for the correct way to behave in this time and place. While we have no guide down this path, it has the benefit that you are now creating the precedent. Whatever action you take now is how things shall be done in the future."

Lucia stared up at the ceiling, *"I just want to tell everyone that they don't need to be afraid any more. That I am going to take care of them instead of taking everything from them."*

Kaius halted her train of thought and made her look at him with new-found appreciation. "Words are fine and well but anyone can bandy them about to win public favour. Your actions will be what define your rule. Show them that there can be a better way."

"A better way would not start with dire threats that everything will remain as terrible as before."

Kaius accepted this meekly. "I apologise. I seek only to do as you will."

She sat up suddenly, *"Kaius, no. Stop it. I am not some goddess to worship. We are partners in this. You and I. We protect each other. We work together. I don't want a servant. I want... I suppose I want a friend."*

He frowned and she sighed, *"A permanent ally. Someone that you know you can trust forever. An equal."*

Religion was not Kaius' area of expertise but he was fairly certain that he was not the equal of an Eater. Any Eater. If he had not already possessed that belief, then a lifetime of having it pummelled into him would likely have convinced him. He was lesser. She was greater. But this was not the first unreasonable demand that had been placed upon him in his career so he spoke freely, cringing inside, "I expect that we will be attacked by the other Eaters before we can secure our power-base. I imagine that they are already on the move. We must secure a military force. With its threat, you can apply pressure to the city's nobles to serve you. Their private armies are not a formidable enough force to sway actual warfare, but they could cause a great deal of disruption. There is already a system of governance in place. I expect that you will want it all burned to the ground."

Lucia grinned at the prospect but he pressed on, "We do not have the time to build a new one before our enemies are upon us. If we use what is here now, we can survive the coming attacks and have plenty of time to reform what you want destroyed."

There was sense to what he was saying but Lucia saw the danger too. *"And what happens when another threat arises. Then another. How long do we postpone?"*

He stared at her with mournful eyes, "You have all of time to make things the way that you want them. I have only those years left to me to protect you as best I can."

Lucia flinched, eternity was not a prospect that she had ever considered before. Now it stretched out before her like an abyss. She stared into it for longer than she should have before she asked, *"What was Negrath like before he died?"*

Kaius frowned slightly, "I believe that it had been driven quite mad. It had been very badly injured at some point in prehistory and the wounds had festered. Have you ever seen an injury turn septic? There is a fever that effects the mind. It believed that you were one of the original Eaters, rather than a new addition to the collection. It loathed the creature that you consumed the remains of beneath the Glasslands. It feared it more than anything else, as did the other Eaters as far as I could tell."

Lucia sighed, *"You don't think that they would accept a peaceful solution?"*

Kaius was quiet as he considered and balanced the information available to him then said, "I believe that every one of the Eaters would destroy the others if given the opportunity. There is not open war only due to the balance of power. My actions have disrupted this balance. There will inevitably be war. And in all likelihood, the majority of the hostile intent will be towards us. Both as the unknown element and as a power that can be quashed before it finds its feet."

Lucia was despairing, flopping back onto the bed with her hands over her face. She let out another long groan. Kaius interrupted before she could generate much volume, "We must be proactive to avert this. If the other Eaters perceive us as too dangerous to tackle head on, then we will only have to deal with assassination attempts and political manoeuvring for a few years. Which should be sufficient time to make the changes that you want to make, and construct effective defences."

She perked up slightly, lifting her head if nothing else, *"So if we can just spook them we will get away with this?"*

Kaius shrugged and tilted his head, "It is not inconceivable."

She spun her legs off the bed and sat up, *"First thing is first. Chosen?"*

Kaius clasped her hand and drew her to her feet, "First the new Chosen. Then call a council of the noble houses to bring them to heel. Finally, we can present you to the public."

She glanced down at her ruined clothes and shifted uncomfortably, *"I don't think I will make a very good impression."*

He considered her carefully, "I imagine that the servants will already obey us without question by now. We could have clothing adjusted to fit you."

She looked him up and down pointedly, *"And you. Scruffy."*

He took in his ruined robes and ruined flesh, "I believe that my armour will be sufficient for the image I am trying to project. I will perhaps adjust the design somewhat to distinguish myself."

She thought on that with pursed lips, *"Can I make armour?"*

He paused to consider the question, "I can't imagine why not. However, it would perhaps be too militant an appearance for meeting the nobles."

She sighed, *"So I should just make myself pretty?"*

The Chosen were fairly utilitarian in their views. Sexism would not have been unknown to them, they did interact with the outside world and it was far from perfect. But holding onto the belief of superiority over another Chosen without evidence of it was poor tactical analysis. Something that was punishable. Kaius was uncomfortable with the topic, "It would not be terrible to appear desirable but it should not be our focus. We should do all that we can to emphasise your inhuman appearance. We must make it clear that you are more than human. To this end, I think that we should endeavour to display the changes to your skin."

She froze, *"What?"* she stood up quickly, *"A mirror. I need a mirror. Get me a mirror!"*

He scrambled across to the bronze tables around the room, knocking incense and finery aside in his hunt for a mirror. He eventually found a full length one tucked away in a recess and dragged it across for her. She put her hands over her mouth and Kaius backed away. Her breathing grew faster and faster, then she seemed to stop altogether. She whispered, *"This is fine. I can live with this. This isn't too bad."* She jumped back, overturning a table, then rushed to press her face next to the mirror, *"What? What is wrong with my eyes. Oh no. Oh no. No. No. No."*

She turned and stalked across the room, stopping with her head resting against the ivory wall and panting, *"This is fine. This is fine. Oh no. This is alright. This is fine."*

Kaius approached her carefully and rested a hand on her shoulder, she flinched. For the first time, he let some of his discomfort be known in his voice, "You are quite beautiful now. If that is your concern."

Lucia smiled and turned her faintly scaled face to him, *"Yep, I am a real looker."*

Kaius smiled back, "You were not exactly stunning before." She slapped his arm playfully and let out what might have been a giggle. Unexpected warmth blossomed in his chest and he mentally sorted it under strange new developments associated with the new words that he was learning. He rubbed his hand up and down her arm in the hope that it was comforting then drew back quickly. He said, "I shall fetch a dressmaker up from the city. Excuse me."

Chapter 14- The First Day

The entrance to the tower was packed with the city's previously Chosen protectors. Metharia had to push her way through them. They were soft compared to her. Used to comfortable duty. Used to giving immediate obedience to anyone who demanded it. She had killed within the last few days.

She was not just going to take Kaius' word that Negrath was dead, that her grandfather was dead. Beyond the throngs of old chosen in their old robes the tower was practically deserted. Servants still sprinted around but they were few and far-between.

She knew more than the common Chosen. Her grandfather had taken the time to talk with her, mainly to gauge the feeling in the Halls and among the Chosen, but the talk turned both ways and she had been educated in a noble house. She knew how to work information out of a reluctant conversationalist. She went down the stairs, noting the soot stains on the roof as she descended. The smell caught her as she went down the steps, sickly sweet and smoky. She had been in ghul encampments out in the dark lands. She had torn them apart in fact. But in each one there had been that same smell of spoiled and roasted meat. She passed by the dark patch on the stairs, slowing in preparation for an ambush but finding nobody there. No servants or Chosen. Everyone was too busy milling around up above. She passed by the furthest she had ever been before.

All signs of the silver door now gone and soon she came across the dead man's torso sitting by the closed door to the inner sanctum. It was discarded and forgotten like everything else that had gone before the rising sun. She gave him a quick kick, partially to check if he was alive but mainly to relieve her frustration, then she opened the door. Smoke poured out and the unbelievable heat inside curled her eyelashes. She staggered back, gasping for air. She spat and it sizzled on the blackened stone. Then she walked in with the heat cracking the cheap leather of her stolen boots. Progress was slow and the smoke was thick and black in the air.

She did not even recognise her grandfather among the mass on the floor until she accidentally rolled him over and exposed a patch of what had been his face. She was not sickened or even saddened, her fury ran too deep. She did not look at him for a moment longer. She just stormed over to the charcoal mass and began tearing at it with her bare   hands.

Her fingernails cracked and tore before she made it through the hard outer layers. Beneath there was pus, thickened into a tar-like thickness that she scraped away until she found what she was looking for. Elbow deep in the remains she found a pulse. She wrapped her fingers around the living flesh and tore it out in one great stringy mess. It was tiny and sickly and grey but it could not die. The power bound within it would not let it die. She sank her teeth into the last remains of Negrath. It tasted foul and bitter and she relished it to the very last bite.

***

Lucia was being swarmed by tailors and dress makers from the finest shops in the city. All too terrified to look at her, hands hovering always a breath away from touching her, flinching at her every word. Kaius had snapped off some commands to them rapid fire as he strode out of the room, trusting Lucia to handle them. Down in the entrance hall, Kaius was making harsh statements and barking out orders. He was bringing all the old obedient soldiers into the new fold. He said the words that had been spoken over him and Lucia experienced an insistent tug as fresh cords of power were drawn out of her and made their new connections.

Soon there were ten. Then twenty. All softly draining at her strength in tiny ways. The light filtering in from outside replenished it all in an instant. The clothes that they were stitching around her were black, not a colour you saw often outside of the Eater's service. They were cut sharp and angular, covering her completely in abnormal places but also revealing the patches of silver now rising up through her skin. When they drew the seams together it was so tight that her breath caught. Her body seemed to be streamlining, her curves, such as they were, were all smoothing out.

Those few assets that she had left were pushed up and out in a manner so aggressive that she wouldn't have looked out of place in one of the city's brothels. It was the same style mimicked by the majority of high society. She would have blended in well if it weren't for the other flairs on the dress. She could feel Kaius moving around already but now each of her new servants was a fixed point in her mind too. It tickled as some drew speed and flew off through the city, out into the lands she had just claimed as her own. At any distance she could sense them through that connection. She realised that the dressmakers, already having given up talking to her, now gave up speaking all together.

One poor girl brushed the back of her hand across Lucia's scales and hissed as her skin blackened suddenly. She had run from the room trying to avoid the Eater's wrath before Lucia even really knew what had happened. The others all froze in place. Lucia looked around their pale and terrified faces, all eyes were averted. She spoke softly, so as not to spook them, *"That girl did nothing wrong and I did not intend to harm her. This new power is... I am still learning to control it. I would not do any of you harm by choice."*

This statement did little to alleviate the tension in the room. Kaius returned to the room, took one look around and demanded, "Why is it not finished?"

The tailors started shuffling towards the door, leaving the seamstresses to complete their delicate stitching with shivering fingers. As each girl finished her stitching she ran for her life. When the last girl left Lucia shouted, *"Thank you."* at the rapidly retreating back of her head.

She sighed heavily. Kaius lifted her face by the chin and said, "You look most imposing. This will do well for the meeting with your nobles."

She leaned away from his touch with a bashful shrug then said, *"I burned one of the girls."*

He frowned and asked, "What did she do wrong?"

Lucia leaned ever further away from him, *"Nothing. She touched me and it burned her. I would never..."*

Kaius had turned away to look out over the balcony as she spoke, he glanced back when she trailed off, "I am glad that they did not displease you. You should come down to the audience chamber as quickly as you are able, the nobles have been stewing there since shortly after our announcement. They will likely have reached a consensus by now on whether they will accept your rule. You should make special mention of the Pontifex. They will be your priests until such time as there is another election. They will convey your laws and wishes to the people. They will be feeling the most threatened with the death of Negrath. Politically they hold little sway but to the commons they will be your voice, it would be helpful in your reforms if they are aligned with your goals."

Lucia's features twisted with anger and heat radiated off of her, *"My 'reforms' will be stripping them and every other noble of their powers and delivering them into the hands of the people that they have abused for centuries."*

Kaius replied flatly, "Better not to mention that part to them at the moment. Bear in mind that while they are somewhat unfair in their judgement they are also the only competent administrators and lawmakers that you have."

Lucia shrugged again, *"So just lie to them?"*

Kaius shook his head, "Be entirely honest about your goals. Emphasise the benefits of the changes to them as well as to others. The important thing to remember is that you are already in control.

If they wish to join you, then all the better. If they do not wish to join you, then the loss is only theirs."

He managed to coax a smile from her and they moved together towards the door. She halted him with a hand on his arm before they passed into public sight, *"Kaius. I need to know that you will support me. No matter if I get everything right or not."*

He smiled, "I serve you willingly and completely."

She gripped his new silk sleeve as he tried to walk on, dragging him to a halt. *"I need more than that Kaius. Tell me why you are doing all of this?"*

He had been wondering something similar. They stopped at the door and he gave it careful consideration. Eventually he spoke, "You sang to me. You sang about things that I did not know existed. That I did not think could exist. It made me believe that the world did not have to be like it was. I fought for Negrath because I was good at fighting. I was forced to do things that I have no pride in. There was nowhere else for me in the world. But now there is you."

She rose on her tip-toes and kissed him on the cheek. He froze as she did it and for the first time she noticed his unnatural stillness. She whispered, *"Thank you."*

They left in silence, both absorbed in their own thoughts.

The conspirators finished their plotting by the time that Lucia entered the room. Everything fell silent as she approached. The nobles who were the most timid literally threw themselves on the ground at her feet. The others still bowed deeply. In their lives they had experienced very brief audiences with the Beloved of Negrath. To be in the presence of an Eater in the flesh was enough to throw some into religious ecstasy, and others into a sin-fuelled panic.

She greeted them graciously as they approached her, whether they were weeping or smiling or quaking in terror. There seemed to be no order in which they came to her so it fell to Kaius' rather limited knowledge of the city's noble houses to inform her who had been in Negrath's favour, and who was of limited usefulness. He was constantly hovering around her and it began to irritate her even more than the obnoxious people that she was trying to play nice with. Eventually she laced her arm through his and they walked together. She ignored his initial stiffening and eventually he seemed to relax into the contact. He was a re-assuring coolness at her side.

The Pontifex sat separate from the rest of the nobles, sitting around the furthest end of a long table that had been pushed to the side of the room. When it seemed that nobody else was approaching her and the Pontifex were not moving she pulled away from Kaius and went to greet them. It was all just a performance and she had been on the stage since she could walk. The Pontifex froze in indecision. They could not decide if they should rise to greet her or fall to their knees in supplication, so they remained frozen at the table. She picked up a chair from the side of the room, set it in the midst of them and sat down. The whole room was silent and echoing. She put her hands flat on the table's surface where everyone could see them and smiled.

The effect was instant, a full half of the Pontifex went pale and the others looked greener. She spoke softly so that they all had to lean in to hear her. It was an old tavern trick but it did wonders. *"You were trusted with a duty to care over the people of Negrath."*

She saw Kaius tense as she spoke, waiting for the hammer to fall and the uproar to begin. She turned her full, wide-eyed attention to the men and women around the table, *"Now they are untended. I need you, brave bearers of truth. I need you to spread the news of my coming. I need you to let the people know that while their old master has passed away from them, I will protect them now."*

She moved her hands to cover those of the two Pontifex nearest to her, one of them fainted and the other trembled. Solemnly Lucia said, *"I will protect all of you now."*

There was a good deal of supplication after that and Kaius faded more and more thoroughly into the background, observing and making what polite conversation that he could muster. His eyes moved always, searching for the assassin's dagger, or the sudden attack from outside but drifting always back to her. Not staring but observing. Her bearing had obviously changed since he found a scared girl in a cave but it was more than just the act. Her physical posture had changed, her shoulders now drew back further and as well as becoming slimmer around the chest and waist she was becoming taller.

It took several viewings to realise it. Spaced out over the course of her meetings with the various noble houses and alliances, he doubted that she would realise before her head started scraping the door-frames. It would be a sensitive subject and he was glad to avoid it for now. He called the two Chosen from outside and set them to watch over the proceedings. He knew them from before the change. They had begun their time in the Halls of Steel just as he had left, but they looked at him with nearly the same worship that they directed to Lucia. He expected no inklings of betrayal from them. Distracted as she was with the dozens of supplicants, Lucia did not even notice him leave until the sudden tug of his called speed alerted her, but there was no time to investigate. The show had to go on.

He stopped first at the lowest point of the tower and dragged the blackened door from its frame. He walked into the roasting heat and pitch darkness timidly at first, but soon called a tiny spark of flame that illuminated everything. He crept across the ashes and the crust of dried flesh and skin until he reached what had been Negrath. The heat must have ruptured the creature from the inside. Its rotten and crispy parts were splayed open to reveal the depth of the decay.

Kaius lowered his head to the dead beast's side and deadened all of his senses bar hearing. He heightened his hearing well past the usual levels of safety and tolerance. He could hear the servant's whispers upstairs and the stone contracting as it cooled. He could not hear a sound from inside Negrath. He let his senses return to more human levels and looked properly at what he had wrought on the world for the first time. He squatted and put his head in his hands and gasped for air. He took that time and let his prized mind run through the meaning of all the things that he had already done in the name of Lucia. He composed himself as much as he could, called speed, and fled.

There was no official caste in the city that dealt with the dead, but there was a place for them. Tunnels coiled beneath the city. The earth was supported by twists of shattered ribs and, deeper still, there were smooth bored tunnels through the stone. Alcoves had been chipped away over the decades in the stone and in the bone. Most bodies lay scattered in the streets to be picked over by scavengers until rot set in. Those few lucky ones who had money and foresight enough paid to have their corpse dragged down into the cool catacombs where they were interred among their ancestors. Kaius crept down the tunnels in his bare feet.

There were candles flickering down here. A ridiculous extravagance anywhere else in the city, but here they were dribbling yellow and reeking things. Nobody questioned who did the work down here, stripping off the clothes for resale, sorting the bones for easy storage and rending the fat into those candles. Deep beneath the city, close enough that heat now rose into the chamber from Negrath's tomb, there was a corpulent banquet laid out. Five dead lay spread out across the table. Rescued from decay to sate a strange palate. The party was just beginning to gather down there.

There were nobles there, less important ones that did not have to attend the new Eater. There was a plenitude of them in fact, and far fewer merchants and commoners. Spaced out among them, having made a slow and dangerous trek through the few pitch-black tunnels that extended beyond the city's walls, were the true savage ghuls. They shook and quivered like Chosen who had called speed. Their skin was cracked and dry, their eyes were sunken and dry. There was a restless energy as they all gathered, looking out upon the feast that had been laid before them. Pontifex Arlia emerged from an alcove in her full regalia with her arms spread wide in greeting.

The religious leader had fallen into deep disfavour among

the proper nobility after her faux-pas at the last feast of Valerius, but here she was still loved. Here she still demanded respect. She said to the gathering, "On this strange occasion we are gathered. At the changing of our times, we gather to worship as only we can. Let us partake of our sacrament and remember the Eater that has passed. Let us feed and give thanks for the Eater who rises."

The words were barely out of her mouth when the gathered ghuls fell upon the fresh meat. Arlia shrugged and sated her own cravings, tearing flesh from bone with her bare hands.

The sounds echoed along the tunnels until they reached Kaius' ears. He did not call his steel before he entered the chamber. There was no need, his face was well known to the nobility in attendance and theirs were smeared with human blood. Only the ghuls from outside the city tried to run, but they barrelled into the others in attendance. Kaius held up his hands calmly showing his peaceful intent and for a short moment Arlia knew hope. Perhaps this new Beloved would be more kind to those of their persuasion. She met his gaze and the hope fluttered and died in her heart. He crossed his arms and gave the gathering a smile,

"Let us talk."

Another feast was laid out, far above the interrupted one and for a more refined taste. Lucia sat at the head of the table, chatting cheerfully with a few noble women that had an interest in songs and history. Their new-found favour was delighting them and they quickly became accustomed to the strange resonance of her voice. Their areas of expertise had never found them much in the way of acclaim under the old rulers, who had pleasures that were more direct. Kaius slipped back into the room after his long absence and it was all that Lucia could do not to jump up.

She lost all track of the conversations around her for a moment and when the women realised and glanced around a couple of them giggled behind their hands. Lucia discovered to her relief that she could no longer blush. She gave Kaius an imperious nod and tried to regain her composure. She took the conversations in a drastically different direction, hoping to rattle the women, but they were more than up to the task. Kaius circled the table, leaning down to whisper some comment to a lesser noble. There was a ripple of conversation in his wake, excitement and the outward appearances of happiness followed him.

Darkness swept over the land once again and, as much as the commons had wailed over the rising sun so much more did they despair at nightfall. Kaius had to rush back up the tower and bellow out reassurance while the party raged on inside. Alcohol had circulated and some of the guests were drifting out of the main room to indulge in marginally more private pleasures together. Lucia looked on it all with thinly veiled disgust. She walked through the room with Kaius on her arm and an abiding distaste for all of her new people. When she caught a glimpse of one of the girls who had earlier been discussing the finer points of string instruments ducking under a table with a salacious wink to the delight of her companions, it was too much for her. Lucia leaned into Kaius and whispered, *"Have we done enough to win them over yet? Can we leave?"*

Kaius gave a barely perceptible nod and they drifted out of the room. Without the sun filling her up with power, Lucia shuddered with every drain now as her newly Chosen called speed or strength as they went about their orders. It made her nervous to begin with but she quickly got a feeling of the depths of the well that she could now draw upon. It would take more than this to deplete her, it would take more than all of them drawing on everything to drain her entirely. The two of them walked up the spiral stairs and they needed no torch between Kaius' night eyes and her faint warm glow.

They came to the chambers of the Beloved and pushed inside without comment from their Chosen guards. Servants had been over the room and it was much more presentable with the majority of Valerius' belongings removed. Clearly some dressmaker had been talking because the servants had been replacing the wall hangings and bed covers with black silk.

The only remnants of the cream colour scheme were the scrimshawed walls themselves. Candles were lit around the room in brass holders, pure and white ones, made from real wax. When Kaius shut the door behind them, they took a long moment to enjoy the silence. The city still bustled outside, their troops feet could still be heard echoing from the top of the walls, the party downstairs was still a whooping and liquid sounding riot, but when they pushed away their senses to the very edge of humanity, it was silent. Lucia smiled at Kaius openly for the first time since they began meeting with her nobles. He tried to return the smile honestly but he had to force it now that they were in the bedchamber and anxiety was churning inside him. She strolled over to the bed and flopped back across it giggling and exhaling all of the day's worries. In a flurry, she said, *"This is actually working. We are going to make it. Those people are horrible in general, but in person they are just people, you can talk to them. Every time I spoke to one of them like an equal you saw their whole world changing. This is amazing. This is everything I could have hoped."*

Kaius walked to the bed with leaden steps and maintained his smile, "You did amazingly well. I believe that you have won many of them over."

She sat up suddenly with a sharp toothed grin, *"Yes, I did! I was amazing. I am amazing!"*

Without having to construct comforting words this time his answer came easier, "You certainly are."

Still grinning wildly she held out her hands, nodding, *"Yes I am."*

Carefully displaying his indifference, Kaius raised his hands to meet hers. She laced her fingers between his and spoke softly, *"Everything is going to be alright Kaius. There is nothing to be afraid of anymore."*

She tilted her head to one side, looking at the smooth lines of his face, already restored by a single day's healing. She tightened her grip on his hands and pulled him down until their lips touched. She kissed him softly but he did not move. He didn't flinch or pull away but he did not kiss her back. She let go of him and leaned back quickly. He was staring past her with an empty expression. She murmured, *"Kaius?"*

He drew away and said, "I am very sorry. I thought that you were... I thought things would be different. I understand now."

He cupped her face in both hands and kissed her with all of the passion that he could fake. Now she was the one who lifted her hands and pushed him away, *"What are you doing. Do you not want this?"*

He froze again and almost imperceptibly shook his head. She rolled her eyes and lolled back on the bed groaning, *"Well I have made a fool of myself as usual."* She glanced down at him with an awkward grin, *"Is there some other girl you have your eyes on? Who should I be jealous of?"*

He shook his head again then with a tremor he whispered, "I don't like these things. I do not want these things."

Immediately she was sitting up again and grasping at his hands, *"Oh my sweet boy I am so sorry. I didn't want to make you feel bad, quite the opposite. I just think that you are amazing too."* She stopped and frowned, *"If you didn't want to then why did you..."*

"Because you wanted to. I was just trying to please you."

She snorted in a very unladylike way. *"Fine pair of fools we are, Kaius. You never have to do something that you don't want to do. I will never make you do something that you don't want to do. Do you understand me? Do you understand that I am not like the monsters you had to bow down to before?"*

He met her gaze with damp eyes, "I am truly beginning to understand now."

The night stretched on. The party downstairs ran its course after several cart loads of liquor and whores were consumed and enjoyed. The nobles drifted off to their houses surrounded by a loyal retinue of guards. The servants scurried around righting the damages that the festivities had wrought. Up above them all, at the top of the tower, two people sat and spoke softly, sharing the stories of their lives and drawing closer. They were interrupted very briefly when the screaming outside began anew. They both rushed to the balcony but stalled when they saw the cold circle illuminating the world. Lucia whispered, *"How many more big, glowing things are we going to find in the sky this week?"*

Kaius shrugged, "However many they hid I suppose."

They stared up at the moon and she took hold of his hand. He did not flinch away from her now.

"How many more ways can the world change?"

Kaius squeezed her hand, "It can change as much as we make it change."

Chapter 15: The Tightening Noose

From the depths of the woods the sound of breaking stone echoed out into the returning dark. The solid slabs of the moss-covered dolmen shook and split. From amidst the tangled roots first one, then two gigantic hands emerged to part the earth. Walpurgan clawed her way up out of the earth, the cracks in her dull grey skin already glowing, but suddenly blazing bright when the moonlight struck her. She ascended through the woods, growing taller with each step until she towered over the ancient, petrified oaks. Her eyes reflected the silvery light of the moon and her silhouette vanished into the glow. She strode through the woods and into a clearing that her servants had spent a sweltering day clearing. By the time she reached her assembled owl riders, the huge birds reached only to her knees.

She spread her arms wide and let out a booming laugh that rippled across the translucent grass at her feet. The owls were pinned in place by her mental domination but even they were uncomfortable. There was a great deal of shuffling feathers and shifting from one foot to the other. Her foot soldiers were already assembled outside the forest and preparing to march. She had been ready to move since before the sunrise. War was an inevitable part of living among the Eaters of the Gods, but the forces being mobilised here represented the entirety of Walpurgan's armies. Her lands stood undefended as she gathered her troops for the long march to the old seat of Negrath's power. The moon's light suffused her and her dwindling reserves once again filled up with power. It did not matter what happened to her lands now. It did not matter what happened to the people of the forests that she had claimed as her own. All of them could be replaced with this power returned to her. Anything was possible now.

With barely a thought she reshaped the tapestries of power that had sat so long unused over her body, expanded them once more to encompass her full girth and through a cunning twist here and a clever word there she gave to herself the shape of an owl, albeit one far larger than the others, and lacking a harness. It would not do to arrive at her prey too soon, but it would be necessary to scout ahead to find a roost for her winged legion. With a thunder of wings, the owls and their riders took flight. The Strangled Forest was abandoned.

Out on the plains an army marched in the sun, shielding their eyes with wide brimmed hats that the camp followers were frantically weaving from long grass. Amongst them, in a shimmer, moved the Chosen applying lash and harsh words to keep them in formation. At their flanks, great beasts of steel walked. These cunning constructs of the Marked were filled with desperate, blinded Chosen following their orders without thought. Many of the Chosen in the field longed for such freedom. At the rear of the columns was a great beast constructed from living sheets of steel. A palanquin for the Beloved of Vulkas. The beast walked on four legs. It had a hunched back and curving horns. No mortal alive had seen one, but the Eaters remembered them from the days before the dark as cattle, indulgently kept for meat.

What the Eaters remembered reverberated in the minds of their Beloved. It was now beyond the skill of the Marked to construct this machine for her so she had done it herself. They came out onto the blinding plain of glass as the sun dipped sullenly towards the horizon. They were over a thousand strong with forty Chosen amongst them. There were another two thousand in the militia, though they would be of little use in prolonged combat except as a buffer. It was one of the most impressively large armies that could be fielded by any Eater.

The progress had been slow, though they set off on the same day that the letter from Walpurgan had arrived. Their supply lines were harried every step of the way. Many of their servants and peasants had been carried off in raids through the nights. It had been five days now since they mobilised, five days for this new Eater to entrench herself.

Vulkas had been certain that was the course that she would take. Certain that the field would be left empty and they could lay siege to the Ivory City. They had planned accordingly, arranging for great shipments of food and construction materials that were being lost during the ceaseless attacks. They suspected in the beginning that it was some commoners uprising in support of the new Eater but as time went on and they started to find the camp fires and the well chewed bones around the camp fires it became clear that Negrath had never come down on the ghul problem in its lands in a significant enough way.

In the path of the army stood a man. He was clad in called steel, shaped in a pattern never seen before, sleek and almost seamless, patterned with fine scales. The march drew to a halt and the man gave a formal bow. He walked, unchallenged and unafraid, through the ranks of soldiers. The metal constructs drew back as he approached the great steel bull. When he stood before it he gave an even deeper bow.

In a shimmer of liquid steel the Beloved of Vulkas emerged and fell to the glass with enough force to send a cobweb of cracks over the surface. She was a hulking creature, as were all the people that dwelt in her lands. While other Beloved made all efforts to appear dignified and perfect, the better to win over their nobility, Hulia was a creature of war, and she strove to appear as intimidating as possible. She was dressed in called armour but instead of robes it was accented with the thick fur of the albino moles that were a constant nuisance in her lands. Her hair was a faded red, turning to grey and bound in huge braids down her back. Her yellow teeth were on full display when she sneered down at her visitor. "Are you the new one then? Why shouldn't I just have you cut down?"

Kaius released his armour and met her gaze, "I am the Beloved of Lucia, and you should not have me cut down because it would cost your army dearly. And because we have a common cause."

She spat at the glass by his feet, "How's that then?"

Kaius glanced around at the many listening soldiers then shrugged, "Because Walpurgan seeks both of our deaths."

She considered this casually, "Aye. She's been trying to kill us since the dawn of time. What's your point."

Kaius came a step closer and the great metal beasts of Vulkas' siege machines shifted to loom over him until Hulia waved them back, "I have heard whispers from within her camp. I have taken some of her owl riders, blinded by the light, and extracted information heard from their mistress' lips. When the three of you come to lay siege to the Ivory City, her army will turn on yours."

Hulia grunted her disdain, "Such an obvious ploy from you, trying to divide us."

Kaius kept his eyes on hers as though they had bare blades in their hands and were circling, "The one that I serve will be mighty soon but for now she is new to these arts. Walpurgan does not consider us to be a threat, merely an excuse."

Hulia's eyes were small compared to her expansive face, but they narrowed further still as she tried to find the flaw in his logic. Kaius pressed on, "We are warriors you and I. We have more in common than you have with that witch. My mistress does not seek war with Vulkas, the mightiest of the Eaters. Think of the peace that we could make together if you held Walpurgan's lands as well as your own."

The glory of finally crushing this old foe would ensure Hulia's place in the war-songs of her people for all of eternity. She kept on searching for the deceit, obviously this Lucia would have to be destroyed, but did it need to be now? Could this opportunity be used to clear the field? Hulia remained silent for a long moment, trying to draw more out of Kaius, but sighed when he smiled at her placidly. "What do you propose?"

Kaius said, "When the siege of the Ivory City begins she means to strike at your flank. Her army will turn to face you, and while my people are occupied defending themselves from Ochress' forces, she will tear through you."

Hulia leaned forward, "What about Ochress' army? What of them?"

Kaius resisted the urge to smile. "When I have your word, I will go to them and speak. I will try to draw them into this alliance of ours. But even if they decline and remain ignorant, I believe that we would be better served working in concert. When Walpurgan turns on you, we shall come out from the city and strike her newly exposed flank. Between the two of us we will destroy her."

Hulia closed the distance so that Kaius could smell the sour wine on her breath, fury simmered behind her eyes, "Then what? You just let us take her land?"

Kaius shrugged impassively, "The Glasslands serve as a natural border between our lands, and I understand that my master wishes to direct her attention elsewhere."

Hulia's eyes flashed wide again at the prospects. This newcomer meant to wage war on Ochress. The Ivory City, and all of its lands would be the exposed rear of the chain of supply. It could be seized. It could all belong to her. And Vulkas, of course. One thing still troubled her. "And you will just trust my word?"

Now he smiled at her, "Of course. As I said, we are warriors, not backstabbing politicians."

She spat into her hand and held it out to him. With barely any signs of disgust or reluctance he did the same. They shook hands in full sight of every man, woman and child in her army. They all heard his words. She smiled drily, perhaps he was not as foolish as he seemed.

In the tower the finest of her Chosen were in attendance of Lucia. They had been selected by Kaius as the best and brightest, the ones whose fluid loyalty had solidified under her caring approach. The march of days, just waiting for the invading forces to arrive, was beginning to weigh on her. Kaius reassured her every night when they found their peaceful time together that the city would be safe, that the people would be protected and she watched from the tower as the farmers and miners of the exposed lands around the city flooded in, having received their warnings from her Chosen.

She was taller than before, towering a head over Kaius now, and her already slim frame was becoming spindly and lithe. The fine silver scales covered her entirely now, her hair receded away from them and while it maintained its new lustre, it seemed to be thinning and disappearing at an alarming rate. Her eyes, in Kaius opinion, were the most changed. They had slowly elongated, first into the almond shapes of his own eyes and now longer still. The changes happened mostly at dawn, but through careful examination and experimentation, he believed that they could be exacerbated by drawing upon more of her power. She had attempted a few of the simple creations that she half recalled from her time beneath the glass. Tiny flames drifted over the Ivory City, illuminating it at night and driving on her metamorphosis.

To begin with she had been afraid of the changes, but as time went by and she accepted that her personal changes at least were inevitable Lucia pondered what her final appearance would even be. Sometimes the little flames would explode upward, searing an owl and sending Walpurgan's spies fleeing back to her. Sometimes they would burn hotter and brighter and drift down over the slums on cold nights. It was not much but it was all that she could do for now.

Kaius had explained that feeding the impoverished would actually become much easier once the siege had begun and they could begin rationing. If they established it early, and it was shown that it was successful, they would face much less resistance to their other plans for the future. This was the direction that their night-time conversations were heading now. More and more often. What were they going to do with the peace when the other Eaters had been driven back. Kaius pressed her to do more than drive their attackers off, to hunt the other Eaters and spread her influence, but something in his sensible strategies made her uncomfortable. The words sounded too similar to the ones she suspected that the other Eaters and their Beloved were sharing.

Lucia laid a many jointed finger on the brow of each of the Chosen in attendance and pushed some of her will through that smoking connection. Her mark was physical as well as spiritual, each of these men and women left the audience chamber with a fresh black burn upon them.

Each of them went off to the special duties that Kaius had already assigned them. Lucia felt the tug increase as the power she granted them grew. Between them and the new lights, she was starting to get a feel for this new ability. She kept her eyes locked firmly on the real world except when she was summoning her lights. Staring at it too long did not give her a headache as such, but it left her disoriented. It made navigating in the real world difficult. It made her question her own use of the term "the real world" as a means of contrast. The longer she spent staring out with her new vision, the more she suspected that the world she had spent her entire life looking at was just the front end of a more complex machinery.

She shook the thought away and tried to be practical like Kaius advised, but she wondered if this is what happened to the other Eaters. If this was how they stopped thinking like people, and stopped caring about people. On that practical, real world level that Kaius kept on dragging her back to, she understood that the defences of the city were being dutifully reconstructed. That her soldiers were being trained day and night, that her Chosen had been given special orders and new stratagems, and that she understood less and less of it every day.

Her time spent with the nobility was surprisingly relaxing, she truly enjoyed talking to these people with all their privileged education and fine manners. Compared to the life that she had before, this luxury alone made up for quite a bit of the suffering she had to endure to get it. They were not easily swayed by her humanitarian arguments. But the fact that she was making arguments instead of pronouncements, and the fact that they could argue back without fear of execution, had made her many friends in the court.

Families that were long out of favour quickly adopted her

new policies. Charity was spreading out like an infection despite the larger noble houses digging in their heels. The tide was beginning to turn. Now all that she had to do was let time bring the rest around. Just that, and defeat three all-powerful immortal monsters from the dawn of time. She took each small victory as it came to her.

Lucia had been happy to see Kaius appear back in the tower each night, even if sometimes it was long after the sun had set and he was smeared with dirt. She did not know the entirety of the work that he was doing, the fortifications being built or the tunnels being collapsed, but she acknowledged her own limitations readily. He knew how to wage war and whether she willed it or not, war was coming for them. Nothing drove that home as clearly as the sight of the owls bursting into flames each night. That and the ominous cloud of dust rising over the Ashen Dales as what Kaius described as a colossal army approached.

Ochress was moving more slowly than the other two, and she had heard rumours among her Chosen that there were not any signs of him moving against them at all. Kaius considered it to be a wistful hope. Ochress' troops had not been seen because they were moving with stealth, not because they were not there. The opportunity was too great to pass up. That was how Kaius always described the death of Negrath, as an opportunity. Lucia was not sure if he was a perpetual optimist or if it was some sort of combat term, an opening in an enemy's defences.

She had watched him going through the motions of the Forms of Bone early one morning in a little courtyard garden and when he had finished and realised that she was there, he had playfully led her through the movements saying, "You must learn to defend yourself." while nudging her off-balance constantly. After the third fall she had conjured a ball of flame and chased him back into the tower with it. It had all been in good fun until a servant spotted her stalking the halls with the blue hot flame dancing in her hand and fainted dead-away.

Three more days and nights passed before the armies of Walpurgan and Vulkas came into sight. Any one of their Chosen could have cleared the distance far faster of course, even a merchant dragging a cart of his wares could make the trip faster because an army is more than just the individuals it contains. It is a great slow lumbering beast, dragging a fat tail of whores and merchants and a long chain of messengers and supplies all the way back to wherever it came from. Not a single man could take a step without every other man taking the same step and it slowed things to a crawl. It had given them time to prepare but also too much time to think about what was coming. Kaius had warned her about the war-machines, so she was not too startled when she caught her first sight of them. But as they drew closer they got bigger and bigger, her mind struggled to accommodate the sheer size of them.

Walpurgan's army lacked such extravagance. It merely held thousands of highly trained killers and hundreds of giant swooping death birds. As Lucia watched them from her tower a particularly large owl circled over that army then plunged down into their ranks. Lucia covered her mouth to stifle the gasp. The creature had fallen so fast it must have died and likely taken a few ranks with it. Lucia peered out, trying to make out the result of the fall through the clouds of dust it had thrown up. Walpurgan rose up amidst her soldiers, at least twenty feet tall and emitting shocks of green-blue light from her cracked and stony hide. Lucia stepped backwards into the room and had to sit down. This was too much.

How could anyone contend with a creature like that? How could anyone dream of fighting against it? The heat of anger flushed the despair from her. These thoughts were what had kept people cowering in fear before these monsters for centuries. This could be the end of all of that, if she could just be brave. She walked back onto the balcony and looked down at Walpurgan. Walpurgan look straight back at her and waved. Then she threw her head back and musical laughter rolled over the city. The pitch growing higher and higher until the commoners quaked, the Chosen covered their ears and the rare panes of glass shuddered in their fittings.

"Will you come and parley with me, Lucia of the Cowering Flame?"
Walpurgan's words shook her where she stood. She tried to shield herself with anger at the slight but it wasn't enough. Dread was sinking into her. She blinked her eyes a few times, making sure that there were no tears there. For just a moment she let her gaze slip into the other world. She saw the complex masses of will tied around Walpurgan, stretching off to her servants and in a hundred different directions. She traced the path of one, thin as spider's silk that seemed to come all the way to the tower. She followed it along until she reached up and touched where it connected to her own temple. The anger chased away the despair this time. With a flick of her wrist she severed Walpurgan's connection to her and all of the fear

vanished. She would have to remember that particular trick and try it out with Kaius if she got the chance. Her vision was still on the other world and she watched Walpurgan closely.

The giant woman was immobile but her mind was moving tirelessly around, twitching a construct here and expanding a weaving there. There were rich and dense tangles of power all around that it would take Lucia all day just to discern the purpose of. In this arena she was clearly outclassed. It seemed time to gamble heavily on Kaius' much vaunted tactics. She wondered what his reply would have been. She could hear him in her head after their many hours deep in conversation, "You cannot let this insult stand. It will affect the morale of your soldiers. You must make some impressive display. Startle the enemy, make them back down."

It was like he thought that people were wild animals, just barely tethered by the commands that the Eaters passed down. She heard the voice again but this time it was more urgent.

"Make your display now. It would be better if it did not initiate hostilities. We cannot afford to take the field without all of our enemies arrayed, but you must do something."

She furrowed her brow and then realised that this voice was not her imagination. He was not the voice of reason in her mind. He was reaching out across their connection and speaking to her. She tried to form a reply but couldn't even work out how to send words down the cord to him. He must have detected her confusion and doubt through the link because his next message came through with the force of a roar, "Are you the coward that she claims you are? Fight back!"

Walpurgan's sniggering voice travelled over the city once more, *"See how this weakling cowers behind her walls. See how pathetic this domain has become. See how feeble are its defenders."*

Lucia staggered under the impact of the words and the same spark of anger that had let her shrug off Walpurgan's insidious attack the last time ignited once more. She stormed out onto the balcony and glowered down at both of the collected armies. She snarled when her vision narrowed in on Walpurgan's smirking face. In her ire, she had not grasped the balcony's balustrade. Her hands were wrapped around the copper posts that Valerius once used to light the city. Her face split into a razor toothed grin and she unleashed her power in a torrent. Starting at the tower and then rippling out, the galvanic lanterns that the city had once held as a great achievement exploded and great gouts of flame burst upwards.

A cloud of smoke blossomed out and darkened veins appeared all over the ivory of the city as the copper running through them carried the heat. The entire city lit up like a bonfire for a long and glorious moment before her anger abated and she realised that she may have inadvertently burned her citizens. She drew the power back within herself. It was difficult and almost painful to swallow it all back down now that it had run free but when the worst of the smoke drifted up into the sky, she saw that every man, woman, war-machine, and giant had moved back from her city walls and showed no desire to move closer again.

Kaius' pleasure washed over her through their link and she briefly wondered if there was a way to close this connection now that it had been made without severing their bond entirely. It wasn't that she did not see the value of it or even that she did not like knowing Kaius' thoughts, it was just that she did not know if she wanted him to know every one of hers. In the city, she heard the first cries of alarm from her people as they discovered their homes alight, but quickly the cries blended together into a roaring cheer. Somehow, they knew, they had recognised that she was here for them. A warmth spread through her body that had nothing to do with the flames licking up all around.

Night fell over the city and the armies around it. They had not laid siege just yet, they were waiting for the final third of their number to arrive, but it was only the very brave, or desperate, farmer or trader that would run the leery gap between the armies. There had never been peace between any of the Eaters. Only that tremulous halting of hostilities that came from forces too evenly matched, and an unwillingness to expose their back to the third party's knife. As united in purpose as they wished to be now, it was only the stern discipline of the Chosen stalking the ranks that kept the soldiers from charging the other's lines.

Lucia sent up her flames, far greater in number than any of the previous nights and it was lucky that she did. Walpurgan's Chosen riding on owl-back were out in force, swooping down into the city streets and scooping up any person foolish enough to break the new curfew. Some of the owls fell to the flames drifting in the sky like lily-pads. Others were dragged down by Chosen, House Guards, and desperate commoners, and hacked apart when they came close enough to the level of the roofs. Soon Lucia emerged from the tower again and launched lances of blue hot flame into the sky above, striking down the circling owls before they could make their assaults.

The fires burned so bright that they left after-images in the eyes of anyone looking up, which was every person that could hear the dreaded and petrifying shriek of the owls. In desperate need of rest, it was with ceaseless complaints that the armies of Walpurgan and Vulkas rearranged themselves into ranks before morning. Vulkas' war machines formed a safe buffer between the soldiers. Cold fog rolled over the plains, giving the troops in the field a very poor night's sleep. It also masked the approach of Ochress' army. When dawn arrived the three armies were arrayed around the city walls. Walpurgan's cackling could be heard as far away as the Glasslands

Chapter 16- The Turning Wheel

Ochress army were not clad in armour except for the called steel of a few Chosen. They wore leathers and silk, things that would not drag them down, if they fell overboard. Ochress' naval forces were the envy of the other Eaters but they could not be brought to bear here, so close to the centre of the continent. They served well as troop transports along the rivers, but even the rivers were now left behind. Water in the Ivory City was found falling from the sky or pooling deep under the earth.

The other armies seemed quite civilised by comparison. They were trained soldiers rather than a loose assembly of raiders and pirates. No leader was visible amongst Ochress' rabble, which was just as well because neither of the other leaders seemed moved to converse. Only the Chosen and Walpurgan had senses sharp enough to make out Lucia's appearance on the balcony of her tower. She was alone once again, her Beloved probably already fleeing for the hills or trying to inject something like morale into the doomed defenders. Lucia stood for a long moment, her quaking invisible at this distance, then did as Kaius had asked. She raised both hands and unleashed a plume of flame into the sky.

Immediately her enemies sprang into motion, just waiting for some sign that hostilities had begun. Walpurgan shrieked with delight as her soldiers began pressing forward. The whooping sound reflected back to her from the Chosen as they raced ahead of the lines and began making impossible high leaps. The owls, stirred from their daytime slumber only by the barbed coils of power that Walpurgan had snared in their minds, took flight in a flurry. They snatched the Chosen from the air and carried them up towards the battlements.

At the top of the city walls, Lucia's own Chosen had gathered. They had not called their steel but they had armed themselves with ropes and hooks which they flung skywards now, dragging any owls foolish enough to fly too low from the sky and letting the gathered foot-soldiers butcher them. Some flew high enough, some made it past that first line of defence, only to be confronted by the incinerating wrath of Lucia in her tower. There were still flames drifting all over the airspace above the city, nearly impossible to see in the daylight. Some of the owls struck those and exploded in a shower of sparks. Others were lucky enough to avoid them only to find themselves being herded together by the drifting clouds of flame and annihilated in the great blue lashes of fire erupting from Lucia's outstretched hands. It was not complex, it was not a fraction of what any of the other Eaters could do with their power, but it was certainly direct.

Walpurgan snorted in disgust, to see an Eater reduced to artillery was distressing. This must have been her Beloved's influence. Walpurgan was glad to be above such things. She started to walk forward alongside the tight-knit formation of Chosen around her, she would tear down the walls with her bare hands if she had to. Her magic was woven densely in the air around her, reaching out to every dying bird in the sky, to every Chosen in her retinue and to a thousand lesser workings that she could bring to life with barely a thought.

Walpurgan's Chosen rained down into the city, scorched and maimed. No army was required to dispatch them. Lucia had won over the people of the city with a fraction of the kindness that she fully intended to give in time, and they fell upon the armoured women with butcher's cleavers, kitchen knives and pieces of furniture. It lacked elegance, but it was certainly effective.

From her position so close to the city, Walpurgan could not see Ochress' or Vulkas' armies, her own men stretched out too far, and she was too intent on the creature before her. She did not realise what was happening until she heard the screams from her own flank, her connections there were severed. They had been betrayed.

Vulkas' war-machines were wading through her ranks. Each of their four razor legs were double edged and bloody all the way up to the joint. She sent a pulse through the link to all her remaining Chosen but she could do nothing but watch in frustration as they sprinted among the other soldiers, trying to turn them from the enemy on the walls to their brutally exposed flank. Many soldiers fell under the slashing legs of the machines and those that were missed were hacked to pieces by the charging ranks of soldiers. Vulkas' Chosen were held back, only lunging into the fray when it seemed that some of Walpurgan's army was crystallising into some semblance of a defence around a particularly effective leader. Before it had even begun, the tide of war was turning against them.

Hulia was itching to join in the fighting, she could not believe that Walpurgan had been so foolish as to take the field herself. If that giant could be brought down and bound ,it would make for the greatest offering ever laid before Vulkas. She could feel him in her mind. She could hear the grating stones of his voice reverberating through her. *Bring down the witch. Bring her to me. Steal her strength.* Even without the voice she was already frothing at the mouth in anticipation. She held herself back and snapped out commands in her booming voice and watched her great victory unfold.

In the midst of her turmoil she even felt some iota of gratitude towards this Lucia and her Beloved. Without them none of this would have been possible. Hulia called her steel into the form of the great bull again and leapt up within it to get a better view of the battlefield. Her soldiers had pressed a third of the way into Walpurgan's army in a wedge. A huge arrow pointed straight at the giant woman presiding over them all.

She was close enough that Hulia could practically taste her blood. She frowned for an instant at that odd thought then shrugged it away. The battle fury made the mind chaotic, that was why she had to keep a clear head and direct her soldier's wrath. There was an uproar from the rear ranks and she chortled. Men desperate for glory were screaming out for the charge. She laughed aloud, spraying the inner side of the bull's helm with saliva. Let them have their charge.

Let her have blood and glory. Let her wipe the smug smile from that crusty old statue's face.

The bull bellowed and charged, trampling through Vulkas' troops and Walpurgan's alike. The head swept low to the ground and the horn's dragged through the masses of bodies, flinging them into the air. Those not destroyed were trampled, those not trampled were fallen upon by the rest of Vulkas' army as it poured into the gap in the enemy lines. The bull charged on. Coming to almost within striking distance of Walpurgan before she casually raised a hand and the air around it solidified.

Metal shrieked as the artificial muscles strained against the raw force of will. Hulia grit her teeth and pressed forward with all of her might and step by agonising step the bull crept closer to Walpurgan who seemed blissfully unaware. Her attention instead turned back to the city, keeping watch for the inevitable strike. The two giants drew closer still and Walpurgan finally sensed the pressure in the air. She rolled her eyes and flicked a wrist in the direction of the bull. There was thunder without lightning. A concussion lifted the bull off of its front legs and drove it staggering back into Vulkas' ranks, crushing a dozen men as it staggered. Hulia roared and the bull let out another bellow.

The back ranks of Vulkas' army fell easily to the marauders. These were men and women who learned to attack in silence as soon as they could hold a knife, to slip from still water and slit throats in the night. They carved their way along the rear ranks evenly. Cutting down a soldier, waiting for the body to fall then moving forward a step. Five ranks were down before the uproar began, before the screams picked up and the army of Vulkas tried to fight back. It did no good, the only defence against the skirmishers would have been a solid formation, ranks lined up and shields locked together. As it was, the soldiers fell just as easily facing the enemy as with their backs turned. The front of the army, so intent on cutting down Walpurgan, and deafened by the bellowing of their Beloved, went on about their bloody business. The divided attention meant death to many in each army.

Now that all pretence of stealth was surrendered, the Chosen of Ochress leapt deep into the ranks of Vulkas' army, dropping like falling stars and slaughtering indiscriminately. Soon a wide circle had formed around each of the Chosen. Terrified men were held back beyond the reach of their thrusting spears. Just as resistance seemed to be forming, they leapt again, plunging deeper still into the heart of Vulkas' army. The honeycombed ranks were distracted for too long and they were swept away by the charge of the rest of the marauders.

Hulia may have lacked social graces but nobody knew how to call steel like her. Muttering the equations to herself she started thinning her armour and pouring more and more steel into the flowing liquid muscles of the bull. The outside of the bull crumpled as the pressure of the air increased until suddenly the tipping point of applied force was crossed and the bull lunged forward again. Hulia hooted and snarled as she stamped through the ruined formations of her army and Walpurgan's alike. Her eyes were fixed only on Walpurgan herself and foam flecked the corners of her mouth.

Walpurgan was casting her head around, seeking the things that were hidden from her sight by the spider-silk thin threads of power stretching out from the city. She traced them back from the Chosen positioned on the wall to Lucia in her tower but she could make no sense of the wavering connections that stretched out all over the battlefield. She nudged aside her gathered Chosen with a bare foot and strolled casually over to where one of the threads dipped under the surface. She crouched down and brushed the top layers of dust and ash away, ignoring the clamour all around her. She dug down deeper until she uncovered a criss-crossing of ancient bones. With a twist of her wrist and a tug she pulled them out and looked at them in confusion. The mix and mash of parts reminded her most of tangled roots. She lowered her face to the hole she had made and peered inside.

Lucia looked down on her city. The few fires that the falling owls had caused were stomped out rapidly. She cast her gaze beyond the city walls and watched as the huge armies turned around the axis of her tower. All of her dread was gone. Everything that Kaius had promised was coming to pass. She could not count all of the people dying outside her walls and she almost drowned in the empathy that Kaius had warned against over and over. War was not the time for sympathy.

When the fighting was done, she could welcome all of the injured and afraid with open arms. She could show once and for all that she was not like the Eaters that they had known before. Kaius presence was just a tickle in the front of her brain as he used her eyes to judge the course of the battle. Apparently enough chaos had finally been created by the circle of betrayal that they had orchestrated because she heard him clearly in her mind, "Send out the signal."

Rolling her eyes, Lucia grasped the blackened metal bars and sent a pulse of fire across the city. For an instant a spark of flame appeared in every lantern. Her Chosen arrayed around the walls had been waiting for this sign.

They had been waiting with the desperate energy of tethered beasts. Every one of them called their steel. The tunnels that they had been expanding frantically since the first day suddenly fulfilled their purpose. They were not high enough for a man to stand up in. They had barely been reinforced, and indeed many of them had already collapsed on their contents. As was intended. The tunnels that had not collapsed were problematic as the called armour laid to rest there had begun crawling along, seeking the Chosen that had summoned it over the past few days. They had pinned the errant armour to the ground with piles of stones and hoped for the best. With Lucia's signal, every set of armour was a silver arrow now, darting up out of the earth and tearing through the soldiers and Chosen above on its way to its master.

Walpurgan fell onto her backside, wailing as the armour burst from the hole that she had dug and ripped through her head. A splatter of black ichor struck the few Chosen around that had not been crushed as she fell. She turned her remaining eye up to the sky and shrieked. The sound swept the battlefield, knocking armoured men to the ground, bursting the eardrums of those too close.

The sound struck Hulia as she charged and she roared right

back. Suddenly freed of the air's hold, the bull lurched across the battlefield and one great curved horn rammed into Walpurgan's side. Baying in triumph, Hulia raised her head and dragged the giant woman off her feet.

The effect on Walpurgan's army was instant, they broke and fled for their lives. Vulkas' army cut them down by the hundreds as they fled. Finally, they realised that Ochress' army was sweeping over them. Finally, they turned to fight back.

The great war machines lurched over the entire battlefield and began carving into the massed warriors. Black and oily gore rained down on Hulia, falling through the eye-holes of the bull and coating her as she roared and giggled. Walpurgan's remaining eye bulged and she flailed her arms around. No sound escaped her lips, only an explosive release of yet more blood. In her panic she severed the connections around her. All of her Chosen became powerless. Those who had been leaping to her defences fell naked from the sky onto the waiting blades of Vulkas soldiers. Others just stumbled and died beneath the bull's staggering feet. The owls, freed of her control fled the chaos of the battlefield, dragging those few Chosen still mounted on them away from their floundering master. Many of the owls even twisted their heads around to peck the irritating weight off their backs.

The connection between Hulia and Vulkas was too strong to be severed by Walpurgan's spells, but it was throttled to within an inch of its life. The steel of the bull became liquid and rained down onto the battlefield. Hulia nearly drowned in the flood. She rose up still clad in armour with the excess steel pouring off. She spat a mouthful of liquid metal into the face of the first of Walpurgan's soldiers, who was foolish enough to approach her. Then she cut him down with disdain.

Walpurgan's broken body hit the ground and knocked the mere mortals off their feet. Hulia rocked but stayed upright, then let out a belly laugh, reshaping her hastily made sword into a thick length of chain. She whipped Walpurgan's side and roared, "Get up so I can beat you some more!"

Over and over she struck Walpurgan's twitching hide, roaring and laughing all the way. She began to sweat. None of her officers dared to approach her, to tell her of the losses at the army's rear or to intervene. She whipped at Walpurgan's side until the bark-like flesh sloughed away and the old creature's ribs were exposed. She swung out the chain again and entangled it amongst the bones. Hulia hauled with all of her called might but while the ribs creaked, they would not break. Instead Walpurgan was dragged breathless across the ashen field. Hulia barked with laughter through her exertions. "I shall drag you back like a side of meat old witch. Vulkas shall feast on your heart!"

The sweat was pouring off her now, many of the soldiers still milling around were falling to their knees, gasping in the heat. The battle rage abated long enough for confusion to show. Then the fire-storm exploded up from the tunnel beneath them.

Lucia staggered back into the tower when Kaius unleashed his fire from beneath the battlefield. She had not experienced such a drain since before the sun first rose, since those awful moments when he had used her power to kill Negrath. She moved forward again to put herself directly into the sunlight. Power filled her just as quickly as Kaius drained the life from her. She had never realised how much trust she was putting in him. The fire rose higher than the city walls and carried above it the charcoal bodies of a hundred men or more. The dead fell back into the torrent of flames. Their screams covered by the roar of its burning. Vulkas' army, already reduced to a fraction of its initial strength, routed in the face of this otherworldly power and scattered across the farmlands around the city.

The tower of flame abated, leaving behind a black plume of smoke. The reek of molten fat swept over the city as sooty bones began to rain down. Kaius pulled himself up out of his bunker beneath the battlefield, one of a half dozen that had been dug out in a circle around the city, so that no matter where Walpurgan approached, there was a way to take her by surprise.

Only Ochress' army remained. Though some of them had succumbed to instinct and given chase after Vulkas' fleeing soldiers, the Chosen were whipping the rest of them into shape and readying themselves against a counter attack from the army within the city. An entire army held in reserve as their enemies slaughtered one another. An entire war turned on a lie.

Kaius looked around himself at the desolation. A crater of blackened earth, sharp outcropping of glass where there had been enough sand trapped beneath the surface and the ruined bodies of his enemies. Most of the bodies were just twists of molten metal wrapped around a few bones, some were not even that. They had simply exploded in the face of the sudden heat.

The only body that still had human form was that of

Walpurgan. One of her arms had been charred clean off her body, as had half of a foot. The injury on her eye had been sealed by the heat. The rigid surface of her skin was thick with soot where it had not been melted clean away. The light that had been pouring from her body before was reduced to a dim flicker emerging from her countless gaping wounds.

Kaius' face was locked in rapturous joy. Walpurgan did not move, but he had his suspicions. He lashed more flames across her back and delighted as she moaned and tried to drag her ruined body away from the heat. He called his sword and crept across to her. He leaned down to the blackened nub that may have once been an ear and whispered, "See how feeble its defenders."

She whimpered, whether in pain or fear he did not care. It filled him with vigour. Across the connection, he called out to Lucia, "Come down. Bring out our army. Let them face off against Ochress' little remnants. Let them feel the victory too. Quickly my beloved, before some other fool tries to take our prize."

Chapter 17- The Divide

The city gates had been cobbled together in the last week from pieces of furniture and ancient bones but they swung open smoothly as Lucia's army emerged. The Chosen worked furiously to keep them in formation but it was a struggle. Each of the noble household's guards had their own agenda. Each one of them was still trapped in the old mindset and they intended to win glory and favour on the battlefield, blissfully unaware that killing for Lucia was the last thing that she would have wanted. Added to that press, were all of the citizens of the city, driven into an adoring fervour, that had snatched up anything that could be used as a weapon and formed their own militia.

They were at the rear, by Lucia's direct command, kept as far from the fighting as possible despite the more experienced commanders' suggestion that they be used as a human shield on the flanks. Once the army had emerged it wheeled about to face Ochress' army. The pirates and ravagers that were left of Ochress' army were forming up into a loose formation, ready to break apart at any moment to pour around the flanks of any group that pressed their luck too far. Lucia walked away from them with pronounced disinterest. She was not concerned that the battle would turn against them now, not after so much had happened. Besides, if Kaius did not care, then she wasn't going to concern herself. He was standing at the centre of a huge blackened dip. The impact was centred on the only solid object that remained, other than his shining form. The limp body of Walpurgan.

His grin had not abated when he turned to Lucia and in a rush of excitement he swept her up in his arms and spun her around. It was the sort of thing that he would have called undignified if any of her Chosen saw them. He set her down with a flourish. Walpurgan hissed at Lucia and tried to lash out with the blackened stumps of her massive clawed fingers, only to find her hand sliced off at the wrist for her troubles.

Kaius tutted at her like she was a spoiled child. Lucia took in the ruined mass of flesh with a pained sigh, *"What shall we do with it? How do you keep something like this captive?"*
Kaius smiled slipped, "You do not, Lucia. You destroy it before it can regain its strength and seek vengeance."
Lucia looked out over the roasted flesh of her enemy and shook her head slowly. *"We can put it down in Negrath's hole for now. I can bind her, I think. Keep her powers contained."*

Kaius stared at her in dismay as her pupils divided and she began to weave strands of will together. He reached out a hand but the heat radiating from her gave him pause. Long slim coils of flame encircled Walpurgan. Flickering between the threads there was a cobweb of tiny searing filments, so fine that a human eye could not have seen them. As Lucia's weaving was completed, it snapped into place on him. He felt before he saw the long leash of twisting, living flame leading to his hand. Lucia turned to him, *"Can you drag her in by yourself?"*

He looked at Lucia, then at Walpurgan. There was no expression on his face, he had reverted to that blank mask that had been a necessity for his years of service in the name of Negrath. He whispered, "No."

Lucia frowned at him and said, *"Do you need me to give you more strength? Or shall we call over some of the Chosen to help you?"*

He raised his free hand and she stopped speaking. Then he said more emphatically, "No. I will not bring a viper into our home. I will not let you do this. It is madness."

He called fire and it poured down the length of the leash. Walpurgan thrashed and shrieked as the mesh tightened around her. She threw out her power in any form it could take, but each time the coils of flame dragged it back within her. Walpurgan burned and wailed and wept while Lucia just stared in horror. The net tightened as there was less and less of the old Eater still intact. The roar of fire was still not as loud as the inhuman noises Walpurgan made while she was burned but it was close. Lucia panicked and tried to close the connection between her and Kaius but by then Walpurgan has stopped wailing and was making a wet warbling sound as she was crushed within the net. Lucia severed the wrong connection as she panicked and the net fell apart, letting the charcoal remains to crumble out across the ground.

Undaunted, Kaius started pouring fire directly out of his

hands onto the tattered flesh that remained, scorching it down smaller and smaller, blasting away everything that had made it look human until there was only a twisted leathery hunk of flesh left. Lucia stumbled as the torrent of flame drew strength from her then managed to pinch off the thread of power leading to Kaius. He reached into the broiling mess with one hand and tore a hole in the withering sac of flesh. He pulled something tiny and brown from inside. It was a heart, cooked through but still beating. He bowed down before Lucia and held it out to her. She backed away from Kaius with horror etched on her face.

Across the field, the two armies clashed head on. with the raider's screaming and the noble soldiers setting their stances as they had been trained through agonising rote. The Chosen of Ochress were powerful and skilled but the Chosen of Lucia had been watching them fight all day. When Ochress' Chosen launched themselves into the air, they were slapped back down to earth by Lucia's, armed with heavy hammers. Crushing armour and dashing them back into their own lines. When the rest of the army came on into the lines of the Ivory City's defenders, it was with a clash of steel but no movement. The defending soldiers did not take one step back towards their home. They held the line. As more and more of the marauders pressed in against them, so tightly that they were crushing their own men, so tightly that they could not swing a weapon. Still, they held the line.

This was war at its most simple. Two lines with an army behind them, pushing for all that they were worth because the line to break, would be the army opened up to their enemy. It was why soldiers did not train for strength or skill at arms above all else and instead trained for endurance. The weight of Ochress' savage killers against the shield wall grew heavier and heavier as more of them flung themselves against the back of their companions. It was a game that they would likely win. Even weary from their clashes with Vulkas' forces, each and every one of them were trained killers. They had been making good use of that training for years when all that Negrath's armies had done was drill and practice. The armies of the Ivory City would look far more refined on the battlefield, they would look far better organised and far more polished, right up until the moment that they began dying.

The Chosen were each worth a dozen men but Ochress' army had more than a dozen men to spare. Every time Lucia's Chosen burst out of their formation to try to break the enemy lines they were dragged down under a mass of bodies and butchered. More bodies pressed in. Each side had to expand their lines to stop the enemy from slipping around their flanks. On this open plain with no obstructions, the lines could keep on expanding out until there were no men left. Each expansion brought more death as the few moments before the lines reformed gave enough leeway to cut a few of them down.

In a war of attrition Lucia's people would win. Ochress army had fewer numbers. But war is not a game of numbers, and the militia could not hold the line against Ochress' raw brutality. They were kept away from the fighting until the line stretched too thin. Then in desperation the untrained civilians were flung into the fighting, armed with only chair legs and devotion. The militia fought bravely. They fought with joy in their hearts to be serving Lucia. They died in droves. Ochress' army swept around the flanks and in a lethal pincer movement they drove into the heart of the defenders. The line broke.

The front lines tried to fight their way free and failed. A second line formed further back in the formation, behind the pincer point, with everything ahead of it left for dead. The raiders bellowed their triumph and trampled over the scattered defenders, striking the new line with renewed vigour. The new line had fresh men but they were already frantic. They glanced back over their shoulders, they considered defeat for the first time since they took the field and they moved in little steps back towards the city gates. Ochress' army could smell their fear, they were practically salivating as they pressed against the line of shields. Victory was close enough to taste. The servants of Ochress could not take their eyes off of the flinching defenders and the rich city of spoils peeking out tantalisingly from behind their banners. The invaders did not look back. They did not even glance at their rear ranks. If they thought that their training in stealth was impressive it was nothing compared to the talents of the dark lands' ghuls.

The ghuls had not just killed the rear ranks, they had already started dressing their corpses for an evening meal. The press of flesh made their work easy. The armies of Vulkas and Walpurgan were scattering across the land. Some were reforming with their camp followers, hiding at the distant edges of the farmlands, while others scattering in little groups to try and make a life for themselves, far from the disgrace of defeat. It would have taken the ghul hunting parties a long time to seek them out and round them up and this battlefield was a buffet.

A cheer of victory from the ranks of Lucia's army would have been enough to draw attention to the attack from the rear but Lucia's army did not know if these were allies at all. They watched the invaders fall beneath the rough stone axes of the ghuls and did not know if they would be next.

Lucia heard her people crying out in pain. She turned her back on Kaius and all the confusion that he carried with him and fled, stumbling across the battlefield. The press of bodies was too tight for her to fling bolts of fire as she had before. Not without the risk of incinerating her own soldiers. With a flick of her wrist she threw out a line of that searing thread once more, a simple trick now that she knew how. It ran between the press of shields and left a charred line along them. She wove a quick, fine net of power and then called strength into her throat and bellowed out, *"Stop!"*

Her own soldiers scattered away ,but Ochress' troops still had their orders and tried to press through. With disgust she pulsed more flame into the line. She stretched and skewed it into a paper-thin wall of flame between the forces. She swept her arms across the field, scorching the earth, and drove Ochress army away from the city. They fled backwards across the field, pursued by the flickering wall of searing light, but even then they did not realise that they were being cut down by the sniggering ghuls behind them. Only when they decided that the day was lost, only when they were down to fewer than a thousand did they turn to the chattering peg teeth, spiked clubs, and ravenous hunger of the ghuls. Then it was their turn to show fear and the ghuls' to show their ferocity. The rout did not last long.

Lucia banked the flames of her wall, building it higher and hotter. She had never knowingly crossed paths with a ghul during her travels. She had probably unknowingly sung for dozens of them. Possibly even slept under their roofs when it was offered. Even so she classified the creatures beyond her wall of flame to be an entirely different species of evil.

These were the haggard, wild ones that lived out their days far from the eyes of humanity. Far from the morals of civilisation. She built up the heat and was ready to wipe them out when Kaius caught her arm. She let the heat abate and turned her face to him, she let him see her fury, *"I am busy killing, just like you demanded. What more do you want from me?"*

He shook his head, "These are our allies. We promised them that their crimes would be forgiven, and they would be welcome to trade here in the future. They are the reason that we had the time to build defences."

She burned his hand where it was still clasping her upper-arm. Smoke billowed, and while he did not cry out at the pain, would never cry out at pain, he still let out a loud gasp.

In his unburned hand Kaius still held the throbbing chunk of meat. Hoping to placate her he held it out, "This is all that is left of the old witch. If you eat this, you will gain all of her powers. You will recover your strength by night and day. You will have mastery over all wild beasts. You will call the four winds. With this power, you will crush the other Eaters. You will remake the world. You can free every man, woman and child."

Lucia backed away. Her concentration faltered and the wall of flame disappeared. She tripped over the naked corpse of a nameless Chosen of Walpurgan, landing heavily on the ground. One hand covered her mouth and she was wide eyed. She whimpered, *"Not like this Kaius. It isn't worth anything if we do it like this. Walking through a world of corpses and eating out their hearts? How could you want this? How could anyone want this? This is a nightmare."*

He was pressing against the hindquarters of Lucia's brain, trying to force his way in, to let her see the obvious truth of his way. With a furious lash of her will she snapped the connection between them. It was Kaius turn to stumble. His turn to fall to his knees. He stared at her, shocked into silence.

"Go away Kaius. Don't come back. I can't spend all of my time worrying that you are going to kill everyone the second I look away."

"But... you told me that I didn't have to do whatever you said. You told me that we were equals."

She rose to her feet and glowered down at him, heat radiating off her in waves, *"That was before you took the power that I gave you and killed thousands of people with it."*

He stared beseeching into her alien eyes, "For you."

She spat on the ground in front of him. It sizzled. *"I don't want you to kill for me Kaius. I don't want any more death. You thinking that it is alright to kill for me is the problem. So please. Please just leave."*

He lifted up the still beating heart to her and she turned her back in disgust. She walked away, leaving him kneeling in the bloody mess of victory that he had made for her.

Chapter 18- The Wounded Heart

Safely enclosed back in her chambers, far from the eyes of subjects and spies, Lucia wept. Her shoulders heaved and she gulped in air but no tears came from her eyes. Even that had been taken from her now. Night had fallen as the wounded were sorted through. Her own soldiers could not understand why they were sparing the enemy. Her nobles could not understand why she had their expensive doctors looking over common soldiers' injuries. If Kaius had been here there would have been a few barked commands and worrying glares and her will would have been done. Now there was endless debate and interpretation of her words. Every noble was in conflict with every other one, every merchant with enough wealth to register in their estimations tried to slip bribes to get their way. The only thing that they could all agree on was that her opinions were deeply flawed, and her policies were unenforceable.

There had been less than an afternoon and two dozen arguments. She tried to push thoughts of him away but it dawned on her that he would have to be replaced, and soon. She was confident that she was clever enough to be a singer, probably clever enough to run rings around her nobles, but how could she hope to keep ahead of every enemy without some ingenious strategist whispering in her ear every step of the way. Her knowledge had limits. The night was not dark, the city was encircled by camp-fires. Cooking fires.

Lucia had not let the ghuls into the city despite whatever promises Kaius had made but she also could not drive them off, not without putting another knife at her own back. At least now she had the Pontifex on her side. They had come in screaming at her about her unholy alliances until they realised that she was in complete agreement with them. She sat on the bed and buried her head in her hands. More hair came away and she gave a strangled laugh. Just another kick while she was down.

There was a gentle knocking at the door and Lucia frowned, she had given the Chosen clear orders that she was not to be disturbed unless there was an emergency. She pointed vaguely to the door and cast out a fine thread of her will, tugging it open abruptly. The girl outside looked startled but she steeled herself and crept into the room. Lucia was still sitting on the bed, glowering at the intruder through the stringy remnants of her hair.

The girl tried to bow down while still creeping forward and nearly ended up in a heap on the rug. She whimpered and grovelled, "Sorry to trouble you mistress but I knew that if I didn't come to see you now I would lose all my courage before heat-rise."
Lucia looked at the girl trembling on her floor and sighed. She patted the bed beside her and the girl stared, not at her but at the bed, in disbelief. Lucia noticed the girl's bandage wrapped hand and recognised her at last, *"You were the seamstress that I burned. I am so sorry."*

The girl shook her head vigorously, eyes still averted, "I just wanted to say that I am sorry that I thought ill of you mistress. I am sorry that I believed you would have hurt me on purpose. I've been hearing about all of the things you have been doing. All of the wonderful things you've been doing to help folk. I saw what happened out in the fighting. I just... I just wanted you to know that I'm grateful. That everyone is grateful. For all the things you have been doing to keep us safe and to help us. I know we are all yelling and making a fuss but you are... Well... You are much better than all that came before, and no mistake."

Lucia stared at the girl. Tears would have been flooding down her cheeks if she was still capable. The girl half walked and half crawled across the room and kissed the dusty hem of Lucia's dress. Lucia caught the seamstress' chin in a cool hand and tilted her face up until their eyes met. The girl shook but she did not pull away. Lucia whispered, *"Thank you for reminding me that this was worth doing."*

The girl's face broke into a crooked grin and in that moment Lucia wanted to keep her. She stroked the girl's hair with some envy and then shook herself out of her reverie. *"Go and find whoever is in charge of my treasury. Tell them I have commissioned you to make dresses for me. Lets say, six dresses to begin with. They are to pay you in advance, and you will have to visit with me many times in the coming weeks to make adjustments and take measurements."*

The girl's eyes dropped back to the floor and she moaned, "You are too generous mistress. It will be an honour to serve you."

Lucia sighed and smiled politely as the girl scuttled back out of the room.

***

Without speed to call Kaius was shockingly slow. Just another abandoned soldier on open plains that were scattered with them. He had found an axe and a belt on a body and it seemed to be enough to convince the other deserters that he was too much trouble to kill. He had shared one of their spluttering little camp-fires shortly after nightfall and had fallen asleep for a few hours. He came awake gasping, he had forgotten how the weight of exhaustion could drag you beneath the surface. By the time he awoke, there were even more soldiers and whores gathered around the fire. Lost and far from home, he pushed his way out of the crowd and headed towards the Ashen Dales. It was familiar territory for him. It gave him comfort and he honestly did not believe that Lucia would send anyone after him. She really didn't have the mind for any strategy more than a few steps ahead. He would have seen the value in what she had discarded so carelessly.

She would see his value before all was said and done. Then she would beg him to come back to her. He felt the first bite of hunger as he waded through the ash dunes. It was the first he had experienced in more than twenty years. He had a solution hidden in a twist of silk in his pocket. A solution to his hunger and all of his other problems. Just as soon as he could find somewhere isolated and safe, somewhere he could rest while the change took him.

***

It was quiet again, in as much as the city was every quiet. Lucia sat alone with her thoughts and, although they were brighter now, she longed for company in a way that she never had while out walking in the dark for days at a time. She rose frm the bed and tried to shake it off. The arguments that she had to deal with were evidence that the changes she was making were working and, more importantly, the people recognised what she was doing for them. It was only a matter of time before she could pass the power to them.

Her first revolutionary thoughts of exiling the nobles and re-distributing their wealth had been tempered by contact with them. They were not evil. Not any more than the starving thief was evil. They were all just trapped in the same web that the Eaters had woven. The nobles could keep their wealth. It seemed like fair recompense for the fact that they wouldn't be allowed to pass laws to shore up their positions of power any more. Lucia thought about the merchants and their bribes. She thought about the entire machinery of the noble houses all suddenly resorting to slipping bribes and striving fruitlessly to turn back the clock to their glory days. She realised then that she was going to be fighting them forever. Kaius would have just lopped off their heads and gone about his day.

There was another knock on the chamber door, much firmer than the first. It echoed around the dim chamber and Lucia realised that she had not even bothered to light candles. Why would she when she could see just as well in the dark? She must have been quite the imposing sight for that poor dress-maker. The knocking came again. Lucia realised that the fine cord of will connecting her to the door had never broken, only become inert like the mess that had covered Walpurgan.

She brought it back to life and pulled the door open gently

this time. Lucia was standing in the middle of the chamber, illuminated only by the flicker of torches from the hall. The figure in the doorway stood stock still, light shining off its bald head, and for a terrible moment Lucia thought that Kaius had come back. She quickly summoned drifting balls of fire around the room and realised that it was just another one of her Chosen. She reached out for their connection and found none. She frowned and readied herself. The Chosen in the doorway gave a majestic bow, keeping her eyes fixed on the shimmering creature at the heart of the tower. It was only when the front of her robes gaped open that Lucia realised that her visitor was another woman. It was strange how much of a difference hair made.

Lucia called out, *"Who are you and why are you disturbing me?"* This seemed to be all that the woman in the doorway needed, she stalked into the room with a polite smile, "I served Valerius before you killed him. I served Negrath too, I suppose, though we never met."

Lucia watched her dispassionately. *"So now that the fighting is done you have come to sign up again? Is that it?"*

The woman halted abruptly. "To my sorrow, no. I have no heart for violence. I did not come to you before for that very reason. I saw how Kaius was behaving. I feared for my life if I spoke out against him, powerless as I am."

Lucia swallowed hard on that uncomfortable truth and the woman went on, "I have observed you Eater. I have learned what I can of you from a distance and now that you have cast that monster out I felt safe to approach you. I would not become Chosen again if you gave me the choice. I regret everything that I did in service of Valerius. But my knowledge, the education that I received, I still have it. I want to use it for something good. That is what brings me to you."

Lucia stared at this woman, her face the picture of innocence and, now that she saw her properly, of elegance. There was a faint familiarity there, something in the tone of voice that reminded her of the early days after she fell beneath the glass. The voice was all clean tones and education. Lucia tried to focus. *"You wish to educate me?"*

The woman strode closer, eyes lighting up, "I wish to support this wonderful world that you are creating. As long as you promise to me that I will not have to kill for you, I will take the traitor Kaius' place. I have been trained in strategy by the same teachers as him, my mind was ever as quick as his. I know that you only kept that monster with you because you were afraid. I know that you needed someone who could advise you, someone to talk with. I could be all of that for you. If you will have me. and if you will give me your promise."

She ended her little speech standing directly in front of Lucia. She showed not one trace of fear, not for an instant.

Lucia's face must have given something away because suddenly this stranger lunged forward and embraced her. Held close, Lucia began to sob once more, this time in relief. The woman held her close and stroked up and down the scales of her bare back. She shushed her and whispered, "Everything will be alright now. I am here for you."

Lucia clung to her and wept once more. Through gasps she whimpered, *"I don't want you to hurt anyone. I don't want anyone to hurt anyone."*

A hand slipped down to the small of her back and the woman whispered, "I know. I know. I will take that as your promise. Don't worry. I will take care of you now."

Lucia pulled back from the embrace and tried to compose herself, *"I am sorry. I don't know what came over me."*

The woman smiled softly, "It is all too much. Far too much for one person to endure alone. No wonder the Eaters have their Beloved. No wonder the Beloved have their Marked. The burden must be shared somehow."

Lucia found herself nodding at this stranger's words, *"I do need somebody. I do."*

They clasped hands, "Then you shall have me."

Lucia let the beginnings of a smile creep over her face, *"I don't even know your name."*

The woman reached up and stroked the wild strands of hair away from Lucia's face, "I am your humble servant. I am Metharia."

Chapter 19-   The Longest Peace

That year seemed more pronounced than those that had come before. Most of it was the cycle of light and dark. Everything that came before seemed like a living dream. Mankind clearly was not meant to live in darkness. It had preyed on their minds. Some of the year's distinctiveness was the slow grinding gears of progress that Lucia was forcing around in the city. The notable changes as repairs were undertaken, when slums were swept aside and new towers of cheap housing were thrown up as quickly as the noble houses could finance them. Now that they could see the profit in renting out property instead of letting people freeze to death in the streets, they were at the forefront of the efforts to rebuild.

When they were stopped in the streets by their new tenants and blessed in Lucia's name, over and over they began to develop an entirely new perspective on life. Some of them went on as they always had, treating the commoners as something to be endured, and sometimes trod on. But other took very kindly to this new adoration. Their properties were the ones that were becoming well stocked with firewood now that the cold season was coming in, theirs were the ones with doors that locked and windows with real glass. Their properties were the ones that were already full to capacity with a waiting list started. They were also the ones who always had strangers ready to run an errand for them, or shine their shoes on a street corner without demanding a penny. The other nobles learned from their example. Especially after the incident in the market.

Change always brought tension, and for one unfortunate nobleman it erupted when he casually backhanded a merchant who was haggling with him. It ended in murder, and ultimately in the merchant's execution by the Chosen who intervened, but the nobleman's family was forced to sit in silent fury throughout the court sessions as the events were laid out clearly and a vote was taken to judge where guilt lay. The merchant was not turned over to the nobles for questioning, he was not turned over to them for punishment and the entire system of justice was changed behind their backs. From that day forward the noble class seemed to be aware of how precarious their balance was at the top of the social pyramid. Many retreated to countryside estates where they could still carry on as they always had, but even out there, far from the eyes of Lucia, her presence was still felt.

The bows were not deep enough, the grovelling was insincere, and the fear was gone. These peasants, these dirt farmers and ash-sifters, thought that they were safe. They thought that they would be avenged. It was intolerable to the inflexible minds of the oldest noble houses. Lucia never moved against them openly. She barely even acted against them in secret. She merely let the other houses know how much their efforts were appreciated. One by one the voices of dissent fell silent.

It was only a few short weeks before the air began to turn to poison. The insect farmers noticed it first. Their charges became lazier and lazier as the days went by until one day they could not be convinced to leave their burrows to graze. Out in the dark lands it struck people first. In the city peoples' lives were slower paced, they were not running or straining themselves so they gulped down far less of the air. Soon though, they were struggling with tasks that had been simple mere days before. It struck the ghuls worst. Their encampment outside of the Ivory City had gone from places of loud rustic celebrations at night to desolate silence.

Lucia had no trouble drawing breath, nor did her Chosen, and Metharia remained stoic throughout the gradual decline. Before long the nobles coming to pay homage to Lucia, and indulge in their ceaseless nagging, were fainting if the conversation became too intense. Corsetry was abandoned and couches were scattered throughout the audience chambers for visitors to recline on. It grew worse and worse until Lucia and her Chosen alone could walk freely through the city. After Metharia's eventual collapse, Lucia had laid the woman down in her own bed and walked among her people for the first time.

Fear was rampant in the city and it carried with it rumours and whispers. The poisoned air could not carry the whispers far, but even the Chosen were human and guilty of gossip. At Metharia's request, one of the Chosen fetched a woman from out in the slums by the walls, where she had lain down to die. Arlia, was much fallen from her position of Pontifex. Despite all of the other changes, she still had not been accepted back into the fold of her peers. She had pinned all her hopes on Kaius raising her back up to grace and his exile had been the final blow to her aspirations. She had not been cast out of the city to live among the feral ghuls of the dark lands, so she supposed she owed Kaius for keeping that one secret at least.

She was draped on one of the overstuffed couches by the throne and Lucia crouched down beside her. Arlia croaked, "Thank you for this audience Lady Lucia. Words cannot express my gratitude."

Lucia shook her head sinuously. *"Do not waste your words on platitudes. Tell me what the people are saying. You live among them and they have no fear for you."*

Arlia grimaced, "It is a curse, by their reckoning. Their reasoning is that Walpurgan had mastery over the winds and she meant to drag us all down into death with her."

Lucia had been in court long enough that her expression did not change. Had Kaius doomed them all?

Arlia reached out with a shaking hand. Her fingertips brushed against the shimmering scales on Lucia's cheek, "I told them that you will save us. Always, when they come to me with their fears and doubts I tell them, our lady of flame will save us. She will burn our troubles away. Do not doubt my loyalty sweet Lucia. I beg you." Lucia jerked back from the wheezing woman, she could smell foulness on Arlia's breath. Arlia had passed out by the time Lucia looked back at her. Lucia sighed then turned to the Chosen by the door, *"Did you hear that?"*

The smooth helms nodded up and down almost imperceptibly. She chewed on her what was left of her lips, how would Kaius act? How would Metharia? Lucia met their gaze and set her shoulders, *"Then repeat it. All of it. This is a curse, but I am going to end it."*

Since the air began to turn, she had not slept in her chambers. Metharia was interred in the bed and the need for sleep had been waning since the first moment sunlight had touched her. Lucia stroked her palm over the woman's smooth head and sighed. At least she was not sickening as swiftly as the common folk.

If she woke, then Lucia would offer to make her one of the Chosen, to protect her from whatever this curse was. If she had not been so terribly aware of the way even the few chosen she had were tapping her strength, she would have offered it to everyone in the city. In the sunlight she had infinite resources, but in the dark of night she could be drained to a husk far too readily. Metharia had been clear that she did not want to be Chosen again. Just the thought seemed to fill her with revulsion.

Lucia would not force it upon anyone. Not after the transformations that had been forced on her by her ignorance. An oil lantern burned by the bedside but it grew dimmer and dimmer with each passing day. Whatever was spoiling the air was doing the same to fire as it was to people. This made it all the more sinister to Lucia's mind. This was clearly a direct attack on her. There could be no doubt about it. With Metharia taking up the bed, Lucia drifted out onto the balcony and looked out over her domain. The moon had slowly shrunk at the same rate as the air turned bad. Now it was gone. The nights were darker than they had ever been. The people were too weak to light fires. Those that the Chosen managed to get alight in their humanitarian efforts spluttered and died moments after they had moved on. Lucia stood staring up at the distant light of the stars. They were so familiar but so dim compared to the new lights that had come to dominate the sky. Then she did the same thing she had done every night since this fresh nightmare began. Her pupils divided, then divided again as her vision wavered out of the spectrum that humans could see and into the higher level of perception that she shared only with the other Eaters. She began her search again, looking out across the world for whichever tangled cord or misshapen word that had been woven in the underpinnings of the universe was turning the very air against her.

The Strangled Forest was abandoned. The people who had followed Walpurgan through the ages had come up from beneath the earth and scattered across the world to isolated settlements or whichever heretic strongholds would take them in. The forest itself was sickening. The thick vines that had held it strong through the ages at Walpurgan's behest were no longer being fed their diet of fresh corpses. They had been withering in the sunlight without their creator tending to them. Their flesh was starting to fade, the darkness was seeping out of it as the blood and sap separated. With each passing day they became more and more green. The pods that had pulsed out air through all of the centuries, the ones that had made the forest breathe, were swollen to near bursting now. By all rights it should die now, as it should have died the moment that the sun hid away, but survival is a difficult habit to break, and the memory of plants run far longer than the fleeting thoughts of animals. Evolving to survive was difficult, but returning to what you had once been, that was like coming home.

To the south, Lucia banked the fires of fury within as her people gasped for air. She could not pray, because who would an Eater pray to, but she hoped with all of her might, and the forest answered.

As the sun rose, the pods burst open. From within them huge white flowers unfurled. A thick cloud of seeds and sticky yellow pollen swept out to catch in the breeze and drift off across the Land of the Gods. The earth had not lost any of its life-giving capabilities, despite the long rest that it had taken. Everywhere the seeds fell, they took root. The Strangled Forest began to draw in a steady breath once again. The sunlight fuelling its transformation as it had the vestigial green in every plant across the surface of the world. Moment by moment, now that they had returned to their purpose, the plants of the world drew in the breath of the human race and returned it as fresh air. By Metharia's bedside the lantern flame grew stronger.

Those that survived that last night were overjoyed when they rose up and could breathe again. Arlia was overjoyed to have returned to court in any capacity, even if it was only as Lucia's spy among the common people. In the coming elections that flicker of acknowledgement would probably be enough to secure her a position as Pontifex again, even if it was out in the provinces. Metharia was one of the last to come around. Lucia had sat on the bedside and let her fingers brush softly over the girl's bare scalp. Tracing little circles there and smiling softly despite herself. Metharia had been invaluable. She had been exactly what Lucia had needed when she had needed it the most. When her eyes snapped open there was a dreadful moment of fear in her expression before her eyes met Lucia's.

Metharia leaned into the other woman's touch and drew in an unsteady breath. She whispered, "You did it. You saved us. Just as you promised that you would."

With obvious effort she pulled herself up onto her elbows and before Lucia could help her or move aside, her lips brushed against Lucia's. She slipped back and her head thumped against the hard pallet.

Lucia stared at her as if she had been struck. The corner of Metharia's mouth was turned up, "I apologise if that offended you, my lady. I cannot lie and pretend that I regret it, but I will not do it again without your permission."

Lucia leaned close and planted a peck of her own on Metharia's dry lips. She drew back a hand's breadth and smirked, "*I am glad you're alright. We can talk more about kissing when your strength returns.*"

Metharia's eyes sparkled at the prospect and the knot of tension between her shoulders immediately loosened. This had been a dangerous ploy that could have backfired badly. She had lain there through those long dull days thinking it through from every angle, adding up the sum of all the sideways glances and smiles that Lucia did not know that she had noticed. What else were you supposed to do when you were faking a coma? This would cement her position. It wasn't as though anyone else would be lining up to fulfil the carnal pleasures of whatever scaly, malformed thing Lucia was becoming.

Life returned. Both within the city, in its usual routines and to the lands outside the city walls where green was spreading across the landscape at such a speed that it seemed virulent. The vines sprung up across the north, hardy enough to shrug off the worst frosts while other plants, long forgotten and assumed dead, were beginning to spring to life. Even the Ashen Dales were losing their uniform grey colouration as seedlings sprouted from the virile soil below the ash. Meetings and councils and audiences started up once again. Every moment of Lucia's life was filling up to bursting with them.

There were days when Lucia wondered how much more she would even need to do. Her people were learning to do right by each other for the simple reward of their good behaviour becoming known. She knew that she could not leave them to govern themselves yet. But time was firmly on her side. She was coming to understand just what immortality meant. She could not trust this generation of nobles, their offspring would likewise be tainted by stories of the good old days when they were free to do as they wished. But the generation that followed? Could she leave them to care for the Ivory City?

She could ease her control and observe them for a time. There was no need to do things rushed and bloody when you had endless days.

Time passed and with it the cycle of seasons. Each night Lucia crept up the stairs to her chambers. As much as she had become accustomed to her new lack of sleep the rest of the city still needed time to recuperate. All except for Metharia, who seemed to subsist on cat-naps during the meetings and audiences Lucia believed that she could handle herself, or that Metharia had no stomach for. She avoided meeting the Chosen studiously. She would not speak to them, she would not acknowledge them. The Chosen themselves seemed to consider her something equivalent to a deserter, but her obvious favour with the Eater kept them silent. There were not many Chosen left in the city, those that remained were more of a police force than an army. Under Metharia's advisement Lucia had sent them all out into the field. To begin with, they were meant to be an early warning system for when the other Eaters finally gathered the resources to attack once more. As time went by their roles shifted. They no longer just enforced edicts, they carried Lucia's words to the people in her domain. They carried the meaning of those words along with them.

The Pontifex for all the territories were re-elected. A huge shift to smaller noble houses had inevitably occurred, but they often found themselves struggling to find a community that needed their preaching and interpretation. The Chosen were spreading the news faster than human legs could carry them.

There was a slow, steady flow of immigrants from the lands of the other Eaters. As word spread of Lucia's treatment of her people, the more defectors she received in her open arms. Several of her Chosen that she had employed as lesser generals in the siege had gathered the necessary courage to inform her that there were dozens, if not hundreds of spies for those foreign powers slipping in alongside the genuine freedom-hunters. With a smile, she had informed them that she hoped everything done in the Ivory City was being reported back to the other Eaters. That every detail was passing from lips to ears and growing with the telling. This was the warfare that Lucia was confident engaging in, these battles to win the love of the commoners with kindness. It was all one long glorious performance.

The meetings where she discussed such things, albeit obliquely, with her people were amongst those that Metharia did not attend. It was outside of the Chosen's areas of study. Metharia never contradicted her publicly and even in private they never butted heads directly. If Metharia disagreed with a course of action, then they would discuss it and discuss it, she would insinuate herself around her point until Lucia had assumed the other side of the argument. The first few times it had happened Lucia had felt a spark of anger at the manipulation, had even said as much, but gradually she realised that this strange relic from the old order hated any sort of direct conflict. Metharia hated to do anything that might make Lucia unhappy. She had practically fled the capitol when Lucia got annoyed with her. Even after Lucia dragged her back, even after Lucia had apologised to her she was still stiff, formal and quiet for weeks.

When Lucia entered her chambers, there were dribbling masses of candles illuminating the area around the bed. Metharia was never in the dark. everywhere she went she carried a candle. A little eccentricity that she attributed to having spent years alone out in the dark lands. Instantly, Lucia dropped into a crouch and silenced all the noises of her movement with a quick exertion of will. She made her way across the chamber, eyes darting around the shadows. She did not make a sound. She knew that she did not make a sound. Yet still Metharia was lounging awake and smiling on the bed before she got close enough. Some day she would catch the infuriating bald woman sleeping again and she would fetch out some ink and draw on her head. This was a fantasy that had been long in development. Initially she had only wanted to catch her out, to see her being human and not the perfect servant. With each thwarted attempt, her intentions had grown more twisted. Metharia must have known. Either she had worked it out or she had known all along. It was the only explanation for her smug smirk every single time Lucia thought she had caught her out.

The smirk was all that Metharia was wearing and Lucia couldn't help but return the smile as she was dragged down onto the bed. The year had changed Lucia further, every moment in the sunlight had spurned it on, she still did not know where the metamorphosis would end but she had grown taller than before, her neck had elongated. Her face had elongated too, the nose flattening down as the rest of the face extended further forward and her eyes shifted out to the sides.

All of her hair was long gone now and the tiny silver scales covered her completely. The changes that had troubled her the most were easily concealed outside of this chamber. Two protrusions grew from between her shoulder blades, angled upwards and getting longer each day. The tail had been a shock too. At first it had just been a feeling of discomfort when she sat, but as her neck lengthened and her flexibility increased, she was able to turn and look at it directly. It was still whip thin but it was broader at its base, tapering to a point. She had locked herself in her chambers for three days after that particular discovery. It was only Metharia's constant coaxing, and their newfound intimacy that had pulled her out of the her panic and back into her work.

***

The bay reeked of spoiled fat. The surface of the water was clogged with foul smelling foam, smears of blood and smothered fish that had tried to steal a free meal. Armoured Chosen patrolled the cliffs above, keeping watch across the grass and swamps, lands that were now growing green once again. Beneath the cliffs, the sea had hollowed out a cave, but it was hidden by the tide for all but two hours each day, when the tide was at its lowest. Those hours were when the Beloved would swim out to commune with Ochress and carry its commandments out into the world. No-one else knew what lay within the cave. It had taken only a few weeks of observation for Kaius to identify the Beloved and learn the patterns. Security was not lax, it was absent.

Kaius swam in with easy strokes. His initial plans had been thwarted by the pus-filled water. The form of a fish was apparently too obvious a choice. He had choked and spluttered on the filth clogging up his gills. He had become disoriented and struck first the sea's rocky bed and then burst out of the water's surface into sight of the patrols. He had finally oriented himself and fled back out to sea where he had constructed a far more complex weaving of power.

There were great hunting beasts in the sea by Vulkas' lands, and he had taken the time to study them when he was passing through, performing his reconnaissance. He took on the form of one of them, delighting in the feel of his warm blood in the cold water, and the buoyancy that his air-filled lungs granted him. As an after-thought. he created a tiny bubble of air and wrapped it around his head. However long he could hold his breath as one of these creatures, he did not want to have to rush.

He chose to enter at night while the moon's rejuvenating light filtered down to him. He swam forward through the murky water until he could no longer feel the moonlight or air above. He swam on until he brushed against something huge. Something that was rubbery and white. It flinched away from his touch. Still blind in the filth, he came to a decision. He let his newly acquired eyes with their helpful transparent lids revert to those that nature had given him, and that the heart of Walpurgan had made so much better.

He let his eyes shift and shimmer out of focus until he saw the vectors of power woven through the creature ahead. With barely an effort, he eased his will inside the thickest of the cords like a parasite and ever so slowly filtered the power flowing through it. If this was as successful here as it had been with the unfortunate Chosen of Vulkas who had stopped him during his pilgrimage from the Glasslands, the gifts that Ochress had given to its Chosen would be blocked, along with any message it tried to send. With that done, Kaius reverted the rest of his body to normal and expanded his bubble of air gradually. First he was enclosed and could only drift through the water by force of will, then until the entire chamber was emptied of water.

Ochress would once have struck an imposing figure. Its tail was like that of some great white whale with a massive human torso moulded seamlessly ahead of the dorsal fin. Its arms were thick and powerful, supporting its tremendous weight when it was unceremoniously dumped onto the cavern floor. There were no fingernails on the hands. In fact, there was very little detail anywhere on the porcelain expanse of flesh. It seemed almost too perfect until Kaius strolled around to the front. Where he would have expected a head, there was only the stump of a neck, the source of the constant oozing of blood and effluence. It had been burned clean off. Kaius nearly laughed aloud.

One of the greatest seafaring empires had this as its ruler. He assumed that there must have been some part of the brain stem still intact to keep the thing flailing around. The hands formed fists and began beating against the solid stone. It startled Kaius for a moment before he realised that it was not an attempt to defend itself, only a temper tantrum at being taken out of its bath.

Kaius strolled up the slope onto the platform where the creature's only caretaker would stand during their visits, then he made some more decisions. The air would not last forever, and the Beloved would be visiting in a short ten hours. There was no possibility of eating the entire thing. But as was proven with Walpurgan, if everything but a single part was annihilated, what was left behind granted the power of the full thing when consumed. Fire was no longer part of Kaius' repertoire, but he had a year of practice and a very flexible, if one track, mind. He created a thread of air and hardened it until it had a razor's edge. He laid it carefully across the top of the huge creature and then began duplicating it, over and over again. The cage of fire had served so well with the last one but this monster would not have to burn. He made a grid across the whole of the ancient beast. He twisted the threads until their ends met and they were just beginning to bite into the flopping monstrosity's skin.

Next came the difficult part. Each point where the lines of will crossed lit up with a shimmer of starlight, each point branched out diagonally to meet every other one. Layer after layer after layer of complex meshes covered Ochress, drew its arms in tight against its sides and made it unleash a reverberating groan with every inhalation as its swelling pressed it against the cocoon. Kaius squeezed.

The flesh was rubbery and soft on the surface levels and the layer of blubber underneath turned into a liquid under the crushing pressure that Kaius exerted. All around him the threads of Ochress power, the entire world of connections it had made, began to blink out of existence. Now someone might recognise that there was trouble. He accelerated the process, crushing the creature until its bones bent under the pressure and finally caved in. He tightened the cage and patched any gaps that the blood was trying to leak from. It was complex beyond any melee he had ever dealt with, beyond any puzzle in any text he had ever read.

A year ago, Kaius would not have been able to maintain the concentration required to add more pressure. But a year ago Kaius was only human. Over the course of the hour, he crushed Ochress majestic white body into a pink soup and contained it in a sphere small enough to be held in his hands. The pressure alone should have destroyed any life within, but Kaius did not think that anything could kill an Eater. The power could not be destroyed now any more than when it was stolen from the corpses of the gods. It only passed along. He let the water wash over him. It filled the chamber again, clean and pure. He kept the bubble of air around his head only long enough to draw the last of it down into his lungs, then he swam out into the ocean, wondering if he could even drown any more.

***

They tumbled for a while and Lucia lost her loose formal robes. Metharia placed gentle kisses where the scales were thinnest. Where Lucia could still feel. The sensations made her writhe on the bed, tail lashing. The candles burned higher all around them, bathing them in light. She ran her fingers all over Lucia's smooth contours and raked her nails down the thick ridge of scales that ran down her spine, catching the base of her tail and holding her still as her kisses trailed lower and lower. Her head dipped down to just below where Lucia's belly-button had once been. She placed a chaste kiss there then abruptly released her.

Lucia nearly fell off the bed at the sudden lack of contact and made a sound somewhere between a purr and a groan when it became apparent Metharia was stopping. The woman was as constant a source of torment as she was comfort. Lucia watched Metharia swaying her hips across the room to pour a cup of water.

She grunted in frustration, watching Metharia's plump lips grazing the cup's rim and coming away moist. Metharia gave her another sly smile and settled herself at the bottom of the bed, just out of arm's reach. Her voice was cool and calm when she spoke, "How did the meeting with the union of merchants go?"

Lucia bit back another grunt of frustration and ordered her thoughts. *"The union was very pleased with the new opportunities, and their wealth will buy enough votes from the noble houses who are having trouble making money these days. You know, the old horrible ones."*

Metharia bowed graciously."That's excellent. With their support, and the more progressive houses already willing to relinquish power, you may have your council of commons in place within a year. I am not certain how the council of nobles will respond after the fact, however."

Lucia shivered a little in the slowly cooling air. *"They will complain and complain. They will see the commons become the place laws are actually passed and they will begin by either denying every law that they pass or by declaring new powers for themselves."*

Metharia smiled at her like a teacher with a prized pupil. "When you deny their new powers and allow every commoner's law, what then? When the nobles deploy their armies against you and the handful of Chosen still in the city?"

Lucia glinted in the flickering candlelight and her eyes widened in faux shock, *"Why, that would be treason. Surely none of them would consider it."*

Metharia just stared at her until she giggled. *"Their soldiers don't benefit from being hired bullies in this city. Not anymore. The roughest of them have already left to find better chances with mercenary companies. The rest will be offered employment in the new city army. Controlled by the council of commons."*

Metharia seemed to relax again, draping herself forward onto the bed, cup still in hand, "I still don't understand how this council of yours is going to work. Can any commoner from the street just stroll in and pass laws each day?"

Lucia lifted her eyes back up to Metharia's face, the woman was deeply infuriating when these teasing moods took her. *"You know how it is going to work. Each year a commoner can put themselves forward for a place on the council. For the first year, the council of nobles will select the best candidates. In future years the existing council will pick. It is very simple."*

Metharia lay flat on her front and placed the cup down on the floor by the bed. "Simple and very easy to corrupt. What stops the council from putting themselves back in place each year? Creating a new noble class that can do as it pleases."

Lucia smirked. She was quite proud of this part. *"The law will stop them. For every year that they serve on the council, they must take a year off. If they have served twice, the gap becomes two years. Thrice makes three years. Besides, even the merchants do not have enough savings to live on indefinitely while their business holdings fall to pieces from lack of attention. They will serve the people. I will see them with food in their bellies and a roof over their heads each night but for anything more they will need to go back into the world and work."*

Metharia tutted, "And when they supplement the nothing that you pay them with bribes?"

Lucia cut her off, *"They will be investigated by my Chosen and tried for trying to subvert my laws."*

Metharia looked pained for a moment, "After you have executed a few, the rest will be too scared to take so much as a fallen mushroom."

Lucia paused for a long moment, said like that it did sound brutal. She shifted uncomfortably, sitting up straight on the bed as she considered all of this. Metharia interrupted by pouncing on her again with her raking nails and nipping teeth. Seeking out the parts of her that were still soft and driving all concern from her mind with a craftsman's skill.

Chapter 20- The Turning World

Lucia's worries returned as they always did when she had time alone to think. She wondered if that was why Metharia stayed at her side for so much of the day when she really wasn't required. The council of nobles had voted on the council of commons and it had been a much-praised idea that had barely scraped by with the required majority. The merchants clearly hadn't wanted to overspend. The first crop of "commons" seemed to contain an unexpected number of noblemen's bastards, and an even greater proportion of commoners who had once been in the service of one of the noble houses that were now out of Lucia's favour but had mysteriously left those positions shortly after rumours of the Eater's latest big idea had started being passed around.

It was pathetically transparent but it would have to be endured for this iteration at least. Thankfully the positions would empty after a year and she wouldn't have to wait for a generation to die out. With all of eternity, a year did not seem so long to endure. Before her change, even a moment of discomfort had aggrieved her, but now everything seemed to be worth the wait. Her anxiety peaked when a Chosen returned from the border of Ochress' lands with a plea from a veritable stampede of people fast approaching. Ochress was gone. That seemed to be the only coherent message. Ochress was gone and Vulkas was conquering the defenceless land with a hunger.

It was the first time Lucia realised the price of her armies and power. It was the first time she considered what Kaius had always tried to hammer into her in his clumsy way. If she was not willing to fight, then she was defenceless against those who were. She could send her Chosen to shepherd these refugees to her city. She was confident that with the new reserves laid aside they could all eat, at least until expansion began. That was not the problem. The problem lay in what her Chosen would do when Vulkas decided to test her. When it threw soldiers and Chosen and war-machines at her envoys of peace, what would she command? There was no time now for careful deliberation. Just an immediate decision that would give life or death to thousands.

Metharia strode swiftly to her side and whispered harshly into her ear. Lucia waved her away and rose from her little padded stool. She shouted through the confusion and the murmurs of her gathered servants, *"Defend them all. Bring all of them to me. Tell them that I will protect them. Send runners to the northern forests and tell Walpurgan's people that they too are welcome to the safety of our walls. Send the message to the people of Vulkas too. Everyone is welcome in the Ivory City. Everyone will be protected."*

The Chosen from the front line was careful to mask the fear on his face but Lucia tasted it and beckoned him forward. She brushed a finger over his filthy face and Marked him. His eyes widened and he looked up at her. *"Send every one of my Chosen within the city to me now. They will be coming with you and they will be Marked."*

Metharia blurted out, "What about the city's defence?" Then she put her hands over her mouth and flushed in embarrassment with a little yelp. Lucia gave her a stern look and answered, *"I can defend this city just as I did when all of the Eaters alive turned against me. When the whole world came to knock on our gates and I burned them away to ash."*

The audience chamber fell silent in the wake of her shouting. Suddenly it was filled with cheers. Nobody heard her quiet little sigh. At least she still knew how to work a crowd.

Lucia had withdrawn to her chamber for the evening when the fighting started. She shuddered at the drain when a half dozen of her Chosen called on her for strength. She gasped as the connections severed. As each of her Chosen died. Her eyes blazed. She paced back and forth across the rugs around her bed until in her frustration they burst into flames about her feet. Metharia had to dart forward from the quiet corner where she lurked to empty a jug of water and put them out.

Her new Marked could feel the deaths too, through the link, they drew more speed from her and crossed the open country too fast for the naked eye to perceive them. It was too late by the time they arrived. Vulkas' Chosen were already wading into the refugees, laughing and hacking them to pieces. Even the brief foray into war last year had not been so brutal to watch. Families were cut apart. Children crushed under steel boots, and the screaming reverberated through Lucia's mind from across the distance. She should have gone herself. There was a fire in her gut and she should have unleashed it on these butchers.

She had the power, why shouldn't she have used it? She poured more of her power through the link to the new Marked. Many of them started to stumble as they ran too fast for their eyes to keep track of the ground ahead. She pushed them recklessly onwards until she could not hear the screaming any more. When the last of her Chosen on Ochress' border was cut down from behind, Lucia picked up a table and threw it at the wall. It did not break. Just clanged and clattered around the room. Even in this she could not be satisfied.

She stormed out onto the balcony and glared up at all of the stars in the sky, at the moon blazing bright above the horizon and helping her not at all. In frustration, she let out a torrent of flames. The city never truly slept. It rested even less easily with the tents and simple huts of the ghuls' sanctuary sprung up all around it, but seeing the flames of Lucia, the people on the streets fled indoors fearing some attack from the sky. Each day had brought more of their trust. Now it was so absolute that they could not conceive of Lucia unleashing her temper or making a mistake.

With the fire gone, she slumped back against the tower's wall. Metharia was there with a gentle arm around her waist, guiding her back into her chambers. She trembled in Metharia's arms then let out a puff of smoke, *"I had forgotten how it feels to have so much of my power used. I feel hollow."*

Metharia shrugged, "Probably why the other Eaters only Mark a few people."

She slipped a hand into Lucia's and tried to pull her towards the bed but Lucia resisted, *"I need to concentrate. The Marked will engage them soon."* Another connection snapped out and Lucia spun around, trying to place it in her perception. One of her Chosen had died and she did not even know where. Another connection snapped, then another. The cords of power stretching out, taut from the core of her being, flailed around uselessly towards the Glasslands. Lucia's eyes widened, *"Vulkas army is coming. They are marching on us in force. They have just crossed the border."*

Metharia flew out of the room, calling to servants and nobles, rallying defenders with all haste. There would be no ghuls nipping at their heels this time. Vulkas army was already mobilised and moving. The people of Lucia could have less than three days and their troops were scattered across the dominions. Lucia trusted in Metharia's counsel and in her military mind. For every minor dispute and skirmish that had arisen with the deserters and bandits roaming her lands Lucia delegated the full responsibility but now that a real battle was coming, she had to resist the urge to jump in.

In her heart, she knew that Metharia was the best choice to make these decisions, but she had known the same thing about Kaius right up until the moment that she didn't. Kaius had spoken about peaceful solutions almost as much as Metharia professed her pacifism. Lucia pondered her new inability to trust while Metharia barked orders and marshalled legions.

The new city regiments did not have banners to call yet. Their soldiers were still employed by the noble houses. Every one of whom was now trying to extract favours in exchange for their support. A thousand deals would have to be struck, and twice as many back-room alliances made, to wage war under Lucia's new regime. The complexity of all of the checks and balances designed to keep the nobles from going to war on a whim slowed their mobilisation to an agonising crawl.

Metharia crouched down in front of her while she jerked and shivered as the Marked drew on her strength to supplement their own. She cupped Lucia's reptilian face in her hands and drew her eyes up until they met. "You must recall the Marked."

Lucia tried to shake her head but found Metharia's grip tightening, "You must call them back so that we can defend the city. So we can protect your people."

Lucia hissed, *"No."*

Metharia's hands slipped down to her shoulders and gave her a shake. "Our people are defenceless. Vulkas marches against us. You told us that. Without the Chosen and the Marked, how will we protect ourselves from Vulkas' own servants?"

Lucia stared off through the eyes of her Marked and she saw the the indiscriminate killing. She wilted before Metharia's eyes, *"I don't need soldiers. I don't need Chosen. All that I need is me."*

She stood up abruptly, sending the other woman staggering backwards and making the assorted nobles that had forced their way into the room jump. *"I will protect every last one of you. All of the nobles. All of the commons. Everyone, everywhere."*

Sparks trailed from her fingertips, searing the bed and the upholstery. All of her power was overflowing, even now when she was pouring it out in two dozen directions and the sun was gone from the sky. Metharia stared at her, half in awe. For one long, glorious moment, she believed that Lucia could do it. But only for a moment.

The new Beloved of Vulkas was a wild man. He stood nearly seven feet tall and was built like one of the oxen that adorned his armour. He had not been selected from the surviving Chosen for his wisdom, but for his fury. He had not been thwarted at the battle of the Ivory City. He had been off in the mountains laying waste to a stronghold of heretics. All that he knew was distaste for those who had failed there, those who had been blinded by ambition, old Hulia among them.

There were no war-machines now. No squandering of fighting men for the sake of a dramatic entrance, and the chance of startling a few spear-waving peasants. His troops marched across the starlit glass already in formation. Discipline was absolute. The soldiers and Chosen he did not trust to obey perfectly had gone to harass Ochress' flock, and to provoke the emotional reaction that Vulkas foresaw from this upstart Lucia. He was reliably informed by his runners that she had not only taken the bait, but was squandering her entire force trying to protect an endless stream of refugees. His grin was fierce. It was all going according to plan.

Dawn found Lucia crumpled on her balcony with her eyes squeezed shut. After the quiet conversations with Metharia, conversations that with anyone else would have been a screaming argument, she had sent the woman away to find a bed elsewhere in the tower.

The fighting had gone on through the night, heavy and brutal in the glimpses that she caught of it, but her Marked had succeeded in driving off the Chosen of Vulkas and slaughtered any of the more human soldiers still trying to have their way with the fleeing fishermen and their families.

When it was so close to dawn that she could taste it, Lucia realised just how dangerous her ploy had been. The reason that the other Eaters had so few Marked was because unchecked, even a few could drain you to the point of enfeeblement. With the chaos of last night, she had shed enough weight that her muscles would no longer support her.

It was like the first few days in the dark again. She was close to empty. It crossed her mind that this probably could not kill her. It might make her wish that she was dead but she seemed strangely resilient. The first hint of sun on the horizon made her gasp in relief. The light and heat swept over her and, with her mirrored scales she seemed to shine brighter than the distant light in the sky. There had been so much power spent that its return was explosive.

The bony protrusions on her back burst open into full wings. The last of the human feeling skin on her shoulder-blades stretched out into nearly transparent membranes across the extended tendons and spindly bones that shaped them.

The agony was immediate. No body was meant to change so suddenly, and dozens of tiny tears appeared as she unfurled the new symbols of her inhumanity. The rest of her body was racked with spasms and aches as muscles shifted to support the new structures and thickened to give her flight. Her neck and tail lengthened and thickened to balance her new wings and she panted for the breath to scream.

Some sound must have escaped, because in a moment Metharia was there, cradling her head in her lap as it continued to stretch. All human features and expressions mangled into this new jutting spear of reptilian madness.

Her eyes, already stretched so thin and narrow by the changes of the prior year's minor exertions, now began to divide until there were three staring up at Metharia, dotted along under the bony ridge of her brow. Each eye was rolling wildly from this new cacophony of pain. She gained bulk, balancing out her increasing length and crushing her against the balcony's edge, twisting her around as she rolled and hissed and wailed. Metharia clung to her as though her life depended on it. She whispered kind words and gentle sounds of comfort into the tiny indentations that may have been ears. Metharia's eyes were dispassionate, her expression calculating.

Lucia would hardly notice something like that in her current state and she needed this information to make plans for the future. She twisted her face back into the appearance of pained concern when Lucia's yellow lit eyes stopped rolling and seemed to focus on her for the first time, two with a slit pupil and one with a double pupil in the shape of a rounded hourglass. She stroked along the ridge of thick scales above the row of eyes with exaggerated care and shushed Lucia. "It's alright now. It's all over."

Lucia's first attempt to speak came out garbled. She could not form words with her new mouth, her voice was missing somewhere down her serpentine throat. She lay curled around Metharia, keening and hissing. The rest of the tower went about its preparations, unaware of any change and devoted to their ignorance.

Metharia kept up her soothing whispers, "Take your time. I think that was your final change. Calm yourself. Just relax."

Lucia trembled as the keening went on, shifting in tone and pitch as she tried to form words again. The sounds were quiet at first but grew louder as she became more desperate. It had a rhythm to it as she warbled up and down and when the words finally took shape they were a song, *"Dance. This is your... last chance. Dance, dragons...dance."* Her eyes did not blink at the same time. Instead they closed in an odd rippling effect along her head from front to back. She drew in breath and spoke, softly but with deep reverberations, *"I am alright. Just... a shock. I didn't know I could change so much. I... hope that is it over and done."*

She shuddered and tried to stand up on her rear legs before promptly toppling sideways into the bannister. She got up on all fours and discovered the new lengths of her limbs. She flicked her tail from side to side and spread her wings to their full spread with a groan. She flexed out her new claws and carved up lines of the balcony's ivory floor.

Metharia shifted her footing slightly and with rapturous precision, Lucia's head snapped around to look at her. She cocked it from side to side, viewing her with all six of her eyes, one side after the other. Metharia whispered, "My goddess."

Lucia snorted and a plume of smoke emerged, drifting up into the sky, *"Let's not get carried away now."*

She moaned and a shiver ran down her spine, waggling her long neck, back and tail all the way to the tip. *"It feels so good to be finished! To be complete instead of that strange, half-human mess. I feel like I am myself again. Even if it is a different self."*

Metharia smiled up at her, "You are beautiful."

Lucia twisted her neck around to look along her new form, and then snapped back to Metharia, *"Not to be too vain, but I think that I believe that for the first time."*

Lucia roared and Metharia threw herself back into the room covering her ears. Then Lucia bellowed out across the land, *"Look at your Eater now. Look at what Lucia has become and know. You are mine and I will protect you."*

Chapter 21- The Story of the Stone

The lower mines were flooded, and they had been for days. It blocked access to deepest cavern and while a brave few Chosen had struggled and swum through the pitch-black waters to receive their orders it had been pointless. Vulkas was not interested in them. Its mind was sent far away looking through the eyes of it's Beloved. The man's simplicity made things like that so much easier. He had a name before, and a reputation, but now he was a puppet. Vulkas rode and spoke through him constantly. It was so easy to line up the soldiers when it could all be seen in person. With its mind half a world away, the ripples in the water all around it appeared to be random.

Vulkas was not crippled like Negrath, nor mindless like Ochress but even so, it was not unharmed by the war before history began. It had charred cracks over its stone hide and from within them sharp spurts of transparent crystals had grown. Vulkas still had some mobility despite its injuries. It walked on all fours and while it bore some resemblance to the bulls used in its people's traditional decoration, there was a distinct reptilian pattern to the shape of its head. Huge horns grew from the grey stone of its head. They jutted straight up and shimmered in the dim light that filtered down from the tunnels beyond the water. It did not pace the chamber now, it had wedged itself into the corner, feeling the familiar comfort of the stone soothed its temper.

Even before the change Vulkas had been full of rage. Only time had tempered it and refined it into the soft simmer that could be more easily directed. Kaius rose silently from the water. Today he looked human and he gave the heaving form of Vulkas a friendly smile. Vulkas lifted its face clear of the water and with a rumble it spoke, *"You did well little assassin. You shall be rewarded well."*

Kaius called up a little bubble of air and settled down onto it cross-legged, "Then pay me Vulkas."

The grating slate sounds were Vulkas' attempt at laughter, *"More stories? So cheap a price to do what a thousand cycles of war could not. Where did we leave off?"*

Kaius' smile never slipped, "You had just slain the blacksmith god." Vulkas' hide dug rivulets in the wall as it shuffled around and got comfortable. After a few grunts and groans it warmed to the telling, *"Together we took the god to ground. It had become as tall as the mountains but together we felled it. Together we had to put an end to its power. Walpurgan told us the way but only Haspreth had the courage, young as she was."*

Kaius came closer and settled down on his haunches to listen. So much history had been wiped away, this was his chance to preserve some fragment when this age passed.

Vulkas rumbled on, *"She bit into the god, she swallowed it down and I swear to you that she would have eaten it all if we had not been there to share with her. We all ate of the blacksmith god. So it could die. That was when we learned of the Steel. That was when the rest of our campaign took form. With the steel we could cut them down, we could protect ourselves against all but the Serpent of Storms. That was why it was such a blessing when darling Negrath slew it. We did not share after that first meal, we were all devoted to the cause but there was a terrible greed in our hearts once we tasted that god flesh."*

Vulkas rambled on in their little bubble in the tunnels. It was a literal bubble. The tunnels outside had filled entirely with water and only a sly thread of Kaius' will held it back. Vulkas kept on shuffling its position, unable to find any place of comfort from its injuries.

Its mind was split in three. One part focussing on the endless pain. One part thrown across the land to where its carefully constructed formations were marching. The rest was cast so far back into the past that the memories pre-dated history. It was the only living thing old enough to know these these tales. It had the only mind that held all of these secrets. Kaius wanted them all. The ocean filled the tunnels above their heads, and on the plains before the Ivory City, the armies lined up. Vulkas told its stories.

Metharia had held back her soldiers behind the city gates but they were baying to get out, spurred on again by their noble paymasters. The villages of ghuls that Lucia could not bring herself to run off her lands were not held back by walls or gates. For all of the adoration that Lucia had accrued within the city, it was nothing compared to the blind fervour of the ghuls. Many Chosen told tales of the encampments of ghuls they found far out in the dark lands and of the primitively hewn idols of the Eaters. They whispered of the complex rituals that surrounded the eating of flesh and, most curiously of all, the way that so many of the ghuls would just kneel in supplication when the Chosen came to kill them.

The ghuls of the plains outside the Ivory City did not act so passively. They charged mindlessly out of their huts. The trained soldiers of Vulkas, catching them head on, slaughtered them all without remorse. There were children in those villages, and elders too weak and shaky to hold a weapon. Those pitiful ghuls flung themselves at the city gates weeping and begging for entrance.

Lucia coiled around the top of her tower, staring down at the tight ranks laid out against her. She thought of how easily they would burn. This could all be over without any of her people dying, if she could bring herself to kill. She spread her wings and let out a bellowing roar. It swept over the city. Even the disciplined soldiers of Vulkas army flinched, before their Beloved's barking put them back in line. All eyes were on her, and once more she did not know what to do.

She heard Metharia downstairs. Her voice vibrating up through the bones of the walls, issuing commands in Lucia's name that she would never have even considered on her own. The city was in a frenzy of activity, so different from the last siege when everything was already laying in wait. In each unit of a dozen enemy men Lucia saw the tell-tale glint of a Chosen's armour. She saw the robust twists of energy flowing into them from over the horizon. Her eyes, her new eyes, were adjusting. The information from the real world and this other world of spirits and spells was finally blending together as one.

It was starting to make sense. All that she had needed was

more eyes to see with. The cords of power running from her seemed to hum and thrum. They were starting to sound musical, and music was the one thing she was sure she could understand. Here in the city it was a cacophony but when she focussed on the fields outside, it was a simpler tune. Each of the Chosen was a tremulous murmur, and the Beloved was like the bass note tying them all together.

Lucia let go of her grip on the tower and spread her wings. There had been little time for experimentation before the army rolled over the horizon but she had learned to make little weaves of heat to give her wings more lift.

She swept down over the city in a gentle arc. Rising up over the city walls with another roar, hoping against hope that fear would be enough one last time. She hung there above the wall for a terrible moment of indecision, then it was too late and she was falling towards the enemy. Vulkas' Beloved was screaming out commands as Lucia plummeted and in her fugue she barely remembered to beat her wings. She hung above the soldiers, close enough that she could see their eyes widening in fear and close enough that she could smell the dried meat of their rations on their breath. She weighed them in that moment, against all of the lives of the people inside the city. She breathed in air and breathed out death.

She had to flap frantically as the flames reflected back up at her from the massive concave shields that Vulkas' Chosen had called over their soldiers. The shield dissolved just as quickly as it had appeared, before it had the chance to fall back onto the soldiers.

Vulkas' Beloved roared with laughter and launched a silver lance at her with a casual overhand throw. Lucia snatched it out of the air with her front leg and then hissed as it exploded into a chain of spikes that tried to ensnare her. She puffed out another torrent of flame, using the concussion to knock the weapon away. She made a slow backwards loop in the air, trying to regain her composure, and landed heavily on the road to the Ivory City, splay legged.

Vulkas' soldiers marched on towards her, not even breaking rank in the face of so fearsome a beast. She shuffled on her unfamiliar legs away from them. She unleashed her fire but when the smoke ,cleared every one of them was still standing. Fear found its place in her chest. She had seen Eaters die. It had been in flame and not by steel, but she did not want to try her scales against their weapons. The Beloved shouted out to her, "Flee little snake. Back into your hole."

Anger swept the fear away as it always had and she drew in a deep breath. This time the fire did not cease. She went on pouring it out over the whole army in waves. When she stopped, it was not because she was out of breath. She did not need to breathe. She was realising new things even now. She stopped because the air was growing so hot that it was making her fear for the earth beneath her feet. The smoke cleared slowly and she saw the molten shields, still held up.

She turned and ran until she remembered her wings and then she managed to get enough lift to hit the top of the city walls and scramble over. Metharia, watching from Lucia's place in the tower, started screaming commands that were carried down the stairs and out into the streets. The gates swung open and the army marched out while Lucia was still trying to find her footing.

This was the Beloved of Vulkas' time. This was his joy. His blood-lust and fervour boiled over as he ordered his units forward. With Vulkas in his head he saw the whole of the battlefield. Every one of his soldiers had lost friends on this field just a year ago. Some of them had even felt the stinging shame of retreat. Not a one of them faltered as Lucia's ragtag assortment of militia, regiments and mercenaries tumbled out towards them. At a word from their Beloved the centre ranks slowed in their advance.

There were noblemen amongst Lucia's troops. Nominal leaders of the armies and desperate to make a name for themselves. It was them that urged their soldiers into a charge before the formations had even reformed. They saw the supposed weakness in the enemy line and wanted to take their chances.

Vulkas' army was small. Despite the charge for the centre, many of Lucia's warriors still found themselves clashing with the enemy lapping around their flanks. It was like hitting a solid wall. The tension on Vulkas' shield wall kept on building and building as the tail ends of the army left the Ivory City and added their weight to the press.

The Beloved held back behind the walls of flesh and steel, eyes locked on Lucia as she scrabbled around. He waited until his soldiers were being driven back step by step. He waited until Lucia looked his way before he spoke the command. The Chosen burst from between the shields with great cleavers in each hand, spinning like dervishes and shrugging off the weak blows that the soldiers could muster against them in that tight press.

Lucia managed to keep her grip on the ramparts as she cast

her gaze across the field. She threw out a dozen threads of will to strangle the strength Vulkas was feeding to its Chosen, but this time there was resistance. It was like trying to crush a rod of steel in her hand. She had been learning since the day she emerged from the glass, but it had not occurred to her that her enemies were doing the same.

Guilt churned in her chest. Her people were down there, exploding in showers of gore and bone fragments as Vulkas' Chosen swept through them. And she was relieved that she wasn't down there with them. Her lofty principles, the solid platform on which she had built her rule, meant nothing here. She would not kill or, more honestly, could not kill. It was costing her soldiers their lives. If the battle continued its symphony of loss, it would mean the end of both her city, and the first seeds of hope for the future that she had been planting.

Death was not so frightening compared to what her imagination could conjure. She knew of the things that could happen to a creature that would not die. She puffed out smoke and took off again. Vulkas' Chosen and soldiers were embroiled too tightly in the fighting for her to have any effect on them without burning up her own people along with them. The Beloved stood further back on an incline above the field, barking out his commands. That was something that she could affect.

She gained height until she was looking down, as though from her tower. A bedraggled owl fluttered away from her, still lost after a year and circling the battlefield, waiting for carrion. Kaius smiled to himself at the sight of her, so close to his eyes on the battlefield. He had not realised how much he had missed her, or how much her change had improved her. Lucia pulled her wings in tight and plummeted towards the Beloved with flames trickling from her gaping jaws. The Beloved laughed and called another lance, he braced himself and waited. Lucia fell like a shooting star with a trail of sparks behind her. The Beloved held himself ready for that flinching moment when she would stop to rake at him or unleash her flame, but it never came.

Lucia hit the ground in an explosion so fierce that it knocked the rear ranks of Vulkas' army off their feet. Before the cloud of flames had even cleared she burst up out of it, one wing bent and the other pierced through by the Beloved's lance. Her perfect silver scales were sooty and scraped. She limped away a short distance and let out another torrent of flames into the crater behind her. The soldiers that somehow survived, the ones who were hiding on the periphery of Vulkas army, swore in the years that followed that they heard her sobbing as she did it. She poured more and more fire into the indentation and it burst upwards in every direction, killing any that tried to approach. When the fire-storm ended, there was no body on the cracked black earth, not even bones. All that remained were ashes and a smear of silver.

Lucia wailed and roared. The two sounds blended into a deafening blast that made every soldier pause. She charged, lopsided and injured, into the mass of soldiers. She used nothing more sophisticated than her mass to break their careful formations into chaos. The Chosen broke free from the melee behind the defender's ranks and charged back into their own. At first, they clambered over their allies and eventually just knocked them aside with casual strikes. Their weapons shifted from the heavy slabs of steel to slender pins. Perfect for slipping between tough scales. They swarmed over Lucia, jabbing at her with their weapons, tearing at her wings. Her roar was a shriek of rage, pain and overwhelming despair.

"That was when Walpurgan turned on Haspreth, when she rent her childish flesh and feasted on her innards. That was the true beginning of the war between us. When we realised that we could take the power from each other now. That was when all of our alliances fell to dust."

Vulkas' head snapped from side to side as it tried to see through a dozen Chosen's eyes instead of the simple single vision it had enjoyed until now. It grunted and turned to Kaius, *"Where was I?"*

Kaius shrugged, "Walpurgan had slain Haspreth?"

Vulkas rumbled back onto its topic, *"Yes. Yes. That was when Astarian truly drew our ire. The last tenuous alliance and the blotting of the sun. It was Walpurgan's greatest invention. For all of the..."*

Kaius held up a hand and spoke a simple command, "Be silent."

Vulkas spoke on oblivious, *"...cleverness she had stolen, it still nearly killed us when we first made the attempt, all of our might bound together in her witchcraft. You see, she took the entire sun from the sky, not just the light. We almost froze to death before it could be undone."*

Kaius raised his voice, "I said enough, you old fool."

Vulkas stopped dead and roared, *"What did you say to me?"*

Kaius rolled his eyes and snapped, "You have gone on for too long and we are both out of time. Let us just get this done."

The bubble of air popped. Water flooded in over them and

while Kaius just drifted in it gently, Vulkas thrashed around in a cloud of bubbles until it found itself floating near the centre of the room, far from the soothing touch of the stone. It went berserk flailing around and snapping its tusked jaws at Kaius, who swam gracefully out of reach. Instincts resurfaced and panic kicked in. Vulkas started flailing towards the tunnel entrance, seeking out air but finding none. Kaius swam along, maintaining his distance. Vulkas saw the shimmering mirror surface of the water ahead and knew then how bloody its vengeance on this boy would be. Rage fuelled it as it paddled forward, only to wedge in a narrow point of the tunnel, just as Kaius had planned. It tried to push its way through, to bend the rock to its will, but it had no traction to press against the stone. It could not concentrate well enough to command it to move aside. From beneath craggy brows it fixed all twelve of its beady eyes on Kaius. The man floated still in the water ahead. He breathed it in easily and pulled together contours of power into some weaving of a complexity well beyond Vulkas understanding. Still churning the water and twisting, Vulkas managed to back its way out of the tight part of the tunnel only to find itself in another pinch point further back. The pressure built up until the stone of its hide cracked. That fresh pain along with the rest of its suffering made it gasp out its last lung-fuls of air. The burning of its lungs was nothing to the crushing pressure as the water around it tightened and squeezed.

There was a crack and a pop then Vulkas was cut neatly in two. The water darkened with its blood. The top half was still alive when Kaius dragged it to the surface, bound in cords of razor sharp air. It was still alive when Kaius started eating it. His teeth lengthened inside its flesh, his fingers curved into claws and hooked into the meat below. Vulkas felt itself sliding down his throat and in desperation whispered, *"We saved you all. We were your heroes."*

Kaius stopped with blood smeared around his twisted maw and snarled, *"Now you are monsters."*

Then he fell on Vulkas again with his teeth gnashing and talons rending.

The Chosen fell from Lucia's bleeding hide. Their weapons were gone. Their armour, gone. All their strength and speed had turned to nothing. Lucia moved like a serpent in a nest of baby mice, snapping at the naked little prey all around her, hissing. The Beloved was dead, the Chosen were broken, and there was a dragon behind their ranks. Vulkas' army threw down their weapons and Lucia still had the conscience left to wail, *"Leave them! It is over."*

She struggled to get all four of her legs beneath her. By the time she was standing, there was a wide circle of soldiers around her, both hers and the enemy.

She shouted out, *"All people are my people now. You are now all friends. I will see you all act as friends. Those of you who want to go back to your mines. Go. Those that wish to live in the city, stay and be welcome. But know this, war is over. Killing is over. You will all live in peace from this day forward."*

She looked around at the gathered crowd, all standing silent, and she barked, *"This is my will. Now make it yours."*

Then she coiled up on herself and tried to feign sleep as she constructed the weaving that would put her new flesh back together.

She wishing bitterly that there was so simple a balm for her mind.

Chapter 22- The Needing of Things

Lucia may have been carried off bleeding to recuperate by the most trustworthy of the nobles. The battlefield may have been scattered with the bodies of soldiers from both sides. But the fanatically loyal ghuls had suffered the worse. They had been trampled underfoot by both sides. Their village lay empty, the few children and elders that had survived the fighting by luck alone had been ushered into the city at last. They disappeared cleanly into the mess of refugees that were seeking employment and homes in a clamour at the gates of every noble estate.

Metharia had not left Lucia's side since she had been brought back to the tower. She was too large to carry up the countless flights of stairs, even if weight was not a concern, so they settled her into a courtyard in the sunshine and Metharia held whispered court in the corridor outside. She hissed out the closest approximation of Lucia's orders as best she could, but everyone saw the concern on her face. The way she kept darting out of the door to check on Lucia.

Nobody could say that she did not care for the Eater.

Nobody would dare to say that she had deliberately put Lucia in harm's way when she so obviously cared for her. If there was not so much to do, Metharia would have paused to congratulate herself on so complete a deception. It wasn't hard to like Lucia. She had an easy charm to her and her idealism was infectious. It was a shame that Lucia had not been born into a world where her faith in the good qualities of others was justified.

The city regiments had started claiming pay even though many of them had been little more than a farce on the battlefield. It was with a great deal of childish glee that Metharia denied them that pay. Listing off their failings and denying any one of their representatives the possibility that they had served their purpose.

They saw the worried glances and fretting and they assumed that this anger would pass when Lucia had recovered so they retreated peacefully enough. Night was creeping up on Metharia before she heard Lucia calling to her. She snatched the last letter from a harried courier and dismissed the remaining nobles before dashing out.

At some point through the day it had rained without anyone inside the tower noticing. It had pooled in the hollows of the flagstones and was rising as steam all around Lucia's coiled form now that she was stirring back to life. Metharia's slender fingers stroked over the armoured scales of Lucia's hide, soothing her and seeking the injuries between the hard plates. She found nothing, even amidst the worst of the bloodstains. Lucia snickered, *"Not a mark on me little one. We are hard to kill"*

Her head lolled over the top of her body and her many eyes

narrowed on Metharia, *"But someone has. First Ochress, now Vulkas. Both snuffed out."*

Metharia met the gaze, unflinching and did not even try to dispute what she had suspected all along. "First Negrath, then Walpurgan, now Ochress and Vulkas. Perhaps you showed their vulnerability and old grudges are finally being paid?"

Lucia's narrow head bobbed along to the rhythm of the words, but shook it at the end, *"Negrath and Walpurgan, we know the killer. Do we guess it was the same one who killed Ochress and Vulkas? Am I the next target? I am the last. The last Eater."*

Metharia stepped forward and cupped Lucia's weaving head between her hands, her voice overflowed with passion when she spat, "Kaius is nothing without you."

Lucia stared at her for an uncomfortably long moment. At Metharia's request she had never been made Marked, Chosen or Beloved, but she had a horrible suspicion now that Lucia could still sift through her thoughts.

Eventually Lucia spoke. *"If that man had nothing but the clothes on his back and he was standing in a room full of my Marked, I would give them even odds in a fight. From nothing, he crushed all three of the armies that threatened me. You would be foolish not to be at least a little frightened of him. If anyone was capable of this..."*

She sniffed, then her eyes turned to the ash stained parchment in Metharia's hand, *"What is that?"*

More than half dazed Metharia slowly came to realise that she was holding something. She lifted it up and said, "Just a message."

Lucia cocked her head and Metharia shook off the worst of the effects from that inquisitive gaze. She unrolled it and nearly spat in frustration before she could bring her face back into its tranquil mask. Lucia asked, *"Well what is it?"*

Metharia spoke through grit teeth, "It is from him. It is a letter from Kaius."

Lucia tried to contain her amusement. Despite all of the worry, this funny little jealous streak was almost as good as catching Metharia sleeping. *"And what does it say?"*

Metharia did not trust herself to speak, she just held the letter up for Lucia, who cocked her head from side to side, trying to find the best way to read with her new eyes. It occurred to her that she had never seen Kaius' handwriting. Under the old order most commands were spoken, generally in hushed tones, in dark places.

If she had to guess how Kaius would write, this would be it. Every letter laid out with painful precision, as if any mistake would meet punishment.

Beloved,

I have done for you all that you needed but would not ask for. I have removed all opposition to your rule, and I have won all of your battles. I do not ask for rewards or applause. All that I would ask is that we talk again. For all of my life before we met I was alone and I considered that state to be the best one but after our short time together I find myself missing your company.

I will come to your city in a few cycles time. I have learned much of your new state in my travels, and I feel that you may welcome my advice once more. If you do not want me in your life or your court then you can send me away as you did before. Or you can choose to have me snuffed out as you see fit. If you simply wish my exile, then you can choose the location that I will be sent, so that if you require me in the future I will still be available to you.

In your name,

Kaius

Metharia stared at Lucia's indecipherable face as she read the letter and thought she saw contemplation. She snapped, "You must send him away. He cannot be trusted."

Lucia said nothing. She just stared at the parchment as Metharia crumpled it up in her hands. Metharia spat, "You said it yourself, he is dangerous. He is a killer."

Lucia drew away from her. *"And what am I now? I killed that man. I crushed... I... When I had the choice to die or to kill, I made that choice. Kaius just made his choice faster."*

Metharia was shouting now. Se did not know when her placid mask had fallen away. "You can't be serious! He must be driven off or he must die. You cannot suffer him within this city. You cannot have him here. He will undo all of the hard work that we have done. He will..."

Lucia turned her back on Metharia, and settled down in a coil once again. *"I am resting now. I will think about it."*

Metharia had lived for a long time in the court of the nobles, she knew a snub when she heard it. She had the good grace to leave quietly instead of making a scene. In the corridor, she looked at the little desk she had set up. She looked down at the simple robes she was wearing. Then she reached over to the table and pinched out the candle stub still burning there, surrounding herself with darkness and drinking it in.

The days passed in silence. Metharia would not talk to Lucia. The nobles had learned of their behaviour and every petty matter came directly before the Eater rather than risk having the it become the source of another dispute. Metharia did not have her own room. She had stayed in the chambers of the Beloved for nearly as long as Lucia had ruled. Servants, and the gradually returning Chosen reported that Metharia was still in the tower to Lucia with such regularity that it made her wonder if she had forgotten requesting the information.

Metharia was in the kitchens making herself a snack. She was in the library catching up on her reading. Lucia's thoughts were back in turmoil. She tended to the city's needs with casual disinterest. She curbed the nobles ambitions with ease byt settling the refugees from the other lands was becoming a full time endeavour.

The bravest of the foreign nobles had started to make their own appeals for her assistance in retaking their family lands, in her name of course. Although the winter stockpile of supplies in the city were depleting at a rapid pace, she held off on releasing these nobles back into the wild until they had learned the way things were done in the city. Until she was certain that they were ready to rebuild things in the correct way, in her image. Ego was a part of being on the stage and, until now it had always been a comfortable enough coat for Lucia to slip on and shrug off as required.

Now she could not back away from conflict. She could not mask her intentions because everything that she did and everything that she was remained on display in the silver of her scales and the spread of her wings. There was no going back from this. No way to slip back into obscurity. She had hoped that it wasn't changing her on the inside but now there were dead men on her conscience and she found that she could not only live with it, she felt justified. She was remaking the world, what were a few corpses left by the wayside when compared to that?

On the third day after the battle, when boredom began to overtake her she climbed up the side of the tower and looked out over the fields. Without the ghuls' predation this conflict was taking much longer to clean up, in no small part because the organisers were the nobles. If the job had been given to a commoner or a soldier the whole place would be clear in a day and everything resembling a valuable would have been for sale in the city. As it was, there were mounds of corpses by the roadside, putting off trade and sickening the farmers as they returned to their work after seeking shelter.

Lucia put her newly stitched wings to the test and found them to be passable. She swept low over each corpse mound and set them alight in one pass. It was time to get the world back in order. The sky was thick with clouds so she stayed low, enjoying the gentle patter of rain on her scales. There were few enough travellers, but if she was honest she had been keeping her eyes open for this one. With her new eyes, he shone as bright as the sun. She landed with a stagger on the road, cursing her clumsiness, and faced him.

Kaius was not much changed in his time away from her. His robes were gone, replaced with a merchant's simple trousers and a vest of leather. His scars were gone, every mark of the life of violence was erased from his skin. He had even regrown his hair. It was fine, black and straight. He had it tied in a high ponytail to keep his face clear. She had supposed that her appearance would probably be a surprise, but he did not even seem startled. He started to bow before her, but in some rush of emotion he crossed the distance between them and reached out to her. She was skittish and leaned away from his touch, but after a moment of looking at the adoration in his eyes, she leaned into it and let him run his hand along the side of her neck. He whispered, "You are magnificent."

She could not blush with her new skin but a shiver ran down her at his words. She asked, *"How are you not more changed? I know that you must have eaten Walpurgan's heart and you must have been drawing power all year to have done what you did."*

He sighed and removed his hand. "Walpurgan's gifts were many. I am able to control my appearance. I could take on your form if you wished. Or I could teach you how to return yourself to that singing girl with the silly hair, if you would like."

She paused, *"You could do that?"*

He smiled, "I can do much more for you. I have learned much of the history of the Eaters in my travels. I have learned where they came from. I have learned how much we can accomplish.

Walpurgan could see the parts that make up the world, she could see through the other Eater's constructs to their core. I have inherited her gifts, but they can be taught, just as she taught the other Eaters to hone theirs."

It was all so tempting. She was immediately suspicious and voiced it without pause, *"Why did you do this? Why did you learn these things? Why did you kill the other Eaters? What is in it for you?"*
His eyes were wide as she spread her wings and rose to her full height, looming over him, "Because I knew that you needed these things. I knew that nobody else could give them to you. I am yours to command, even now. Please do not send me away when you need all of the gifts that I have brought you."

She backed away from him with an edge of disdain in her crackling voice. *"So it is just like before? You decide that someone needs to die. You decide what I need."*
He stalked closer as she backed away another step, "There are no more that need to die for you to be safe. I am done."
She lunged down towards him hissing, *"And what happens when you decide that the next person is a threat?"*
He shook his head, "The Eaters are gone Lucia. You are all that is left."
They both stopped and turned. Wild laughter was rolling out from the city gates. The rain grew heavier and thunder tolled overhead. Metharia walked out of the city, dressed up in Valerius' old cream and gold robes. She was cackling. Kaius saw her and froze.

Lucia sprang around to face her, leaving Kaius at her back without a moment's worry. Lucia spoke to her in a low voice,

"Metharia. We are just talking. This does not concern you."

Metharia rolled her eyes and sneered, "No Lucia. This does not concern you. I have been waiting for a year. Putting up with your whining and idiocy. Now shut your maw before I shut it for you."

There was a crash of thunder and Metharia jerked her arm out at Kaius. A blinding bright line of lightning flashed out. It was only with a burst of called speed that he was able to avoid it. He shouted, "Lucia, fly away!"

Another flurry of lightning bolts exploded the charred earth around him. He was forced to dodge and leap for safety. Metharia's laughter grew and grew until it was a coarse and raking sound.

Lucia spread her wings and tried to block Kaius from sight even as she screamed in vain to be heard over Metharia and her storm.

Metharia stopped her onslaught as Kaius slid to a halt, panting. Finally, Lucia could be heard. *"What have you done Metharia? How can you use this power?"*

Metharia snarled at her, "Shut up, you worthless slug. I was the natural inheritor of Negrath. Hiding it from an idiot was so simple. All I had to do was stay in the light and act human. After enduring your pawing and prattling for all this time you have finally given me my heart's desire. You have given me a way to take the only thing that Kaius has ever wanted away from him."

Both of her arms whipped forward again and a crackling blast of elemental fury burst from her fingertips, arching out towards Lucia too fast for human eyes to follow. But not too fast for Kaius.

He had called his steel into a smooth suit of armour and a rounded shield. He launched himself between the dragon and the madwoman. The lightning struck through the shield and danced across the armour. He fell, blackened, to the ground, back arching. A guttural scream burst from between his lips. Lucia tripped over her own legs stumbling away from him. Metharia chortled, "Oh ho. Kaius. Caring? I didn't know you had it in you."

The molten slag of Kaius' armour fell away in a shower. His body pulsed and swelled. His fingers cracked apart and curved talons emerged. His back slit open and a row of mineral spikes jutted out. Everywhere that his blackened skin cracked, a dull green glow emitted.

The features of his face melted away until there was only smooth flesh that snapped open along a vertical slit, revealing dozens of rows of razor sharp teeth. From inside that gaping mouth a grating, warbling, nightmare voice shrieked out, *"You don't know what I have in me."*

Chapter 23- The War of the Monsters

Before Kaius' transformation was complete, Metharia was already readying more lightning. It crackled between her fingers but vanished as she had to duck away from a gout of fire from Lucia. Kaius twisted his torso so that the hole that had been his head faced towards Lucia and he snarled, *"Get away. Fly!"*

He glanced away from her just long enough to send out a

crude lash of wind to knock Metharia from her feet. He snapped again, *"I do not matter. Your people need you. The world needs you. I am a relic. Fly!"*

He called air beneath Lucia's wings and flung her up, whipping head over tail into the sky.

The next bolt of lightning from Metharia deflected away from him after striking a sudden outcropping of rock. Metharia leapt over it with electricity trailing from her fingers and fell promptly into a pit that had just opened on the other side. With a disgusted flick of his head, Kaius drew the top of the hole shut over her.

Lucia had stopped spinning in the air and was plunging back towards him, her head sweeping from side to side as she tried to sight Metharia. With the strange double vision the Eaters of the Gods possessed both of them saw, as much as they felt, the sudden draw of power beneath the earth. It was only then that Kaius realised that he had given Metharia total darkness.

The air all around them hummed with the electrical discharge beneath the earth. The coarse silver hair on Kaius legs and flanks stood on end. The earth shuddered beneath their feet.

A pointed bone burst up out of the earth, bleached white and looking like nothing so much as a spider's leg. An impression that grew more accurate as another, then another, burst out of the soil, trying to impale Kaius as he danced away. The leg's hooked into the surface and dragged Metharia's body up out of the ground.

Her body was still mostly human from the waist up. Her head was more skull than flesh apart from the huge webbed ears that framed it. She leapt from beneath the ground to tackle Lucia from the air. Lucia let out a great storm of fire all around them, inadvertently keeping Kaius at a distance. But that just set Metharia off cackling again. A brutal and fluid noise now that her throat had completely changed its shape. In the midst of the roaring flames and the creaking sounds as Metharia crushed her wings against her, Lucia was screaming, *"Why are you doing this? What did I ever do but care for you?"* Metharia's still human arms broke apart into hooked and barbed bone spurs that she raked across Lucia's scales. She broke from her cackling to shriek, *"You do not matter. You never mattered."*

Down on the ground beneath them, Kaius was muttering and weaving layers upon layers of his will all around him. Remaking himself into a more suitable shape and calling allies from across the world in a sudden star-burst of his power.

Lucia reached the apex of her acceleration away from the ground and they began to fall. Metharia managed to hook a claw under one of the larger scales and plucked it off Lucia with a triumphant snigger. She snapped her spread claws back into a single bony spike and drove it into the gap in Lucia's armour.

Blood rained down onto Kaius and he launched himself into the air, half formed, with a wail of wild fury. Metharia dragged Lucia's lashing head down to meet her gaze as they fell to the crushing earth. Her mutating face froze for an instant in a terrible grin.

A wave of air buffeted them up and then Kaius tore between them sending a spray of gore and Metharia's chitinous body flying off into the farmland. He grasped Lucia's limp body with a single clawed foot.

He spiralled down to deposit her gently on the ground before beating his wings and soaring across to the ruined farmstead Metharia had just ploughed into. He recognised this place. He knew that the nobility had favoured it, and when he unleashed another torrent of threads of his will, they fastened on to the creatures he knew would be there.

A storm of carrion birds followed in his wake. He was the point of the arrow and they flooded in behind him. He snapped his wings in against his feathered body to increase his speed and managed to catch Metharia as she was scrambling out of the shattered timbers of the farmhouse.

He hit her as a bird, raking claws first, and drove her back into the ruined building. By the time she was scrambling up again his body had shifted. The feathers were melting away into fur and he looked like nothing more than a huge black cat.

She reared up with her dagger pointed front legs poised to impale him. All of the birds in the sky converged on her in a flurry of violence. They pecked at her eyes and clawed at the joints of her chitin. None of them did damage, or at least not enough to stop her, but every one of them distracted her while Kaius circled around in huge lopping strides and pounced onto her back.

The added weight drove her from her legs but she hit the wet ground and sank in without any real injury. She snorted in laughter until his jaws closed on the soft skin of her neck. Then she flailed at him and poured out a fresh storm of lightning that danced all over her body. Kaius leapt howling back into the mud. She climbed back to her feet with more confidence. She was about to rush forward at the still stunned Kaius when a curious prickling sensation crept over her new body. She opened and shut her eyes slowly. She felt... good... in a queasy kind of way.

She staggered and knocked over the last wall of the farmhouse. With painstaking effort, she turned her gaze downward and saw the insects latched onto her body. Their stingers were painlessly penetrating her flesh just as they had been bred to do. Recognising the drug infiltrating her blood, she let out another pulse of lightning. She fried every one of the beetle larvae still attached to her and let them fall in a shower all around her.

This time Kaius made no attempt at subtlety. His front claws raked down her chest, finding purchase in the ribs just below her breasts. With that point of leverage, he raked down at the connection between her soft stomach and chitinous lower half. He locked his jaws under her chin and tore out her the pale skin of her throat. Even coated in her blood, he did not stop raking at her body until the soft flesh tore to shreds and the chitin was laid open.

Beneath the hard armour and the mask of humanity ,there was a rubbery black leather hide that turned away his claws with a screech. Metharia barely even flinched as her flesh sloughed off. Plates of chitin still covered her arms and she dug their barbed points into his back, extended barbs from them and then used that grip to lever Kaius off and fling him into the air.

Kaius tumbled up, changing shape as he flew. He looked almost human by the time Lucia caught him. Her flank oozed red but she had enough sense to heal her wound before plunging back into the fighting. Lucia twisted in the air after catching him in her forelegs and unleashed a torrent of flame to keep Metharia at bay. With the shell of her back already cracked and clawed Metharia shrugged it off. She extended a pair of leathery wings to match her fresh-grown skin, with more ivory spurs of jagged bone protruding from their span.

Her laughter had finally stopped after her windpipe was torn out, cast away, and trampled into the mud. The stings were effecting her more than the violence had. The entire world spun in a graceful spiral around her, colours were brighter and sounds were louder. She was not sure how much of it was her new senses suddenly developing, and how much was the recreational venom and she did not care.

She belched out a maelstrom of lightning across the fields and staggered after it with Kaius' location still locked in her head. She gained a little speed and then began flapping her wings. Her many limbs dangled beneath her like a squid dragged from the water as she took flight. In Lucia's arms Kaius called out, "Hold me still, I am trying something."

Around Metharia's lumbering flight he wove slim bands of air and swiftly worked them into a mesh. Just like everything else, it grew easier each time he did it. It wrapped around Metharia, as it had all of the Eaters before but with a discharge of lightning, the complex designs that Kaius had woven together dissipated. His sigh of relief became a grunt of disbelief. At least now he understood why Negrath had been considered a threat through all of the unfathomable centuries and wars. He drew in a deep breath and shouted over the whipping wind, "Gain height. She cannot fly as well as you. She has not learned yet"

Lucia grit her teeth and beat her wings faster. They rose ever upwards above the city and the lands all around. They flew higher and higher until the air was growing too thin and Kaius had to drag a huge column of it up with them. Metharia trailed behind. Apparently, her throat was healing because she bellowed up, *"You destroyed me Kaius. You took everything away from me. All for her? For this mewling waste? I should have killed her a long time ago."*

She began to close the distance as Lucia tired. In her drug fuelled frenzy she was salivating and ranting, *"That first night I should have gutted her instead of rutting with her. I should have greeted you wearing her rotting entrails."*

They left the clouds far below and the blue sky faded into stars. Kaius looked up past Lucia into the dark and a smile cracked his face. He made a connection between their minds, just like it was before, because he did not know if he could draw a breath to speak up here. "Let me go. I will lead it away from the city."

Through the same connection, he heard her old sing-song voice whispering back, "If I let you go you will die."

She tightened her grip around him and he stroked his hand across her scales with something resembling love, "If I die I will be remembered kindly. This place that you have made. This new world. It does not need warriors or monsters. Let me do this for you. Let me go."

Her talons gripped him tighter as they broke the surface of the sky and they drifted there in the dark. His last word came to her as though from a great distance, soft as a whisper, "Please."

Lucia let him go. The pull of the world, so distant beneath them dragged Kaius down as she watched in horror. From this altitude he could see the entire continent encircled by its bitter oceans. The Land of The Gods. There were the mines and mountains of Vulkas. The vine ridden forests and overgrown pastures of Walpurgan. The sweeping ocean empire of Ochress curved around the southern coast. At the centre of it all there was the cataclysmic blast radius of the Glasslands and the Ashen Dales. The wastelands that had been his home.

Rising with arthritic beats of newborn wings came Metharia, gasping for air. Kaius looked human again and muscle memory re-asserted itself. He called steel around himself, smooth and perfect. It began to glow as he fell faster and faster. Metharia must have spotted that tell-tale glow in the pitch darkness because she drifted into his path.

With a jerk of his hand he tore the last of the air from her lungs. The lungs themselves burst out of her mouth in the explosive change of pressure, lolling around like fat tongues. This far up he could not call on any stone to block the lightning that she lashed out at him and in the jittery haze of called speed he watched the electricity curve and arc towards the metal of his armour. He was struck and once again the calculated and pressurised lines of will holding him in this shape disintegrated.

He managed to dismiss his armour before it could crush him but it was ill timed. He was just passing Metharia as the liquid metal fell away. She lashed out with eight barbed black limbs and ripped tatters from his golden flesh. Gobbets of meat whipped away from him into the sky and he would have screamed if he had the air. Instead, he locked onto the rear leg closest to him with crushing jaws and bore down with all of the might that he could muster. He broke through the remaining chitin and tore the limb off at the joint.

It was cold up here, chill enough to freeze the blood as it left her, but not quite enough to numb the pain. She kicked him off, and for a glorious moment he was falling freely away from her again. She realised that her wings were still extended, fighting against the push of the wild winds that were nearly tearing them from her back. She dragged them flush against herself and fell after him.

Kaius quickly wove a more human shape for himself. He was still faceless and clawed. Still stony skinned, many winged and gigantic. But the underpinnings were familiar. He launched spikes of air at her but all they did was slow her momentum.

They both fell, burning bright towards the rapidly expanding world. Kaius spun in the air, slowing their descent with a cyclone of wind, and throwing Metharia away with its spinning force. They both fell silently for a time, bolts of lightning crackling wildly all around Kaius as he angled from side to side to avoid them. They struck the layer of clouds and the blazing heat dissipated them with a hiss.

Kaius called the water from the clouds and added it to the whirlwind. Each time Metharia launched another discharge of lightning at him, it was caught by a sudden burst of water and dragged into the tempest.

He was faceless still, but Metharia could swear that he was mocking her. She spread out her wings to control her fall and to bring her closer to him but she was too close to the outside of the huge spiral. The wind snagged her wing and she whipped around. The water battered at her as she tried in vain to push through to the other side. Her own lightning, still leaping around in the darkness of the storm, hit her and she lost all of her senses.

Metharia tumbled out of the cyclone so Kaius braced himself and slowed the spin. The water fell as though dropped from a bucket. Buffeted by the winds, Kaius descent was much more gentle. He touched down on the surface of the glass so softly that it did not make a sound. The glass, once so thick that it could support an army on the march without a creak was broken.

Cracks as thick as his arm extended out in every direction. Metharia was nowhere to be seen. She was lost beneath the surface. Kaius drew himself back into a human shape. Being small would make it easier to navigate under the surface, if it was as he remembered. He called a sword and leapt down into the dark.

He need not have bothered. Metharia was impaled on the titanic spikes of crystal, just a quarter mile's drop beneath the surface. Her new body was spread-eagled, like a pinned moth, where the angled spires of glass entered her oily flesh. Each time she slipped down, the angles of the spikes pulled her limbs and wings further apart. Stringy flesh was exposed and Kaius, hanging from the side of another spire of green tinted glass licked his lips in anticipation. Her massive, bat-like head hung halfway off her narrow shoulders, attached by only a quivering tendon and a stretch of skin.

Even now her blazing green eyes narrowed in fury. Lightning crackled all over her length and she began to laugh again.

It was a bitter, gurgling sound coming from a ruined throat and a mouth never meant for speech. Small patches of gas, drifting around in the enclosed air, popped into bright bursts of green flame around her. She gathered up the last of her might. There was opportunity here.

Kaius did not flee the coming storm. He did not leap for the surface, he just watched as Metharia grew brighter and brighter with gathered electricity, shuddering and sparking. He called the air. He called all of the air across all of this underworld, sensed the fuzzy patches that were not like the rest, the bad air, the gasses of corruption that had been trapped here since the city beneath the glass had died. He drew all of those pockets of flammable gas together into one and herded it up towards the electric mass of Metharia. Beneath the surface of the earth, far from the sunlight, the gas and crackling lightning touched

Chapter 24- The Ballad

Lucia drifted slowly down towards the ground, keeping a safe distance from Kaius and Metharia as they brawled and unleashed their fury upon each other. She saw the coloured lights flashing under the Glasslands but she felt the explosion as an impact on her wings. A circle of ash blew out from around the glass, expanding across her lands, and knocking her people from their feet.

The glass shattered into huge shards and fell into the pit beneath, exposing the blackened and ruined civilisation buried there. The earth shook and she held herself there in the sky, waiting to see if the monsters would emerge and continue their brawl. After countless long moments, the glass finally stopped falling, although a hissing stream of ash poured in from every direction. She flew closer and peered down into the void. She opened up all of her senses, all of the layers of vision and scent and sound that this final form afforded her. Nothing moved and nothing lived in that crater. With a sob caught in her throat, Lucia flew back to the people who needed her and buried her choking regret.

The city was silent at her approach. The people could not

meet their master's gaze. Even the proudest nobles would not look at her directly. She launched herself from outside the city gates and coiled around the top of her tower. With a hiss of frustration and exhaustion, she tore the balcony doorway open and forced her way inside. She spread cracks across the ivory surface of the tower and blackened it with soot in her anger. There were no questions that day. No nobles made entreaties, and the council of commons was silent until nightfall.

She flew over the pit again when the moon had risen far enough to give illumination, but there was no sign of Kaius or Metharia. For a moment, down in the pitch blackness beneath the glass, she caught a glimpse of movement. Faster than she even knew that she could move, she dove into the city below.

It was a shifting pile of ash that had drawn her attention. There was nothing alive down there. Slipping across the collapsing dune, Lucia caught a glimpse of something dark and familiar. She padded over, the ash playing softly through her talons as she drew closer. Her head snaked down until it was level with a dark cloth case that she had not seen since another lifetime. She reached out with a claw and hooked the strap of her sickle-harp case. She was not capable of tears, but a great heaving motion racked her body. Terrible gouts of flame spilled past her jagged teeth as she tried to gulp her sorrow back inside.

By dawn she was back in the Ivory City, working out the details of dissolving the council of nobles with the few councillors that had independently exhibited radical ideals. She broke from that discussion to invite the union of merchants to make bids on the salvage rights to the black city that had been the Glasslands. It was an essential debate as every human working salvage on the glass was now dead. The noble families that had members interested in history were invited to accompany the expeditions and above all to write their findings down. For too long history and truth had been the word of the Eaters, tempered only with the subversive songs that she and the other bards had kept alive.

To the sound of her deep breathing, as other jabbered on and on, the strings of her sickle-harp thrummed. She had been glancing at it through the proceedings. Trying to fit an instrument she could no longer hold without shattering into her new life. As an offhand thought, she commanded that a school of history and music be constructed in the city. After many hours of unexpected debate it became a fully-fledged school. It would housed in the Halls of Bone and Steel with details to be confirmed. The Forms would now be considered an art-form and would be taught to anyone with an interest. Side by side with more abstract and practical subjects taught by noble experts and tradesmen. There was immediate speculation about new entertainments to replace the Trials. That debate drew out for pointless hours too and it was only just before nightfall, and her traditional retreat to solitude, that Lucia realised what would soften the ache in her chest.

The sickle-harp case had sat propped against her side all day, unexamined and unthought of by the nobles, merchants, and petitioners alike. But every time that she had spoken the strings had vibrated softly in accompaniment. She was something new now, something that her old self could not have even dreamed of. She was the ruler of the world and the wielder of power beyond mortal imagining, but she was something old too. Beneath the scales and flames, she was still Lucia. She hummed in the empty chamber, letting the sound echo out through the tower. The harp thrummed along with her. She was not ready to abandon everything that she had been.

Servants and Chosen fled through the city streets rounding up vagrants and questioning them harshly. It was an hour after nightfall that the rag-tag assortment of the most dishevelled and downtrodden citizens of her new world assembled before the tower. Many of them were quaking in fear, others were faking bravado, and every one of them clutched a small box or bag containing their instruments.

The dragon descended from the top of the tower, scurrying down head first and causing some of the more nervous performers to faint. Lucia settled herself in the courtyard and began auditions. The city was drawn to sound and light. Soon a festival of sorts had sprung up around the singers. Each gave a rendition of a song that every singer worth their salt knew, belting out the Ballad of Kurgan Hall with gusto. The street people of the city sang along to almost every chorus. The musicians were then challenged by Lucia to perform an original song. The singing went on through the night. At dawn, the nobles were as exhausted as they had ever been from Valerius' old parties, but they were otherwise none the worse for wear.

The city had come and gone through the night, but there was no real anger about the disruption of sleep. Music had been a rare treat before Lucia's reign. She was intent that it would not be so unusual in the future. The best five musicians received chambers in the tower, a pouch of silver and instructions to rest well, because their nights were going to be full. That night they began composing the Ballad of Kaius, starting with the grand finale and working backwards. They received a great many interruptions from the silver beast they did their best to pretend did not exist. Gradually, they came to realise that despite her appearance, she was more than familiar with their craft. The song came together over the course of the nights and new plans were pushed through with unexpected energy throughout the days.

Many of the musicians who had not been picked by Lucia were instead composing their own songs. They pieced together the story from hearsay and rumour as their kind always had. Revelling in an untold upturn in popularity, those musicians were hired in taverns and noble houses to perform every night. Even their apprentices were roped into action for the lower paying events. In the Ivory City, life went on.

Kaius lay in pieces, buried beneath mounds of razor sharp glass. His lower half seemed to be more jelly than flesh, and he left a red smear as he dragged his way to the still blinking eye that remained in the half skull of Metharia. He pulled himself across while more shards dug into him, slowing him down. It did not matter. He had forever. His teeth lengthened as he neared Metharia's remains. He managed to wheeze out, *"Was your revenge worthwhile? Did you get what you wanted?"*

She was in no position to answer. He hauled himself up and bit into her eye. It burst in a shower of vitreous fluid and blood. He let out a startled laugh, dislodging some of the glass in his lungs, making him cough and splutter. He tore into the spongy, tenderised flesh of her face. It took four days to finish eating her. His health declined each day until at last he finished. Then he lay there for a while absorbing the new power and rasping blood from his mouth. In his memory, he had a single image fixed and when he wove strands of power together it was not to return him to his old flesh and restore him. He wove new flesh to pursue that perfect memory.

While he was still small enough, he crawled his way back out through the crystal chaos. He emerged into the cool night air and stared up at the stars. He finally knew what he wanted, and he knew what Lucia needed. What she truly needed. The two things were one and the same. He completed his crafting and rose up on all fours. He spread his jet black wings to their full length and stretched out his sinuous neck. He turned his gaze towards the Ivory City, all lit up with her fire. Kaius took flight. He drifted up through the clouds with steady beats of his wings, gathering air to carry with him. Kaius rose above the sky until he was a speck crossing over the moon. Then he was just another star, another shimmering spot in the sky, disappearing into the darkness that was his home.

Biography

G D Penman writes... a lot. At the last count he has ghostwritten over thirty books in various areas of interest and he shows no signs of slowing down, but of course he can't tell you what any of them are. He lives in Scotland with his partner and children, some of whom are human. He is a firm believer in the axiom that any story is made better by dragons. His beard has won an award. If you have ever read a story with monsters and queer people, it was probably one of his. In the few precious moments that he isn't parenting or writing he likes to watch cartoons, play games, read more books than are entirely feasible and continues his quest to eat the flesh of every living species.

If you want to be more invasive into his personal life, he jabbers on Twitter almost constantly @gdpenman <https://twitter.com/GDPenman>

CPSIA information can be obtained
at www.ICGtesting.com
Printed in the USA
FSOW01n0319150917
38524FS